I0631333

Fellow Travelers

Bonnie Elise

Published by Bonnie Elise, 2023.

FELLOW TRAVELERS

First edition. September 4, 2023.

Copyright © 2023 Bonnie Elise.

ISBN: 979-8987696613

Written by Bonnie Elise.

Acknowledgements

Risk something or forever sit with your dreams. – Herb Brooks

I've thought about writing a book for ten years. And once I am excited about a new creative endeavor, it's hard for me to let the idea go. For years the dream rolled around in my brain as a "One Day" project. After my mom passed suddenly in 2022, I started asking myself, "What are you waiting for?" My new mantra became, "I don't waste a day." In 2022 I put all my dreams down on paper, and *Fellow Travelers* was born.

I wrote the first draft in November 2022 as part of my own NaNoWriMo (National Novel Writing Month). I finished it on November 30th with the realization that it felt effortless. I loved writing that much. And then I spent the next few months learning HOW to write a novel, revising, and revising again. A big thank you to romance novelist Jessica Kate for recommending two books that were a tremendous help, *The Story Equation* by Susan May Warren, and *The First 50 Pages* by Jeff Gerke. I loved learning a new skill – novel writing – and both books made a huge impact on the way I thought about character development.

My endless gratitude to friends who read early drafts and provided comprehensive feedback. I spent a lot of time with their ideas during my revisions. And I felt such *love* that people with their plates so full would take time to read my story and help me make it better. Big hugs to Kim, Pia, Sherry, Laura, Sarah, Lezlie, Diedre, Lindy, Jennifer, Ginger, Sunny, Jessica, Candy, Victoria, Lisa, and Eva. *You are simply the best.*

Finally, a big thank you to David who supports all my dreams, never questions my sanity when I start a new project, and joins in on most of them. He understands my inability to shelve something I'm passionate about, and he encourages me to see what it's all about. I am very, very lucky.

If you have a dream of writing a book, I hope you will do it. I hope you love yourself enough to follow all your dreams and see where they take you. I'm so glad I did with this one.

Thank you for reading my story,
Bonnie

PROLOGUE
Cam

I'm just like my dad.

Cam Anderson steals a look at the man in the driver's seat. His dark, somewhat unruly hair, always in need of a cut. Cam glances in the side mirror and attempts to tame his own hair. Even the clothes they wore this morning in Cisco, Utah before starting the fourth and final day of their road trip - shorts and graphic tees. Cam's is advertising a bar just off the campus where he (legally) had his first beer. And his dad's, a Boston music festival souvenir that is probably as old as Cam is.

"So have you ever thought about moving to California?" Cam ventures, hoping his tone reads nonchalance. It's something he's wanted to bring up for the last three days, but the time was never right. His dad is currently working in Pittsburgh and seems to be loving it. He doubts he'd want to leave his new position at the hospital, but there is probably similar work in Los Angeles.

"Nah, I don't think so," George answers. "What about you? After school are you going back to Maine?"

Cam takes a moment, surprised by the question. He is studying at UCLA and assumes he'll stay in the area after graduating to pursue work in the entertainment field. His acceptance into their school of Theater, Film and Television is his greatest accomplishment. And where he belongs. His dad would understand that.

"Do you think I should? I feel kind of bad leaving Grandpa Ben and Granny, but I go back for the holidays and during the summers. And Grandpa has been out to visit me a couple of times. He's coming back in a few months if Granny is doing OK."

"Oh yeah, how is she?" George asks.

"You know she stopped working. He says it's early dementia and it was hard for her to continue working at the school. She's the one who made the decision to retire so that's good. It's probably good that she doesn't have the extra stress of work."

"She seemed OK when we picked up the van."

"She has her good days. So do you think I should go back to Maine and look for a job there?"

George changes lanes and waves at a group of men on Harleys. "Not if it's not what you want. You have to live your own life. Work becomes like your family at some point. Your grandparents would understand."

Cam thinks about his grandparents in Maine, on their own. "What about you? Did you think about going back to Maine where your family is?"

"What? No. I've been gone since your mom. I go back every few years, but I gotta live my own life too. You'll see. Once you leave, it's hard to go back." George nods his head in the direction of the motorcyclists they just passed. "Have you ever thought about getting a motorcycle? Might be easier than a car with the LA traffic. I hear it's brutal."

"No, I hadn't really thought about it. Not sure Granny would be happy about a motorcycle. My new apartment is close enough to campus that I can walk or bike. One day, though, I'll need to get a car if I have a job off campus or if I move away from campus." Cam secretly hopes his dad will offer to help with the car. He knows his grandparents would, but he hates asking them since they're covering his outrageous tuition.

George smiles at a distant memory. "I've always wanted to do a cross-country trip by motorcycle. Maybe visit all the national parks. Take a summer off and hit the highway. Your mom and I talked about it once, but by then she was expecting you. You've never thought of a motorcycle road trip?"

"Uh, no, never have. So, it looks like we've got just a couple hours left before we get to my dorm. I pick up the key to my apartment tomorrow morning. I'll pack up the rest of my stuff in the dorm tonight and we can make a few trips tomorrow before you head back east with the van?"

"Yeah, I told Bill that I wouldn't be at his house in Santa Monica until tonight because I wasn't sure when we'd get in. We made better time today than we have the last couple of days. I guess all this stuff we can take tomorrow to your apartment and then go back to your dorm for the rest of your things."

George motions to the back two-thirds of Cam's grandmother's minivan. They loaded up a small desk and bookcase, boxes of books, high school memorabilia, dishes, linens, clothes, and artwork three days ago. His childhood bedroom at his grandparents' home looked strangely different with mostly just the furniture left. That feeling of regret returns as Cam remembers waving goodbye to them. This feels a little more final than when he and his grandfather flew out to move Cam into his dorm freshman year.

Cam realizes he hasn't answered his dad, but his dad doesn't seem to mind. "Yeah, let's do that. Hey, I'm 21 now you know. I told a couple of friends you'd be in town. Can we take you to this bar that we like to go to? Maybe tonight? I want to introduce you to everyone before you have to go back to Maine."

"Wow, 21! Yeah, sounds good. Maybe lunch tomorrow. I don't know if Bill has set anything up tonight. Not sure when I will be leaving but I've got a long drive back. Didn't you say you have an internship starting soon?"

"I interviewed for three and I'm waiting to hear back. They would be for this summer." Cam glances again at his dad. They even hold the steering wheel the same way, right hand resting comfortably on the bottom of the wheel. Left elbow propped up on the window ledge.

"Is there one you're interested in?"

"Two were with movie studios, so that would be cool. I think those were in the office though, not on sets. But it wasn't clear. The other one was with a casting agency. They're new, but one of my professors said it was a good group to work with. They work with producers to find actors for movies, tv, and commercials. I don't know much more about it. I'm supposed to hear back in the next couple of weeks."

"Great, great. Yeah, I don't see you going back east. I think you're going to make a life for yourself in California. I know you're worried about your grandparents, but they want you to be happy. That's the most important thing."

"Yeah, I guess," Cam says softly, watching the landscape turn green as they leave the desert and enter the very outskirts of Los Angeles. "I know they've got friends there but I kind of feel like I should be there for them. I mean, they're family."

"They wouldn't want you to feel responsible for them. You have your whole life ahead of you. You need to chase your dreams. That will make them proud," George advises.

"Yeah, OK. Hey, thanks for doing this with me. Not sure Grandpa would have been able to with Granny's health." Cam looks at his phone's GPS to guide them through eastern Los Angeles and the rest of the way to UCLA.

"You know I love to travel. I've been all over the US and Canada and I love a road trip. That's probably the reason your grandpa asked me to help."

"Was it hard to take time away from work?"

"No, not really," George tells him.

"It's been a while since we've seen each other. I think you're going to like my friends. You should tell them about some of your favorite places you've traveled to." Cam glances over again when his dad doesn't immediately respond.

"Ok. Sure. So, what time tomorrow morning at your dorm?" George seems distracted. Probably burned out from driving the last several days.

"I can't get the apartment key until 10:00 so maybe we can get some breakfast first?" Cam suggests.

"Yeah, yeah. Sounds good," George responds, with a faraway look in his eyes that his son doesn't recognize.

***

At 8:30 the next morning Cam gets a text from the dorm lobby that he has a package. He finishes taping shut the last of his cardboard moving boxes and takes the stairs two at a time to the lobby mailbox area. He retrieves a bulky envelope with his name on the front written in marker. He opens it to find a set of keys and a note hastily written on the back of a hotel receipt.

Cam, I bought a motorcycle last night! I am going to ride it back to Pittsburgh and let you keep the van. You and your friends can use it to move into your apartment. Maybe your grandpa can fly out and drive it back to Maine if he still wants it. Can you let him know the plan?

Chase your dreams! ~ George

"Nobody – that's my name."
~ Odysseus to the cyclops Polyphemus in Homer's *The Odyssey*

Seven years later

LOS ANGELES, FRIDAY
Cam

"Great," Cam assures Jacob Coleman, flipping back to the first page of the scene. "I think we got that one. Did you want to go again?"

"Not if you're happy with it," Jacob rolls his shoulders back and stretches his neck side to side. He glances at his agent, Cooper, sitting quietly at the back of the room. "I think it's the scene in the shop where I might want to try it a couple of different ways. If that's OK."

"Let's move to that scene. Karen, let us know when you're ready on video." Cam looks up and smiles.

"It's ready, Cam. Did you want me to play the second person in the shop in this scene, along with the Elizabeth main character?" Karen asks.

Cam quickly reviews the pivotal scene. "Yes, that would be great. Appreciate your stepping in. Jacob, we're ready whenever you are. I'll read the narration in this one, so you'll be doing the scene with Karen."

"Video is rolling Jacob, whenever you're ready," Karen tells the young actor.

Jacob takes a moment to prepare himself for the scene. He knows how critical this meeting is with Cam Anderson. He has not read for James Casting before and he wants to make an impression. If not for this role, then to make sure Cam remembers him for future movies. Jacob straightens to his full 6'1" height and assumes the voice and characteristics of a 1946 English shopkeeper.

***

Cam, Karen, and Jacob lay down their scripts and Karen turns off the recorder.

"Thank you for that," Cam says to Jacob. "I think I have what I need. Did you want to try anything different?"

"Why don't I try it shy-er this time?" Jacob offers. "I got the notes from Cooper that you are looking for slightly more affluent in tone and manner. Would he be less self-assured and maybe more timid with her?" Jacob watches as Cam checks the recording in the playback screen and nods to Karen who makes notes on a laptop.

"I don't think so," Cam responds. "Elizabeth is strong-willed and old enough not to want to play any games. If she is going to be attracted to someone after the love of her life dies and years of war finally end, she is going to want him to know his mind too. Let's go once more and maybe even more confident this time. Karen? Can we go again?"

"We're recording, guys. Start when you're ready."

***

Cam takes the stairs two at a time and stops on the second floor when he hears Cooper calling his name. Cam was hoping for a quick escape but pauses and gives the talent agent his full attention.

"Thank you, Cam, for the extra time today. I think Jacob would be perfect for the role. I thought he nailed that last scene."

"I'm going to send my casting recommendations to Bachman when I send in the other supporting cast recs. They'll let us know soon if they want him to read with the producers."

"I know he doesn't have a lot of experience outside commercials and the one show, but he's good Cam. I see him doing more leading work at some point."

"Yeah, I know you do," Cam smiles. "Remind me, has he done any voice work?"

"No not yet, but he has done two national commercials."

"Encourage him to consider it. He could get a lot of voice work given the accents and lack-of-accent I've seen him pull off."

"I'll tell him that. He's worked hard at it, given his Massachusetts upbringing."

"Really?" Cam asks. "I'm from the northeast too. I don't hear it in him."

"And I assumed you were born and raised in California," Cooper says.

"No, just the last several years. Hey, I've got to run. I'll get back to you by Monday, I hope. I know Bachman's team has updated Breakdown with new shoot dates," Cam says as he backs toward the door.

"Ok, good to know, I'll take a look and make sure there aren't any potential conflicts. Just in case. Have a good weekend, Cam."

"You, too." Cam lets out a deep breath and climbs into the maroon minivan. It's been a long week, busy few months really, and he's looking forward to a quiet weekend. *Maybe a run?* He calls the office while he checks emails on his phone.

"Show me the money!" Chelsea greets him in her best Rod Tidwell.

"Nice," Cam unbuttons the top two buttons of his patterned dress shirt and runs a hand through his thick, wavy hair. *Maybe a haircut this weekend?*

"How was Cooper's guy?" Chelsea asks in a weak attempt at indifference. Cam imagines her twisting her blue-tipped hair around her finger.

"Oh, you know his name. You've seen his show."

"Was he any good? Tell me he was good."

"He was great. Takes direction well too. Karen will send over the videos in a few minutes. I think the third version is more what they're looking for. Can you make sure Alison sees them this weekend? I'll send Bachman the recommendations when she has a chance to weigh in. I told Cooper I'd get back to him Monday with an update. I need to make sure we're still within budget given the changes they sent in."

"Yep, I'll get it to her today. What's up this weekend?"

"Nothing," Cam tells her. "What about you?"

"I'm going out with Marcus's friends tonight. Not sure about tomorrow," Chelsea adds.

"Marcus, huh? I thought that wasn't going anywhere."

"I don't know what I'm doing there," Chelsea admits. "But tonight, we're going to dinner and probably to his friend's bar after. This group is into sports so not sure I'll make it past 9 p.m. I know better than to invite you along."

"Yeah, need some quiet I guess."

"Hey text me if you send anything else my way, OK? She's got a full week next week so I'd rather take care of it or get it to her this weekend if I can. And try to get out and have some fun, OK?"

"Sure, sounds good. Hey, who do you go to for a haircut? I just walked into a place last time."

"I'll send you Kristen's number. Just text her times when you're free and I bet she can fit you in."

"Ok great. See ya." Cam responds to a couple of quick emails and heads home, past the Cathedral and Echo Park before entering *his* LA. He never gets tired of the sidewalk lined streets and orange trees in every yard. Unfortunately, he also has to witness historic homes being torn down and replaced with postmodern blandness. But he loves residential Los Angeles, with its sunshine and blue skies, brimming with optimism.

Cam pulls into his driveway and drives all the way to the back of the property to the little guest house he calls his own. He walks to the 1920s Spanish-style main house, knocks on the side screened door, and calls in.

"Mr. Franks, are you decent?"

Jeremiah Franks calls from the living room and Cam follows his voice.

"I haven't been decent in years," he laughs. He turns down the evening game show he's watching and peers over his readers at Cam.

"How's Hollywood?"

"Just as you left it," Cam says. "What's for dinner?"

"Well, Paige made me grilled cheese and soup like I asked."

"I see a salad there too."

"Yeah, you want it?"

"No, you eat it."

"I'm not eating it. What's up? You got big plans tonight?"

"Not tonight," Cam says. "You need anything?"

"Yeah, I need a hot date. You know anyone?"

"No, afraid not."

"I know you've got them lined up, Cam."

He laughs, "Maybe, but I'm not sending them over here."

"Alright. Hey, why don't you come over tomorrow when Paige and the family get here? We're grilling some steaks."

"Hate to interfere with your family time."

"You know the kids love it when you come over. We'll have plenty so stop by if you aren't busy. And maybe you could get me some figs."

"I'll bring some over. Thanks for the invite. Call if you need anything."

"Alright, I will."

Cam returns to the guest house and looks around. Two years ago, Mr. Franks offered his neglected guest house at a reduced rent if Cam would fix the place up. Cam hesitates to look too closely because he knows he has not made good on his end of the deal.

The guest house is so much better than the two apartments he lived in during college and after graduation. But he doesn't pay much attention to the furnishings or appliances, and he rarely has people over. His last couple of relationships were brief, as they all have been. He and his dates typically meet up at a restaurant or event, and eventually go back to her place if things are going well. Now Cam takes a moment to look around his home.

The stucco walls could really use a good sanding and coat of paint. There are water spots on the living room wall that may be new, or maybe Cam just never noticed them before. *Should I be writing all this down?*

The curtains in the main areas of the house are heavy and dark, and God knows how old. Cam got a new mattress for the double bed that was in the bedroom when he moved in, but he really should sell all the outdated furniture in the guest house and give the money to Jeremiah. Or maybe donate it all. Cam could afford new furnishings. But then, why? It all works just fine. Cam pushes it out of his mind for now.

After changing into shorts, he heads out for a run through his eclectic neighborhood with its modernist homes quietly tucked away behind iron gates that are draped with fall jacaranda blooms. Since moving to California for college Cam keeps thinking he'll start to miss the changing seasons that so many people look forward to in Maine. But so far, he hasn't. Los Angeles suits him.

Cam takes a shower and opens the ancient, yet serviceable, fridge in his terracotta-colored kitchen. Dinner is leftovers from yesterday's lunch out with Chelsea and a bottle of seltzer in front of an old movie. Not the way most 28-year-olds spend Friday nights in LA, but not a bad life either. Without family in the area, Cam has gotten used to a quiet life. Maybe tomorrow he will consider a project to start fixing up the place.

He puts a Blu-Ray in the player and gets his remotes ready. Many of his favorite films are streaming, but Cam prefers the satisfying whir of the DVD, along with the menu of options, including the Director's Commentary, that he can't get from streaming. An old soul, Mr. Franks calls him. Cam sits back in the aging recliner and glances at his phone, noticing several missed texts. None from James Casting so the rest can wait. As he lays the phone back down, he sees Ben Young's name light up the screen. Hesitating only a second, Cam answers his grandfather's call.

LOS ANGELES, FRIDAY

Cam

"Grandpa, hey."

"How are you doing son?" Grandpa asks, his tone somewhat strained.

"Good, good. Everything is great here. What about you?"

Grandpa Ben laughs. "How about you give me a few more details?"

Cam smiles, never big on providing specifics but knows his grandpa is sincerely interested. He walks to the kitchen to get a beer.

"Life in California is good," he says. "Still working at James of course. We have three movies right now and I'm working on supporting actors for one of them. You may know the book it was based on. A big bestseller, WWII."

"*The Forbidden Fable*?" Grandpa asks.

"No, is that being made into a movie?" Cam asks, interested.

"No idea - you tell me."

"No, the one I'm working on right now is *The Bridge of Valor*."

"Ah yes, I heard that was going to be a movie or a TV show or something. Good for you. You still enjoying it?" Grandpa Ben continues his questions, drawing out more than Cam would provide otherwise.

"Yes, definitely."

"Good, that's good. And what else is going on in your life?"

"I stopped by to see Jeremiah Franks earlier. He's about the same," Cam adds.

"He's been good to you. I still can't believe you are living in his neighborhood." Cam's grandfather was surprisingly star-struck in Los Angeles. They saw three celebrities at lunch one day on his first visit, and Cam, of course, introduced him to Jeremiah Franks on his most recent trip. Grandpa Ben recognized him from several old movies.

"Well, his guest house actually. I got a deal." Cam guiltily remembers the deal for the second time today and commits to start making those improvements.

"I suspect you'll want to buy your own place one day soon," Grandpa states rather than asks.

"Hmmm, we'll see. Real estate is expensive out here."

"Let me know if you need any help. You know I'm good for it."

Cam laughs and knows he will never, in a million years, ask his grandparents for a house loan. And while this catch-up has been nice, it's obvious Grandpa's called for a reason. Cam is quiet so he can spill it.

"So, I was wondering when you could come home?" Grandpa Ben gets to the point.

"Um, well, I've got a few projects I'm in the middle of, but I think I could. I mean why? Is there something going on?" Cam asks, surprised by the request.

Grandpa is quiet. Cam wonders if he is with his Granny or if he's stepped away from her.

"No easy way to say this," Grandpa says in a softer voice. "Granny has pancreatic cancer, and we don't think she has more than a couple of months left."

Without realizing it, Cam slides down the wall in his kitchen and doesn't respond. He takes a sip of beer.

"I realize all this is happening fast, but I'd appreciate it if you could be here sometime soon. You might have been waiting for the holidays but, well, I was wondering if you could just come on home earlier than that." Grandpa stops talking and waits for his grandson's response.

Cam hadn't, in fact, been thinking about going home for the holidays. Like he hadn't the last couple of years, partly due to the pandemic, he told himself. And his work was always busy, no matter the time of year. But his grandparents are about the only family he has, so he has tried to be there for them as much as possible. Cam still hasn't spoken so Grandpa continues.

"I've got to work on some details with the doctors and our lawyer, and I want to spend as much time with her as I can. Even though she is sleeping more now during the day," he adds.

Cam notes his grandfather sounds drained and resigned. Grandpa Ben continues in a gentle voice.

"Granny isn't going into the hospital and we're not talking about treatments given all she's going through. She's at home and we have help around the clock. But I still want to be with her."

Grandpa pauses again to let Cam ask the questions he must have. Still no response.

"I know you're not ready, son, but the time is coming. It's not a rush but when do you think you can be out here?" Cam wonders if Grandpa Ben had anyone with him when he received the news about Granny's health.

Cam finally asks, "Um, how are *you*?"

Grandpa Ben chuckles, "Well, ha, I'm tired. I haven't been fishing in a long time and I don't really want to take any time away from your Granny, you know."

"When do you need me?" Cam asks quietly.

"Now I know you can't just leave work, but maybe within a couple of weeks? I know this is hard."

Cam can't get out any more words and Grandpa seems to understand.

"Ok," Cam finally says. "Can I call you tomorrow after I call the office?"

"Sure, and again I'm sorry to have to give you this news."

They both say quiet goodbyes and end the call. Cam stretches his long legs out. It's quite some time before he gets up from the kitchen floor.

LOS ANGELES, SATURDAY
Piper

Piper hustles from her yoga class to the salon, texting friends while she walks. Her oldest friend, Abigail, is venting about her coworker again. Piper responds with the thoughtful advice that her friends appreciate and expect.

Ask her out to coffee to talk about it. Tell her you're concerned about her attitude. Be a good listener but be direct. Running in to see Andres. Talk soon.

Her mother's text is about the DVR and it's not clear what the problem is. Piper takes a deep breath and calls her.

"Hey Mom. Tell me what you're seeing on the screen... OK...It shouldn't be blue. What screen are you on? OK you're on one of the subscription sites... Can you go back to the main TV screen? Right - just normal TV... Ok. What do you see at the bottom of the screen... Guide is the one you want. Go to the show that you want and click record...No, they're asking you how long you want to keep it. Unless you delete it, it won't go away...Mom...OK, good...OK I'm running into the salon. Love you."

Piper enters her sanctuary, the industrial chic oasis where the receptionist greets her with a kiss on the cheek and Beyonce's voice fills the air at the perfect volume. She says quick hellos to the stylists she knows and plops down in Andres's chair, accepting the sparkling rosé he hands her. Piper takes a moment to sip and breathe before launching into her questions about his latest date.

Andres has known Piper for more than a decade and manages her energy smoothly. "Sweetie, I love this color on you," he says, complimenting Piper's yoga top. "You are definitely a fall." He drapes her in black and answers her questions about his latest dating debacle. "I think I'm taking some time off from the apps. I'm not meeting anyone worth my time that way. I'm going to do a reset."

"I agree. Delete your profile and spend time with people IRL for the time being. Let your friends know when you're ready to be set up. See if you can meet someone organically. You're such a catch Andres. Don't put up with any more dating fiascoes."

Piper finishes her flute of wine and Andres sets it on the counter. She's scrolling through Insta stories when a text comes in from her friend Cam.

Hey Piper. I'm going to Maine in a couple of days. Are you OK to check on Jeremiah and maybe check on his fig tree while I'm gone?

Immediately Piper responds.

YES Do you need a ride to LAX? Happy to take you

There is no response from Cam, which is typical. Three minutes go by. Then four. Piper considers calling.

No Thx

Piper immediately responds with:

Cam it's not a problem. When is your flight?

Again, no response from Cam. Andres finishes Piper's color and moves her to process under the dryer. Minutes later still no word from Cam. She catches herself drumming her fingers on the arm rest.

"OK, now I'm getting worried," Piper mutters. And then three little dots...

No flight. Taking Odysseus back.

Piper moves to come out from under the dryer to call Cam, but Andres points her back. She groans and texts.

What? Why?

No response from Cam. He's avoiding her. Again. Typical of their friendship. Cam rarely contacts Piper. He's such a good guy though, and doesn't know many people, so Piper loves connecting him with her friends. *He clearly needs my help.* Her leg bounces while she waits to be shown to the wash station.

"Wait," Piper says, eyes pleading when Andres turns off her dryer. "I have to call Cam."

"Two minutes," Andres says.

Piper bounces onto the balls of her feet while the phone rings and Cam finally answers. "Why? Will the van even make it? That's 3200 miles," Piper says by way of greeting.

"You maps'd it?" Cam asks, surely not surprised.

"Cam, what is going on?" Piper asks with real concern in her voice.

Resigned, Cam sighs. "Grandpa Ben called. My grandmother is not doing well. I need to get back. I want to return the Odyssey."

"Couldn't you just fly? Do your grandparents need the van back? You should have sold it and bought a real car years ago. You deserve a different car, Cam."

Andres interrupts Piper, reaching for her phone. "Piper, I've got to get that color off of you."

"Cam, we'll talk once I am done here at the salon. Bye," and she hangs up, telling Andres about Cam's latest news while he washes, cuts, and dries her hair, styling it into the cutest long bob with golden highlights. Piper barely notices. She pays and kisses Andres goodbye.

And then she drives straight to Cam's.

***

"I thought you'd text me," Cam says, surprised to see her at his door. "I didn't think you would show up."

They hug and Piper looks around at the sad, lifeless guest house.

She shuts the front door with her hip and pushes it again when the heavy door doesn't quite close. "I picked these on the way in. That tree is neglected," Piper adds.

Cam nods a little guiltily. "I will take care of it before I leave." He takes the figs from Piper's arms and places them in a colander in the kitchen sink, running water over them.

"I want to go with you," Piper says suddenly. She moves dishes from the kitchen table to the sink and uses a towel to wipe down the table and counters.

Cam looks at her but doesn't say anything.

"Seriously Cam. It's a long drive and you need a wingman. I will play navigator and DJ and will keep you awake and company. It'll be great!" Piper dances around the kitchen, excited about the idea of a road trip. With Cam.

Cam counters, "What about work?"

"It's under control. Cam, let's do this!" He looks doubtfully at Piper whose wheels are spinning, packing and planning a playlist in her mind.

"What about your mom, brunch, advising everyone in the greater Los Angeles area?" Cam asks, clearly stalling. He looks surprised to see the clean kitchen table now with a vase that Piper has arranged while they talked.

"Seriously I'll be fine," Piper assures him, rearranging books stacked on top of a bookcase. Cam shakes his head and places the figs on a towel to dry.

"I'd really like to go. You know I work remotely 95% of the time, anyway." Cam doesn't respond but doesn't say "No" either.

"This trip could be good for me. I'd really like to go."

Cam nods his head "Yes" but doesn't say anything. Piper squeals, gives him another hug, and walks into the living room to open the heavy curtains.

LOS ANGELES, MONDAY
Cam

It's a gorgeous early fall day as Cam walks over to Jeremiah's home with a bowl of figs. The older man is sitting on his porch, watching birds in the avocado tree.

Cam joins him and takes a seat, turning his face to the sunshine. "I'm going on a trip today. I meant to stop by this weekend to tell you and drop these off but had to get a few things done for work before I left." Cam rolls his shoulders back, noticing again that they've been tight since Grandpa's call on Friday.

Jeremiah squints up in the sunlight, "Is this about family?" he asks.

"Yes, I'll be gone for a couple of weeks. You have my number though, right?" Cam is suddenly a little concerned about being gone for so long, especially when Mr. Frank's daughter Paige travels for work most weeks.

"Yep, we've got your number. Don't worry about us. We missed seeing you Saturday when we cooked out. Not sure if you heard but the grandkids knocked on your door."

"No, I must have been out. Oh, I also wanted to let you know that I'm going to start doing some projects around the guest house when I get back."

"Ok, sounds good. You take care of those you love. Safe travels."

Cam stands and places his hand on Jeremiah's shoulder, "Will do." Cam steps inside and places the bowl on Jeremiah's kitchen table. As he leaves through the back door, he asks the housekeeper quietly, "You and the nurses have my number, right?" She nods and he reminds her, "Please call me if anything comes up."

"Don't worry. We'll take good care of Mr. Franks," she reassures him, patting his arm. Cam writes his cell number on the dry erase board on the refrigerator and returns to the minivan.

He packed light for the trip - work laptop, t-shirts, a couple of long-sleeved shirts, shorts and jeans. He added a suit as well. Just in case. After grabbing a bottle of tea from the refrigerator, Cam locks the guest house door and cranks the Odyssey. He considers turning right and going straight to the I-5, but he knows it would break Piper's heart if he went without her. *I never actually said Yes,* he thinks to himself. He should have said no. *Why didn't he?* Something in the way she said she needed this trip made him think he should just give in. Like he usually does with Piper.

After meeting Piper through friends a few years ago, his life in Los Angeles shifted considerably. His focus since college had been entirely on work. He dated some, but no one seriously, and no one he could see himself spending more than a couple of weeks with. Piper, though, never gives up. She seems to have made it a personal mission to connect him with everyone in her vast social network. She encourages him to attend most of the events he gets invited to in order to meet more people, even though he knows these sorts of short-term interactions never amount to much. And while Piper's fun to hang out with, Cam doesn't want to give her the wrong impression. Sometimes he gets the sense that she would be happy being more than friends. But he can't have their friendship end with a fling. Or maybe he's misreading her. He hasn't had a lot of women friends over the years. And there is no one quite like Piper.

Cam resigns himself and starts to turn left toward her condo when Piper honks and pulls into the driveway. She parks in his spot by the guest house and gets out excitedly, a huge smile and a little wave.

"Hey! I thought it might be better to leave my car here instead of at my place, on the street. This way Mr. Franks can keep an eye on it. I texted you. Where should I put my bag?" Piper walks around to the back of the minivan where Cam is opening the door. He holds off saying hello until she's finished talking. Normal for them.

"Hi Piper," he leans in and gives her a kiss on top of the head.

"What snacks did you get? Do you have GPS set up? Can we take some of these figs?"

Cam waits until all the questions are done and asks about her laptop.

"Got it right here," she points to the slim bag on her shoulder. "Do you want me to take the first shift? Are we heading to Las Vegas first?"

Cam picks through the lobbed questions to answer the one he wants. "No, we're headed south since I've got to stop in Dallas on the way."

Piper enthuses, "Oh that's great that you're getting some work in. OK I'll get these figs and we'll wash them and be ready."

Cam walks toward the shed to get the ladder because there's not a single fig Piper will be able to reach. He watches her trying to pick the lowest fruit and shakes his head. Today she is dressed in shorts, a blue flowy top with crisscross strap things in the back and sandals with heels. Her hair is up in a ponytail and Cam thinks she looks more like a college student than a journalist with a national newspaper. They load a bag she pulls from her car and go back inside to rinse the figs. Finally ready to leave, Cam looks up to see Jeremiah waving to them from the kitchen window. Piper runs over to him, and Cam follows.

After a hug she asks, "What are you reading these days?"

"*Harbor's Edge*," Jeremiah responds. "Political thriller. What about you?"

"Nothing right now, I need a new book. I read all day for work but need something completely different than the news. Mind if I go through your library?" Piper asks.

"Be my guest, young lady."

Piper pulls a recent bestseller off the shelf, and he nods, "You'll like it. I'm sure they'll make it into a movie or a Netflix or something."

She gives him another hug, says goodbye to the home health nurse and jogs back to Cam's van.

Mr. Franks catches Cam's eye and shakes his head. Cam grins and shrugs. Jeremiah adores Piper, and Cam knows the older man thinks Cam should be clear about his intentions. *The youth these days*, Cam's heard him mutter, more than once.

Piper climbs into the passenger seat of the Honda and immediately notices there are no snacks. Just the tea and figs. She stares at Cam with her mouth comically hanging open. "Why don't you have road trip snacks? Have you set up Google Maps? Here, I'll hook up my phone to Bluetooth."

Cam pulls out his phone and says, "Piper, the van doesn't have Bluetooth. It's more than 10 years old."

Piper stares at him again. Cam wonders, not for the first time, if this is a bad idea. Piper smiles and says, "Well there will be a Whole Foods somewhere as we head out of the city. We'll stop for snacks."

Cam starts to protest that they've got to cross the entire country and it's already 2 p.m. He turns to his passenger and sees that she's slipped off her sandals, slid on her sunglasses, and snapped her seatbelt in place. *No turning back now.*

"Good luck to you, even so. Farewell! But if you only knew, down deep, what pains are fated to fill your cup before you reach that shore."

~ Calypso to Odysseus, in Homer's *The Odyssey*

LOS ANGELES, MONDAY
Cam

They do indeed stop at Whole Foods because there is one not far from Cam's home on the way to the I-5. The minivan catches the freeway near Stadium Way, where a late season Dodgers game is underway, and then they turn onto the I-10.

Piper solves crises for two friends via text and fills Cam in on the situations. He plays along, asking relevant questions, although he doesn't know the two people Piper is updating him on. Or even worse, he *should* know them and doesn't remember. Either way, Piper always seems to think that Cam is as invested as she is.

"How is work going? What did you bring with you?" she asks when she's caught up on her texts.

"Three movies," he says enthusiastically. He knows that Piper asks about his work because it's the only thing he has going on in LA. And he'd rather talk about work than women. Piper has met a few of the ladies Cam has gone out with, and she was not a fan. She has introduced him to many of her friends, but there is no way Cam is risking that.

"I'm working on supporting characters for all three. I want to send out recommendations to the studios tomorrow but am waiting to hear back from Chelsea with the go-ahead. I had a couple of meetings today that I wanted to be in town for, which is why we're getting the late start."

"That sounds great. I brought work too. I'll be able to do a lot in the car when I'm not driving. So, tell me about this trip. How fast are we planning to get to Maine? How often do you want me to drive?"

Cam responds non-committally, "I'm not really sure, I think I can do a lot of the driving." He's aware that Piper knows he's only answering some of her questions, but she lets it slide.

"Do you have any music in the Odyssey? CDs?" she asks, eyeing the radio and CD player. "How far are you thinking we'll go today?"

Cam runs his hand through his hair, realizing he never texted Piper's friend about a haircut. It slipped his mind after Grandpa's call. He adjusts the air vent and decides to bite the bullet. This is as good a time as any to bring up the hotel rooms. "Phoenix. Hey, listen, I know you really wanted to come but let me take care of getting the hotel rooms, OK?"

Cam feels Piper looking over at him and knows he probably looks particularly uncomfortable. He does his best to pull off casual. The longer her silence lasts the clearer it is that she thought they were sharing a room. Cam has no idea how to ease into that conversation.

He continues, "I need to get some serious work done on this trip, and I can't really do it in the car. I was just thinking that it would be good to have some space to make that happen. I'm sure you wouldn't mind having your own room, too." He wonders if he should have mentioned it before they left. Piper doesn't respond so he quickly changes the subject to another potential minefield.

"And hey, do you truly want to ride all the way to Maine? It's 48 hours just driving time. With any stops I have to make, it could take several days. I mean, it's also a lot to ask given my grandmother's health." Cam wants to give Piper an out and knows that she could easily be regretting her decision to join him right now.

Piper, though, looks at him somewhat stunned and asks, "I was planning to go all the way, Cam. But why are you driving?"

"My grandparents need me, and I want to get their van back. But last night I was thinking that if you get tired of the long drive and me working nights, then I could always take you to an airport and you could fly back to LA," Cam offers.

Piper doesn't say anything but dives into the Whole Foods cloth bag and pulls out baby carrots and hummus.

Not my idea of road trip food, but that's Piper. Piper who also picked up sunscreen for us because "the windshield does not screen out all the UV rays". Cam watches her, knowing she'll eventually respond to him about his idea of returning early.

"Can I put a playlist together?" she asks, clearly changing the subject.

"Of course," Cam easily gives in, although the idea of listening to music out of an iPhone speaker isn't that appealing. They turn on the radio while Piper scrolls through Spotify and they snack.

She crunches a carrot and says, "Hey, I don't think I told you, but I'll need to turn in my 'Today's Ten' column by 2:30 LA time each day for the overnight publish."

"And your manager knows you're going to Maine? I mean, I know you work remotely most of the time."

"Yes," Piper answers, still scrolling through music. Cam notices she is also watching out the van windshield and keeping up a rapid text chain with a friend. She seems to be back in her happy place.

He's relieved to have won the hotel room battle. For now. He also introduced the flying-home-if-it's-too-much idea. He's acquiesced to health food and letting the passenger play DJ since it didn't occur to him to get any CDs together. They should be just fine. Until Dallas, when the whole thing could blow up in his face. But that's a couple of days away. He dips a baby carrot into hummus and watches Los Angeles in the rear-view mirror.

SOUTHERN CALIFORNIA, MONDAY

Cam

Odysseus heads east on I-10 past Pomona where Piper went to college and then bypasses Palm Springs where Cam and Piper met at a wedding.

A Palm Springs wedding is a glorious event. Piper's colleague from the newspaper was marrying his boyfriend of seven years. Cam had met Henry and Ethan at an art show that he was dragged to by a woman he briefly dated. The couple and Cam really hit it off and they started calling him regularly for dinner and L.A. Kings games. Like Cam, they were from the east coast originally. Unlike Cam, they felt if Cam had a special friend at their wedding, it would make it that much more fun for him.

They told their good friend Piper that they had a guy she might enjoy getting to know. They introduced Piper and Cam at one of the pre-wedding festivities in the desert. Piper quickly adopted Cam into her group, and she has been a regular part of his life ever since. It dawns on Cam that he has not seen Ethan and Henry in months. *Maybe I should give them a call?*

"Remember how gorgeous the wedding was?" Piper asks, looking out over the desert. "I loved that everyone wore sunset colors to the rehearsal dinner. Those photos were stunning." She flips through an album on her phone and pulls up one of the groom and groom with Piper, Cam, and a few other friends. She shows the photo to Cam and then gazes out the van at early dusk in Southern California.

"Yeah, I had no idea what that meant when I saw it in the invitation, so I had to get some help. It was one of the best California weekends I've ever been a part of. Sorry you had to babysit me."

"Right. Come on, Cam, we had so much fun, and I knew our friends would love you. It was a magical weekend," Piper sighs.

"It was the first time it occurred to me that I might get married one day. Like it could be a serious possibility."

"What? Cam, of course you'll get married one day! Why wouldn't you?" Piper turns fully in her seat to study him.

"You might, but I'm not sure. I guess I never really thought of it as likely. You know I'm not really into long-term relationships. Too much of a loner, I guess. And I mean, look at my dad. He's doing great and he never remarried. Not sure it's in the cards for me, as they say."

Piper shakes her head, pats Cam's hand, and announces, "The playlist is ready!"

Cam steels himself for bad sound quality but Piper continues, "When we stop at a service station, I want to get a proper speaker. Something we can run through the van's CD player. They've got to sell those."

Audio crisis averted.

***

They ride in silence until Piper sees the sign for Joshua Tree National Park and Cam literally jumps in his seat when she screams, "We have to check it out!"

"Piper, we've only been on the road three hours. We've got three or four more to go," Cam calms his heartbeat down.

"Just for a quick look around? Please Cam, I haven't been in years," Piper pleads.

Cam chooses to give in, knowing there might be bigger battles ahead. He pulls the van off the interstate onto the road to the South Entrance. He's never visited any of the California National Parks but has been meaning to for years. "It looks like it's only a mile or so to the Visitors Center," Piper announces.

Ten minutes later they pull in. After a quick restroom stop, Cam grabs a Coke and Piper insists on a photo with the national park sign, with cactus and scrub brush behind them. The city traffic and urban sprawl of LA have given way to mountains and desert. "OK, let's go!" Piper yells and runs back to the van.

They knock the Joshua Tree dust off their shoes and quickly make their way back to I-10 and on toward Phoenix. Cam finishes off the carrots and hummus as they cross the Colorado River at the California-Arizona line. Piper holds up a peace sign and says, "Two."

Cam looks at her confused and she clarifies, "Our second state."

He wonders how she even saw the "Welcome to Arizona" sign they passed moments before. She had been researching a data privacy debate in Germany, presumably for a future 'Tens' column, and hadn't even looked up. *I guess she did,* Cam thinks to himself. "Two," he repeats.

Piper tilts her head, looking at Cam. "You look tired. Want me to drive? Want me to find a hotel?" she motions with her phone.

"Chelsea booked me at the 3 Palms near Phoenix. I called her back and asked her to add a second room," Cam tells Piper, hesitant to discuss the room situation again.

"She knows I'm with you?" Piper asks.

"She knows I'm not alone. I can't remember if I told her you were with me."

"What did she say about that? 'The First Rule of Fight Club,'" Piper guesses.

"Wait, what?" Cam asks, confused. *Piper knows the first rule of Fight Club?*

"'Don't talk about Fight Club,'" she informs him.

Cam jerks his attention toward Piper giving her his most confused look. "You've seen *Fight Club?*"

"Yeah, it's got Brad Pitt in it. I've seen it."

Cam looks out at the desert that's surrounding them as far as he can see. Occasional small towns pop up and he wonders who lives there. It's nice to be out of the city, but the earth tones and quiet of Western Arizona give off a somewhat eerie vibe. At 10:30 p.m. the Odyssey pulls in to the 3 Palms.

"Old school," Piper says and grabs her bags.

"Vintage," Cam says, clearly admiring the retro feel of the hotel. He sends off a quick text to Chelsea.

Blessed are those who expect nothing for they shall not be disappointed. Great hotel.

Cam checks them in and hands a key to Piper. They put their bags in their rooms and walk to the only restaurant still open and each order a club sandwich.

"Have you talked with your grandpa? Is he OK?" Piper asks.

"I guess. I'm worried about him. But I guess he seems to be doing OK."

"I know they'll be happy to see you. Did they ask you to return the van?"

"No, but I feel bad that I've had it all this time. I mean, they've done so much for me. I know they aren't upset with me over it, but I don't like giving them a reason to be disappointed, you know?"

"No, I get that."

On the walk back Piper asks, "Are you going to work tonight?"

"Yeah."

"Mind if I join you? I'll be quiet. I'm just not excited about being alone when you're down the hall."

"Honestly, I just want to shower, get in bed and get my work caught up before my sleeping pill kicks in," Cam says. He doesn't say anything more and neither does Piper.

They part ways in the lobby with a hug and a kiss on the cheek.

SCOTTSDALE, TUESDAY
Cam

And then all hell breaks loose. The agreement to meet in the lobby at 8:00 a.m. goes sadly wrong as Cam sleeps straight through until almost 10:00. He could sleep another two hours except for the banging in his head. *Oh wait, that's the door.*

A deep voice comes from the other side of the heavy door, "Sir, I need you to please open up or I will have to use a master key."

Cam jumps out of bed and opens the door to find a terrified Piper and an embarrassed hotel manager on the other side. Piper's emotions shift to relief that he is OK after all. The manager mouths a silent apology and Cam waves him off.

"I was so worried about you!" Piper says, walking passed him into the room. "I've been calling your room phone, your cell, and knocking on your door." Cam notices the time on the clock and stands motionless, brain foggy. Not sure what to do first.

Piper takes charge. "Why don't you give me the van keys and I'll pack up while you get ready."

"Thanks Pipe." He grabs his clean clothes and turns on the shower. Piper takes his laptop backpack and goes out to the van.

"I got yogurt and fruit!" she yells over her shoulder.

Odysseus is back on I-10 heading southeast toward Tucson in no time. Cam mentally calculates they are never going to make it to Dallas tonight at this rate. He holds off texting Chelsea about tonight's accommodations.

They've barely finished their breakfasts when Piper says, "Hey you know where I've always wanted to go?"

Cam is afraid to guess and doesn't say anything.

"Cam?"

"Sorry yes. No, where?" Cam asks, already regretting asking.

"Four Corners," Piper says. "You know, where Arizona, New Mexico, and two other states meet up? Let me take a look." Cam glances over at Piper and sees she looks much more focused than he is feeling after a long night of work. She has opted for a knee-length skirt and tank top today and has already slipped her sandals off. *Where does she get all this energy?*

Cam is about to say "no" to the side trip when Piper announces that it'll take them an extra four hours. "Oh well," she says, abandoning her idea.

With the city of Phoenix and the surrounding towns behind them, the landscape returns to desert, cactus, and low shrubs along the interstate. Cam is not ready to admit he would be bored on this trip by himself, but he makes a mental note to look at a map when he has time. *Who knew Arizona had this much desert?*

His thoughts turn to Dallas, and he feels a little conflicted again about that stop when Piper spots the first Saguaro National Park road sign. She grabs his arm, but this time Cam is ready.

"Dallas is like 15 hours away. We have to keep going," Cam says.

"Can we just stop at the sign?" she pleads.

"Piper we've got to keep going."

She looks at the time on her phone screen. "What time is your meeting in Dallas? Are we trying to go 15 hours today?" Piper asks, suddenly concerned with the logistics.

"I thought we could, but I guess not. But I need to get there tomorrow. I'm serious Piper." Cam looks at her again with what he hopes is a stern look on his face. But her enthusiasm is hard to resist.

He caves. "OK. Let's take the first road we can into the park and take a photo. But quick, OK?" If she realizes he's deflecting any discussion about his Texas errand, she doesn't say anything.

Piper bounces in her seat and pulls up Google Maps on her own phone to navigate them. She slides on her sandals and applies more sunscreen to her nose and cheeks. They take a right at Walmart and head toward the park. At the first saguaro they spot they get out and take a quick selfie.

Piper looks around, clearly longing to explore. "I wonder how big the park is," she muses. "It would be awesome to drive around and see what all is here." Cactus, desert, and rather small trees are all they can spot where they've stopped.

"Gotta head back to the highway, OK?" Cam says, sliding an arm around her shoulders.

"We passed an In-n-Out on the way in. Can we make a quick drive-thru?" Piper looks up at him, hopefully.

Great idea, Cam thinks and nods.

Back on the interstate Cam's mind drifts. He is aware he's not talking a lot or being a good road trip partner. Piper is working on her article, doing online research and writing in a notebook. He takes a moment of quiet to try to put a plan in place.

How long will it take them to get to Maine? Where is the best place to encourage Piper to head back to LA? She can't go all the way to Maine. Maybe the Dallas-Ft. Worth Airport before he gets to his meeting spot? He's got 15 hours' driving time to mention this solution, which would probably be for the best.

"Cam?"

"Cam?"

"Oh. What?" Cam snaps his attention back to the vehicle.

"I said I have a playlist updated. Can we stop at a huge convenience store sometime so I can look for an adapter for the stereo? I don't think a small gas station will have anything," Piper asks.

"Oh yeah, can it wait awhile? I'd like to get as close to Dallas as we can tonight. And don't say it," Cam says.

Piper does not mention that he shouldn't have overslept if he's on a schedule. She spends the afternoon reviewing news stories and Cam spends his time avoiding thinking about Maine even though his mind keeps drifting back. *Is there more going on than Grandpa has said? Would his dad be there? Why would he?* He was still in Chicago when Cam last called him.

Three hours and a much-needed restroom stop later, Cam finds Piper back at the van bouncing for joy. She's got something for her phone, but this is more than CD adapter enthusiasm.

"Cam, can we please go to Truth or Consequences? It'll only be one hour out of our way and then we'll get right back onto I-10. I talked to this guy in the gas station, and he said it lives up to all the hype." Piper is bursting with excitement, but her face says she's fairly sure she'll be shot down.

They climb into the Odyssey and resume their interstate drive. "What is Truth or Consequences?" Cam asks suspiciously.

"It's this quirky little town with a space program. It's got hot springs. It's in the middle of all these ghost towns. Come on! I promise I won't ask for any more stops for two days. Please?"

Cam doesn't respond and it occurs to him the main reason he didn't want to include Piper on this trip. He's growing irritated and he will never make it to Maine at this rate. He's going to say something that drives her away, he is sure of it. Time to bring up the airport solution again.

Piper starts to work on the adapter for her phone and the CD player. *Does she just think I'm going to give in?* Another glance at his friend and Cam sighs, deciding it might be fun. He wanted to take a route different than the one he took with his dad all those years ago. Might as well see a couple sights.

"Let me see the map," Cam says, in a voice that is more snappish than he meant.

"What map?" she asks.

"Piper! You said it was one hour out of the way. Let me see where you've got it mapped out."

"Oh, I don't. That's what the guy back there said. Are you angry?"

Cam pulls over at the next rest stop and dramatically changes Waze on his phone.

"This is the last stop. OK?" Cam says, trying to control his temper, giving her a small smile.

"OK fine. I didn't realize you were upset. We won't make it to Dallas today and you never told me when the meeting is. You haven't really seemed in a rush to get to Maine. Sorry."

Waze alerts them to turn off I-10 onto Hwy 26. Piper hasn't started her playlist while there's slight tension in the van, so they continue their ride in silence.

Cam uses the time to calm himself down. They can still make it further tonight so that they only have six or so hours to get to Dallas tomorrow. They can get up early and arrive in plenty of time. He'll work a couple of hours tonight and make it up tomorrow night. It occurs to him that he hasn't looked at his email in hours. Chelsea knows where to call him if it's urgent. Cam attempts a small smile in Piper's direction, but she is staring at the dusty fields and mountains in the distance.

They turn at Hatch onto I-25 and the lights on the dashboard flicker.

"What was that?" Piper asks.

"I don't know. It hasn't done that before. Let's have a look when we get to Truth or Consequences. And maybe some lunch. I could use a break. Half an hour or so?"

"Yes, I think so."

Cam hands her his phone. "Can you check?" he asks her somewhat testily.

Piper frowns at Cam but takes his phone. "Yes, 32 minutes."

They ride in silence and eventually pass an RV park. Otherwise, they are alone on a long, desert highway. And then the interior lights go out. Cam pulls over to the side of the deserted road as the van dies. He tries cranking it, but nothing happens.

Cam groans. "Can you pull the paperwork out of the glove box?" Piper moves the package of face masks that she bought at Whole Foods and pulls out the stack of manuals and papers. He finds the number for the car service and calls. "They say they'll send someone out, but it'll be a little while." He gets out and walks to the back of the van, putting space between them.

It doesn't take long for Piper to join him, her arms crossed across her chest, and her face frowning.

"I'm sorry. I feel like this is all my fault. I feel like you don't want me here and I feel like I'm not being the help to you that I thought I could be. I don't understand why you're upset, and I don't know what I can do to help."

Cam looks taken aback and Piper realizes tears have escaped. She wipes them away.

"Come here," he says and hugs her. "This isn't vacation to me. My granny isn't doing well. I'd like to get the van to my grandpa in one piece. I've got work to do. You're wanting to go sightseeing and I get that. Sorry I snapped. I probably will again. I was probably better off doing this trip alone."

Piper kicks the rocks under her feet, disappointed. Cam didn't reassure her or tell her that he is glad she's here. Piper returns to the front seat, pulls out two waters and hands one to Cam, who wonders where they came from. "I got them for us at that last service station," she says, reading his mind again.

They wait in silence for the car service. Cam resists checking his email to avoid additional stress. He would likely take it out on Piper again. He turns his face to the sunshine and calls Chelsea to check in.

"What do you say to a couple of steaks and a bottle of wine?" Chelsea answers.

"You could start by saying hello," Cam responds, grateful for the banter.

"Where are you?" Chelsea asks.

"Truth or Consequences," Cam sighs.

"Truth!" Chelsea exclaims.

"Nope, that's where we are. Or somewhere near it. Van trouble, car service on their way."

"No! You're still in New Mexico? This is going to be a loooong trip," Cam hears Chelsea typing through the phone line.

"Did you get the recommendations I sent you late last night before I crashed?" Cam asks.

"Yea, I gave them to Alison who wanted to know how you were doing. So how are ya' kid?"

Cam walks away. "About ready to send her back. Is there an international airport in Truth or Consequences?"

Chelsea laughs, "Are you mad at her? Really?"

"OK, maybe not. I'm annoyed the van died in the middle of nowhere. And I'm worried about my grandpa," Cam concedes.

"Piper's pretty freaking great and adores you. Are you OK though? You're frightening me a little."

Cam pauses for a long beat. "If my answer frightens you then stop asking scary questions."

"*Pulp Fiction*. Nice. Gotta run. Good luck." And with that Chelsea is gone.

Piper walks over to Cam. "Everything all right at work?"

"Yeah, I've just got a lot to get to, hopefully tonight. Hey, I'm going to make another quick call." He steps away again to call his contact in Dallas. Then he joins Piper leaning against the front of the Honda.

"Sorry," he nudges his friend's shoulder. "I shouldn't take my stress out on you."

Piper nods and says, "I bet your grandparents really miss you." Cam agrees, recalling the time Piper met his Grandpa Ben. He had not been out to LA since that long weekend more than two years ago. *I really should have been back home before now.*

That weekend Cam declined an offer to go to the Hollywood Bowl with Piper and her friends because his grandpa was going to be in town. Since Cam rarely talked about his family, Piper seemed especially excited for him.

"What are you going to do while he's in town?" she'd asked him.

"I don't know. Maybe take him to the beach. Show him the Hollywood sign. I'll see what he wants to do. He's been here before, but we mostly hung around the campus."

"Any chance I can meet him while he's in town?"

"You want to meet my grandpa? Ok yeah, I guess so."

"Great! How about lunch Saturday? And I'll send you some places you should definitely take him to while he's here. This is so great, Cam!"

In the end, they met up for lunch and Grandpa excitedly told her about all the sightseeing they had done. Cam remembers squeezing Piper's hand thank you because her suggestions had made for a great experience for his grandfather. Her gentle smile and the hopeful look in her eyes made Cam feel uneasy at the time.

An hour later a tow truck pulls up and takes the van, Cam, and Piper to Truth or Consequences. The driver asks where they want the vehicle taken and Piper names the mechanic.

Cam looks at her with mild amusement. "What?" she asks. "I called ahead and let them know we were coming."

Cam looks out the window and quietly says, "Thanks." Piper nods.

The mechanic takes Cam's information and says he'll call when there's an update. They leave their luggage but take their laptop bags to get some lunch. They eat salads at a small cafe and then walk around the town. Piper takes tons of photos. She asks a docent in a tiny museum about the ghost towns nearby. The older woman answers Piper's unending questions and Cam takes a moment to step outside and enjoy the peace and quiet. He is grateful that Piper has someone else to connect with for a few moments.

He checks his email and it's not as bad as he feared. He reassures two agents that their clients are still being considered for roles. And then he sees an email from his boss, Alison James. Nothing inside. Just a memo title "Is it OK or worse than you feared?"

He types back, "Guess you heard I have a guest," and presses send.

Piper comes out of the museum and takes Cam's arm as they walk toward the mechanic. "Thank you for bringing me here. Are you still upset with me?"

Cam resists the instinct to pull his arm away. "Could this place be cursed? I mean, you said ghost towns, right? I'm not mad. I'm just anxious to get to Maine."

The mechanic calls to let them know that he has sent someone to Las Cruces to get a new alternator. "It'll be late tonight before you're ready to go."

Cam's shoulders slump and he sighs deeply. To Piper he says, "Let's just spend the night here. It'll give us a chance to get work done." They walk to the library to get on Wi-Fi.

Piper submits her article and takes off for a tour of the hot springs. "I'm guessing you don't want to go?" she asks hopefully.

"No, I want to finish up these recommendations for Chelsea. I'll get us a hotel while you're gone. Don't worry about me. Have fun."

Cam retrieves their luggage from the van and walks to the small motel that the museum guide suggested. He pays for two rooms, leaving Piper's key and luggage at the front desk. He texts her to let her know where they're staying. He refreshes his email again. No response from the boss. Cam changes and heads out for a run. When he is back and showered, Piper knocks on his door. "I'm going to get some dinner. Do you want to come too?"

Cam yells, "Yeah, give me a second," and checks his email once more. They walk across the street to a Tex-Mex place. Piper does not bring up the two rooms again over plates of chilaquiles and heaps of guacamole.

"How were the hot springs?" Cam asks, feeling his anger diffused. Probably from the run. Or the margarita.

"Hot," Piper replies. "But they were cool to see. Thanks for bringing me here. "

"Hey, I know I've been stressed and taking it out on you. I'll try to do better."

"Is it because of your grandmother? Is it work? Is it me?" Piper asks, clearly worried about her friend. But also, somewhat relieved to see Cam back to normal.

"No, not you. I guess I thought we'd be closer to Maine by now. I admit I didn't do a lot of research, but I thought this would be a quicker trip. And I am not convinced you really want to sign up for the entire ordeal. Seriously, it's a lot to ask."

"You didn't ask. I offered. And I'm committed to the entire ordeal." Cam smiles warily and gets the check.

Back at the hotel Piper mentions, "The mechanic is open at 7:00. Want to meet in the lobby then and we can go straight there?"

"Yeah, we've got a long drive ahead of us tomorrow." Piper hugs him and says goodnight.

Cam buys a beer in the hotel lobby and returns to his room. With *Seinfeld* on in the background, he settles in to take care of the rest of his outstanding work. *It's going to be another long night. And a tricky day tomorrow.*

TRUTH OR CONSEQUENCES, WEDNESDAY

Cam

By 7:00 a.m. Cam and Piper have checked out of the motel and picked up Odysseus with his new alternator. Piper sneakily pays the mechanic while Cam loads their bags. *Did she arrange this with him yesterday?* Their first stop is a general store for fuel and snacks and then they catch I-25, heading north again.

Cam changed from jeans to shorts given how hot the weather has been the last two days. He notices he's wearing the shirt that Piper has told him brings out the green in his eyes. If any other woman had told him that he would chalk it up to flirting. With Piper though, it has always felt somewhat different. And there is no reasonable response to a statement like that. *Thanks? Great? That's why I'm wearing it?* In the end Cam went with something like "Uh yeah".

"Can we skip lunch today?" he asks. "It's 11 hours to Dallas and we can eat dinner and spend the night there."

"Yes, definitely," Piper says, and Cam is relieved to see she too is back to normal after the tension yesterday.

Half an hour, an orange and a bag of almonds later, Piper loads up her playlist.

"All songs about California, Arizona, or New Mexico. I think you're going to love it!" she exclaims with what Cam is starting to think of as her National Parks-level enthusiasm.

As the Eagles sing about Winslow, Arizona Cam wonders if he should bring up the airport again. She just reassured him last night that she was up for the entire trip, but Cam knows he's not going to be able to avoid getting stressed and taking it out on Piper again. *This might get worse after Dallas.* He decides now's not the right time and changes the subject to anything but their next stop.

"So, how is work going?" Cam asks, rather nonchalantly.

"It's good. But if I'm being honest, I'm somewhat over it."

Cam is surprised. "Really? I thought you liked the 'Tens' list and the LA articles they've given you. You seem like the perfect fit for it."

"Well, thanks, I guess. I mean, yes, I'm from LA and I already know some of the people they're asking me to cover or interview. And I like the balance of those articles with 'Today's Ten' since that's much meatier. And I know my article is popular, and they're happy. Maybe I'm just not being grateful enough." Piper centers herself and takes in a long inhale and releases a longer exhale. "I guess I want to write more in-depth articles instead of promoting the players in town, you know?"

Cam nods and Piper continues. "The paper benefits from my LA connections and that's worked well for both of us. I'd like to try other things though. I don't want to still be doing the same kind of work for *The Herald* in two years." She adds in a low voice, "Actually I'd maybe like to write a book."

"You'd be good at that," Cam says. "What kind of book?"

"I don't really know. Maybe romance?"

Cam laughs, "Yeah, you'd be good at that."

"Don't mock me, Cam. I don't want to be the butt of your jokes," Piper says in a teasing voice. But is there a little hurt underneath?

"What? You're not."

"Maybe I am when you talk to Chelsea?" Piper nudges.

"You're not," Cam reassures her.

Seemingly satisfied, Piper sings along with the Beach Boys while reading articles on her phone. Cam knows she tends to go down serious rabbit holes when she's considering a "Today's Ten" topic to include in the next day's article. They're informative but also have a clear viewpoint. She needs to understand the details of any topic before she can choose an angle for her ten brief stories that people across the country read each day.

Cam also knows that she has had mixed feelings about her work at *The Herald*. Piper confided in Cam that her dad tells everyone she's a journalist, which makes her feel almost fraudulent. Her mom, on the other hand, talks about Piper's marriage prospects instead of her ambitions. It seems like her mom wants her to focus on settling down and not so much on her work. Like she did. Which might be more of a deterrent than a strong case.

Piper looks up from her phone and notebook. "Wow, it's really changed in the last couple of hours, hasn't it? More green and less desert." Cam notices the sun is still bright overhead in the cloudless sky.

"Hey, I'm going to make a call, OK?" Piper says in what Cam thinks of as her fix-it tone.

"Yeah sure."

"Hi. No, no, I'm happy to...OK text me the three looks... I don't think you should go dressy... A business suit might be better. It's your deal. Wear what makes you feel powerful and feminine, not just pretty. You deserve to be the most stunning one there. You own that room...Can't wait to see what you choose... Kisses."

Piper hangs up. "That's Maddie. She's got a promotional event tomorrow afternoon and the stylist the company sent her has put her in teal. Teal!"

Cam nods and his thoughts return to Dallas. *Is now a good time to give her a heads up?* Then he sees it - the first sign for Roswell - and he quickly glances at Piper. She's chewing her thumbnail and studying her phone.

"Everything OK?" he asks her.

"Yes, Simon's date did not go well last night. This is their fifth and the last two were lackluster at best. Calvin suggested he end it on the next date. I said to call the guy now. Thoughts?"

Cam is flustered. "I don't know. I don't know Simon. Who is he?"

Piper goes to the next text. "From George's gallery. You know - tall, dark, handsome?"

Cam looks confused, "No."

"Cam I've introduced you twice. He's from Washington State and has great hair."

Cam just shrugs. Piper huffs and goes through her phone.

"Here," Piper says and shoves the photo in his face.

"Oh, got it," Cam says, still not actually remembering Simon.

Piper looks slightly exasperated with him. "Sometimes I feel like you don't want to meet people. Is that true? Or maybe you don't like the people I'm introducing you to?"

"I meet people all the time at work," Cam counters.

"Yeah, I guess. I introduce you to friends every time we're out and I feel like you just instantly forget them."

"I mean, do you really want to talk about this?"

"About what? Friends?" Piper looks at him confused.

"I have never had a big social circle. I don't have a lot of lifelong people in my life except my grandparents. Unlike you. I don't even keep up with high school friends. And they don't seem interested in staying connected with me. I mean, that sense of belonging is nice, but I guess I'm not someone people want to be friends with. I'm content with acquaintances, I guess."

"But I'm in your circle, right?" Piper asks quietly.

"You are." She smiles and then Cam thinks *Oh crap*. Because Piper looks up from her phone at the most inopportune time. A road sign.

"Cam! Roswell!"

"We don't have time. We're behind already and I've got to get to Dallas tonight," Cam hears himself almost whining.

"Can we just drive through? It's right on the highway," Piper again thrusts her phone into Cam's face again to show him the highway on Google Maps.

"Piper, quit I'm driving," he laughs. "How far off the highway is it really?"

"It's literally right on this highway. I'll look at TripAdvisor and we'll drive by whatever we can see. OK?" Piper pleads. She's starting to bounce in her seat, albeit somewhat tentatively. Cam wants the full bounce.

"OK," he says, "but just for a minute." He's rewarded with an extra high squeal.

But as they travel through the town, Piper is clearly disappointed. "This is not what I was expecting." She has a Roswell website pulled up on her phone as well. "This is a huge city. Not LA huge but really big. I thought it was some little ghost town type place with alien signs pointing you to Area 51."

Cam isn't sure what he was expecting to see but he stays the course on Hwy 380.

"No wait," Piper says, looking back at her phone. "Let me look up Area 51 instead. Oh, crap it's near Corona not Roswell. Wait. Aren't Roswell and Area 51 like the same?"

"We passed a turn off to Corona a while ago," Cam says. "And wasn't the Roswell Incident in like the 1930s or 1940s?"

Piper, in bulldog mode, continues researching possible sites before they exit the city. Cam keeps going, heading toward Lubbock and Abilene. He knows she's disappointed, but he's determined not to circle back to some roadside attraction. He glances at Waze on his phone. They've still got seven or eight hours to go. Just then, he sees a green alien painted on the side of a building and pulls in. "Let's take a quick photo."

Piper jumps out of the van, clearly excited, and Cam wraps his arm around her. She melts into Cam's side. The selfie captures their faces - Piper all lit up and Cam realizing in that split second that he's potentially giving her the wrong impression again. Or is he? He checks his GPS and announces they can still make it to Dallas by 7:30 p.m. if they hurry.

The van crosses into Texas and they stop for a stretch, bio break, and fuel. *God, we're never going to make it to Maine*, Cam thinks. Piper returns with water bottles, protein bars, and cashews.

"Great, more nuts," Cam welcomes her back. Piper smirks and gets in. "Give me a second. I need to make a call." He walks to the back of the van for a minute then returns for one last stretch and back to Hwy 380. "Protein bar, please."

Fellow Travelers – Odysseus Returns to Maine

Playlist available on Spotify and Apple Music

"(I Left My Heart) In San Francisco" by Tony Bennett
    "Back to California" by Carole King
    "Back to California" by The Wallflowers
    "Beverly Hills" by Weezer
    "California" by Lorde
    "California" by Phantom Planet
    "California" by Tim McGraw, Big & Rich
    "California" by Tyler Lyle
    "California (There is No End to Love)" by U2
    "California Blue" by Roy Orbison
    "California Country Boy" by Cracker
    "California Dreamin'" by The Mamas & The Papas
    "California Girls" by The Beach Boys
    "California Gurls" by Katy Perry, Snoop Dogg
    "California Kids" by Weezer
    "California Love" by 2Pac, Roger, Dr. Dre
    "California Soul" by Marlena Shaw
    "California Stars" by Bill Bragg, Wilco
    "California Sun" by Ramones
    "California Sun" by The Rivieras
    "California Sunrise" by Neil W Young
    "California Waiting" by Kings of Leon
    "Dani California" by Red Hot Chili Peppers
    "(Get Your Kicks On) Route 66" by Nat King Cole
    "Going Back to Cali" by LL Cool J

"Going to California" by Led Zeppelin

"Hollywood" by Daniel Powter

"Hollywood Nights" by Bob Seger

"Hotel California" by The Eagles

"I Love L.A." by Randy Newman

"I Remember California" by R.E.M.

"It Never Rains in Southern California" by Albert Hammond

"It's a Longer Road to California" by The Wind and the Wave

"L.A. Blues" by Tom T. Hall

"L.A. Woman" by The Doors

"La La Land" by Demi Lovato

"Los Angeles, I'm Yours" by The Decemberists

"Los Angeles is Burning" by Bad Religion

"Me and Bobby McGee" by Janis Joplin

"Meet Me in California" by Plain White Ts

"Paradise City" by Guns N' Roses

"Queen of California" by John Mayer

"San Francisco" by Scott McKenzie

"Southern California Purples" by Chicago

"Straight Outta Compton" by N.W.A.

"Streets of Bakersfield" by Buck Owens feat. Dwight Yoakam

"Surf City" by Jan & Dean

"Surfin' U.S.A." by The Beach Boys

"Sweet Life" by Frank Ocean

"The Fresh Prince of Bel-Air" by DJ Jazzy Jeff & The Fresh Prince

Theme from "Beverly Hills 90210" by John Davis

"When You Get to California" by Hoodoo Gurus

"You" by R.E.M.

WEST TEXAS, WEDNESDAY
Cam

Piper and Cam pass the time singing along to any songs they know on the playlist. At Cam's request, Piper replays the collection of state-themed tunes, but this time skips anything released prior to 1970. And she plays Led Zeppelin and Guns n' Roses on repeat.

Five hours into their day Cam looks over at Piper. He's sure she's researching Texas music since she got to a stopping point with her work an hour ago. She is studiously working on her phone. He smiles to himself when Marty Robbins starts singing about West Texas. He looks at her and she smiles back at him. *This is it. Time to bring up Dallas. But it's 5 1/2 hours to go. That could be a long, uncomfortable silence.*

"Can I get in the back seat and close my eyes for a bit?" Piper asks. "I didn't sleep well last night," she says, and Cam notices she looks away. "After a nap I'd like to help you drive if you'll ever let me."

"Yeah sure," Cam responds, relieved for the reprieve. "Let me find a rest stop."

"No need." Piper climbs over the center console, lays down with her jacket as a pillow and straps in the best she can. "Be careful. Precious cargo back here."

"Got it," Cam tells her. He turns the music down and is happy for time to enjoy this part of the country and not have to deliver imminent news. The desert and distant mountains have been replaced by flat prairie as far as Cam can see. There are a few towns off the highway in the distance and some trees lining the road, but otherwise it's a quiet ride without much civilization to speak of. And still, the bluest skies.

Two hours later Piper asks if they can stop, and Cam realizes he's been thinking about Maine almost the entire time she was resting. Not about work and not about any of the women he's recently gone out with. Family. *What help will Grandpa need? Will I make it in time to spend some lucid days with Granny? Will I see Dad?* Cam thought about the move with his dad across the country a few years ago. *Has it been four or five years? Or more than that?*

After gassing up and taking a quick break, Piper checks out Google Maps. "When did we turn onto I-20?"

"I don't remember," Cam replies. "Maybe back around Sweetwater?"

Piper sounds rested and ready to support Cam. "Three hours to go. Where are we spending the night? Do you want me to find a spot on this side of Dallas?"

"No, we're heading to Richardson tonight. Chelsea may have set up a hotel, I'll call her later to see," Cam lies through his teeth.

"So how is Chelsea? I haven't seen her in probably a year. Is she seeing anyone?" Piper asks, somewhat out of the blue, Cam thinks.

"I don't know," Cam answers.

"What about Alison?"

"No idea. Why? Ready to set them up?"

"Not exactly," Piper says. "Just wondering."

The playlist resumes and Piper finishes her "Today's Ten" article. After she submits it, she calls her editor and puts the call on Speaker. Alex has the same feedback he usually has, but Piper chooses not to engage in today's debate. Her editor reminds her of a time when Piper regularly included a sports or entertainment item in her column of ten top stories. But recently it's been mostly global and domestic news which, sadly, adds up to doom and gloom.

"The *world* is more doom and gloom now. I'll include something else when it's as important," she has told him time and time again. Alex sets the disagreement aside as well and mentions that his new assistant did not work out. Piper turns off Speaker.

"Oh, that's too bad. I liked him...Did you work with Lisa on the job description? Why did Chris not work out? Maybe you need to include the time expectations in your position posting... They have to understand that print is not like a normal office job. There are perks to that, but downsides too. Yes, thank you... It's going well. I will. Call if you need anything. OK...Bye."

Cam looks over at Piper. "Does everyone in LA go to you for advice? Can you address every issue? Are you Superwoman?"

"Yes, that's me. These issues are not rocket science, Cam. People want to be validated for their own choices. Or they haven't thought it through, so they call me for a quick fix," Piper sighs.

Cam reminds her, as he often has in the past, "You don't have to fix everyone's problems you know."

Piper groans then smiles sweetly. "I actually don't think it's a problem but thanks for your concern. Now what's going on with you? It looks like you need to say something."

Cam hesitates and then starts. "OK, just hear me out, OK? I appreciate your coming with me on this trip, but it occurred to me that this is going to take several more days. I think what makes the most sense since I need to focus on work and family right now, is I take you to DFW for an evening flight back to LAX. I could arrange a car to pick you up at the airport when you land. You've been a big help, but I think it makes sense."

Piper studies the playlist on her phone and says, "Cam that makes no sense. If I've been a help, why don't you need me anymore? Am I keeping you from getting to your work? Do you want me to drive? I'm happy to. You just seem to want to do it all. How can I be more help?"

Cam tries another tack. "It's not that. I just don't know that you realized how much of a commitment this would be, especially with a work meeting in Nashville on Friday. This isn't straight through."

"And Dallas," Piper reminds him. "Do you have any other days that you have meetings?"

Cam sighs, "You're changing the subject. Let me get you back to your peeps in LA."

"Cam, I wanted to get the hell out of LA for a while. And I wanted to spend time with you."

"But we see each other a lot," Cam reminds her.

Piper shakes her head, "You know what I mean."

"Look, I've got a lot on my mind. I don't think my grandpa is thinking straight. When I called him back Sunday he seemed off. My head's just not in the right place for entertaining I guess," Cam says quietly.

"I know you're worried about your grandparents. And I know you want to take care of them. It's one of the reasons I'm surprised you're driving instead of flying there. They'll be so excited to see you. Will you get to see any other family while you're in Maine?"

"I don't really have a lot of other family."

"What about your dad? It just occurred to me – did you think of asking him to go on this trip with you? Didn't he drive with you last time?"

"Yeah, we had a great trip. No, I didn't think to ask him. I don't think he could. He's busy with work. I haven't seen him in a long time."

"Well, his loss."

"My grandfather has really had a lot to handle these last few years, and I just want to be there for him. I remember one time, when I was maybe in high school, he said he assumed he'd be the first to go and he wanted me to check in on my grandmother a lot. I hadn't thought of that in years. They are really close. This has got to be hard on him."

Piper reaches for his hand and turns in her seat. "Cam, I chose to do this trip, and unless you don't want me here, then I'm willing to see it all the way through to Maine. Maybe you can take me to the nearest airport after I see your grandparents."

Cam sighs to himself. "OK but if you change your mind, it won't hurt my feelings. I will make sure you get home safely."

Piper pats his leg. "You worry a lot. Hey, do you remember Martin from hiking a few months ago?"

"Yes, I think so," Cam says somewhat warily.

"He'd love to hike more, and I gave him your number," Piper informs him enthusiastically, while reading another article on her phone.

"I don't need you setting up play dates for me," Cam says in a voice he hopes sounds teasing and not annoyed.

Piper doesn't respond directly. "Do you want to stop to get something to eat in a little while and check on hotel reservations with Chelsea?

"It's OK. I'll call her later. Let's get to Richardson before we eat," Cam says, biting on his lower lip.

Cam feels her looking at him, and he knows the stress is showing again.

Piper pulls out the book she borrowed from Jeremiah Franks and starts reading. *She's clearly disappointed that I'm not jumping at a chance to hang with Martin the hiker.* Cam turns the music up just a notch as they sail past Abilene, making good time on I-20.

"I think before we get to the next turn-off, I want to make a quick stop," Cam announces. They head to the restrooms and Cam sends off a text walking back to the Odyssey.

Be there in an hour.

"Want me to navigate in Dallas?" Piper offers. "Where are we going?"

"Let's go to dinner. I know a good spot."

"It looks like I-30 starts in Ft. Worth. We need to take that and then get on 820 toward Plano," Piper says. "We've got an hour. So, I didn't really hear but what projects are you working on?"

"Um, we've got three movies - I'm casting supporting characters for those."

"Well, yeah, I think you mentioned that already. Just wondering what all is going on with your work. You haven't really talked about it much on this trip, and you normally do," Piper adds.

"Yeah, that's about it. Sorry, I guess I'm focused on this rush hour traffic."

They pass a sign for the Dallas-Ft. Worth International Airport. Before Cam can say anything, Piper playfully pushes his arm and says, "I'm on this odyssey with you."

Cam continues following GPS while Piper uses the sunshade mirror to brush her hair and apply lip gloss. "What kind of restaurant is it?" she asks.

"BBQ. Maybe you want to look up the menu. They're supposed to have great sides and desserts."

Piper pulls up the Ten50 website and Cam tries to keep cool. Second guessing isn't going do him any good now. But he probably should have warned her.

The Odyssey pulls into the busy parking lot. There are people walking to and from the entrance. One tall guy in jeans and a button-down shirt slings a bag onto his shoulder and waves goodbye to an Uber driver. Piper spots him two seconds before Cam does. She blows out a long breath.

"Coward," she says between gritted teeth.

"Yeah. I know," Cam responds somewhat sheepishly.

Fellow Travelers – Odysseus Returns to Maine

"Alone in Arizona" by Exene Cervenka

"Arizona Skies" by Los Lobos

"Arizona" by Josh Kerr

"Arizona" by Kings of Leon

"Arizona" by Mark Lindsay

"Arizona" by Scorpions

"Big Iron" by Marty Robbins

"By the Time I Get to Arizona" by Public Enemy

"By the Time I Get to Phoenix" by Glen Campbell

"Comin' to Your City" by Big & Rich

"Furnace Fan" by Robert Earl Keen

"Get Back" by The Beatles

"God Love Her" by Toby Keith

"Havalina" by Pixies

"Hey Willie" by Waylon Jennings

"If you Don't, Don't" by Jimmy Eat World

"June on the West Coast" by Bright Eyes

"Leaving Winslow" by Jackson Browne

"King of Arizona" by Clutch

"Ocean Front Property" by George Strait

"One Way Ticket" by Billy Currington

"Phoenix" by Cady Groves

"Scottsdale" by Chronic Future

"Send Me Down to Tucson" by Mel Tillis

"She Is His Only Need" by Wynonna

"Summer Running" by Billy Idol

"Surprise, AZ" by Richard Buckner

"Take It Easy" by The Eagles

"The Ballad of Boot Hill" by Johnny Cash
"The Painted Desert" by 10,000 Maniacs
"There is No Arizona" by Jamie O'Neal
"This Town" by Reubens Accomplice
"Thumbelina" by Pretenders
"Your Arizona Room" by Everclear
"Yuma, AZ" by Damien Jurado
"Albuquerque" by Phish
"Las Cruces" by Martha Scanlan
"Lights of Albuquerque" by Billy Mize
"New Mexico Kind of Thing" by Billy Dawson
"New Mexico's No Breeze" by Iron & Wine
"Point Me in the Direction of Albuquerque" by The Partridge Family
"Santa-Fe" by Bob Dylan, The Band
"Sunset, Santa Fe" by Dave Barnes
"Taos, New Mexico" by Waylon Jennings
"Worse Comes to Worst" by Billy Joel

"Now I say by hook or crook this peril too shall be something that we remember."

~ Odysseus to his men in Homer's *The Odyssey*

RICHARDSON, WEDNESDAY
Cam

Is it still Wednesday? Cam thinks to himself. *Longest fucking day.*

They pull into a spot not too far from the restaurant entrance and the man with the bag walks toward the Odyssey and abruptly stops.

Piper seethes, "So he didn't know either?"

Cam opts for an overly cheerful voice and steps out of the van. "Hey man, good to see you." The two guys give a back-slapping hug, and the man looks at Cam, and raises his brows.

"Piper?" he says.

"Hi, Theo. Good to see you," Piper responds, getting out of the van.

"Didn't realize you were going to be here."

"Same," Piper says. "I see you have a bag."

"Yes, assuming you've got one too," Theo says, finally shifting his eye contact to her.

"I do," Piper responds.

They both look at Cam who says, "I've heard good things about this place." He starts to walk toward the restaurant and then remembers Theo's things. "Want to put your bag back here?"

Theo follows Cam and gives him a pointed look which Cam ignores. The three walk inside and are seated toward the back of the very full restaurant. Cam immediately picks up a menu and begins to review.

"Really?" Piper says. "You're just going to order?"

Cam loudly greets the server and realizes he's overcompensating. He takes it down a notch and orders water for the table. He asks what beers are on tap and selects a local microbrew. Theo and Piper order drinks and the silence resumes.

"So, Theo, what's good here?" Cam asks, avoiding his friends' eyes and questions.

"Everything," Theo says. "I've only eaten here twice, but you can't go wrong."

Piper hasn't touched her menu, waiting out Cam's silence. The server returns before any answers are given. She orders pulled pork with greens and okra and takes a delicate sip of her tea. No one misses the face she makes, but quickly tries to hide, when she tastes the sweetness of the drink.

Cam sighs and decides to address the awkwardness. "OK. OK. I let Theo know about my grandma and he asked if he could tag along. We decided to meet up here. When I talked to him, I didn't know you were planning to come, Piper."

"And for the last four days? Any idea why you didn't think to bring it up?" Piper asks, pushing her tea aside.

"To either of us?" Theo asks.

"I didn't think it'd be a problem," Cam smiles brightly.

"Got it," Theo smirks.

The server brings the food, and everyone digs in. Cam is suddenly very chatty, talking about basically anything he can think of to break the tension. Theo is over the surprise and the guys enjoy catching up while Piper eats, mostly in silence.

Cam looks over at Piper and sighs. "I know you don't like him. I tried to get you to fly home before we got here. Sorry."

Piper blushes and tries to cover. "I like Theo. Not sure what you mean." She sips her tea again, attempting not to make a face this time.

"The last time he came to LA it's all I heard about. 'Piper is annoying' and 'Theo is a ladies' man,'" Cam finishes with air quotes. "That's Piper's phrase, not mine," he says to Theo.

Theo and Piper silently agree to drop the whole thing.

"So why Dallas if you've been working in Austin this past year?" Piper asks the table, but clearly the question is directed at Theo.

"Because I'm done in Austin and it's out of the way. We thought Dallas made the most sense," Theo tells her. "There are hotels near here unless you're wanting to get out of the area before stopping for the night?" he asks Cam.

"No, I need to get some work done and I've had enough driving for one day," Cam says. He gets the check and neither of them protests. Cam knows he owes them. They head back to the van and Theo moves to the passenger side.

"Old Odysseus. How's he running?" Theo asks, sliding the door open.

"Except for a $600 alternator replacement in New Mexico, great."

Piper asks, "Theo you sure you don't want the front seat?"

"It's all yours," he responds.

They climb in, head north, stopping at the first decent hotel they find.

"So, do we need two rooms?" Theo asks.

"I'm not sharing with you," Piper says sweetly.

Theo looks at her, trying not to roll his eyes. "No, I wasn't sure if you two had been sharing a room or what the situation was." Everyone is silent. "You really haven't talked logistics, have you?"

Cam fills him in, "We've had separate rooms. I need some time to work each night since I'm going to be gone for a while. Welcome to share a room with me Theo if you want."

Piper looks at Cam in surprise. Theo notices and says, "No, let's just get three rooms and get a good night's sleep."

Checked in they say they make a plan for tomorrow and walk to the elevator.

Theo stands across from Piper who is studying the numbers as they go up, up, up. "So, Piper, are you going all the way to Maine?"

"I am. And you?"

"Uh yeah, that was the plan," Theo tells her.

Cam jumps in, "Great. See you at 8:00 if that's OK. I've got three or four hours of work tonight."

Piper gives him a small smile and Theo responds.

"See you at 8:00."

Fellow Travelers – Odysseus Returns to Maine

"A State of Texas" by Old 97s
  "All My Ex's Live in Texas" by George Strait
  "Amarillo by Morning" by George Strait
  "Austin" by Blake Shelton
  "Beautiful Texas" by Willie Nelson
  "Blue Eyes Crying in the Rain" by Willie Nelson
  "Cowboy Take Me Away" by The Chicks
  "Dallas" by Jimmie Dale Gilmore
  "Deep In the Heart of Texas" by Gene Autry
  "Does Fort Worth Ever Cross Your Mind" by George Strait
  "El Paso City" by Marty Robbins
  "El Paso" by Marty Robbins
  "Galveston" by Glen Campbell
  "Girls From Texas" by Pat Green, Lyle Lovett
  "God Blessed Texas" by Little Texas
  "Gone to Texas" by Terry Allen
  "Houston" by R.E.M.
  "If You're Gonna Play in Texas" by Alabama
  "Lone Star State of Mind" by Don Williams
  "Lubbock or Leave It" by The Chicks
  "Luckenbach, Texas" by Waylon Jennings, Willie Nelson
  "Miles and Miles of Texas" by Asleep at the Wheel
  "My Blue Heaven" by Gene Austin
  "My Texas" by Josh Abbott Band, Pat Green
  "Red River Valley" by Marty Robbins
  "Rolling Stone From Texas" by Don Walser
  "San Antonio Rose" by Patsy Cline
  "Screw You, We're From Texas" by Ray Wylie Hubbard

"Streets of Laredo" by Marty Robbins

"Texarkana" by R.E.M.

"Texas (When I Die)" by Tanya Tucker

"Texas Flood" by Stevie Ray Vaughn

"Texas Was You" by Jason Aldean

"Texas" by Charlie Daniels

"That's Right (You're Not From Texas)" by Lyle Lovett

"The Bluest Eyes in Texas" by Restless Heart

"The Mighty Rio Grande" by This Will Destroy You

"The Yellow Rose of Texas" by Gene Autry

"Waltz Across Texas" by Ernest Tubb

"West Texas Waltz" by Joe Ely

"Wheels of Laredo" by The Highwomen

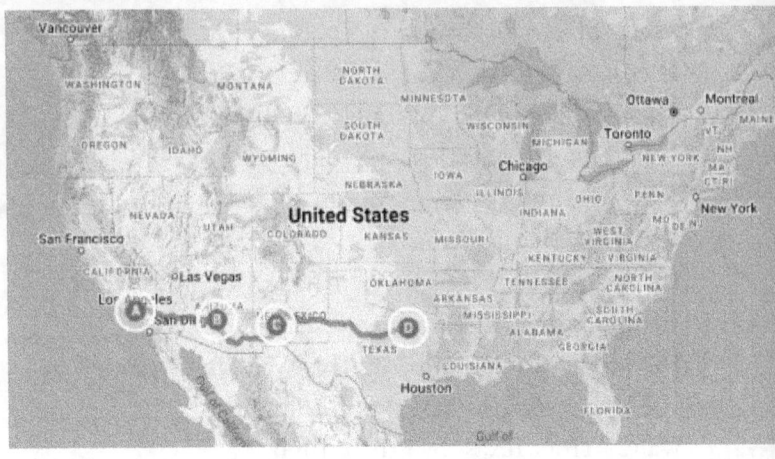

RICHARDSON, THURSDAY
Theo

At 7:30 Theo and Piper run into each other at the breakfast buffet.

"Hello," Piper says, blowing on her coffee. "Mind if I sit?"

"Yeah sure," Theo says pushing out her chair with his foot. Theo breaks the silence after they sip coffee for a couple of minutes. "So how are you, Piper?"

"I'm great thanks! I'm a little surprised at our friend right now but you know, he's not one to divulge information unless he has to," Piper smiles a bit too brightly, not hiding her annoyance well. *Or is it nerves?*

"Yeah, I guess," Theo responds, watching her.

"I'm not really mad at him," she clarifies. "So why did you want to go on this trip? Surely you have work that needs your attention."

Theo takes his time. "Not right now. I finished my latest contract which was with the South by Southwest film festival, and I haven't accepted a new gig yet. I thought I'd support our friend in his hour of need. Plus, I love a good road trip."

Piper nods, "Well maybe we can discuss how this is going to work."

"No need Piper. I'm not going to change a thing. I'm just along for the ride."

"How is that helping Cam?" Piper asks.

Theo shakes his head. "You know what I mean. I'm not going to change anything you've got going on."

"Great," Piper says. The pause stretches out for longer than she is clearly comfortable with. "So, aren't the women of Austin going to miss you when you're gone?"

Theo is thrown by the question but recovers quickly. "Uh, I haven't been seeing anyone seriously. I knew I'd only be there a few months."

"That hasn't stopped you before. I remember a couple of times when you'd come to LA for only a weekend and yet still were able to break a few hearts," Piper winces at the tone in her voice.

"Oh, you do?"

"Yes, word travels fast in LA."

"Strange. I don't hear much about your love life when I'm there. I assume you've got one. Who are *you* seeing these days?"

Piper shoots him an exasperated look just as Cam walks off the elevator and sees the two of them sitting together. Theo knows he looks relaxed, leaning back in his chair, sipping a coffee. But Piper is wound tighter than last night, looking like she is trying to formulate the perfect response. Theo can't help but smile.

Cam walks up to them. "Hey. Let me get something to drink and we can go. I'd like to make it to Nashville if possible - meeting tomorrow afternoon."

"Who wants the first shift?" Theo asks. Piper doesn't respond.

Cam says, "I will," and they load the van to leave the Dallas area. Piper returns to the front seat and Theo gets in the back. She watches him stretching out his long legs and turns back to look out the window.

"How do you usually split up the drive time?" Theo asks. Piper glances over to Cam but doesn't answer.

"We'll figure it out," Cam says, somewhat evasively.

"I assume you're OK if I play some music Theo?"

"Yea, of course," Theo answers her, shaking his head at her formal tone.

"Can we hold off for a little while?" Cam asks. "This traffic is brutal, and I want to get back on the interstate."

"Sure," Piper tells him, puts on her sunglasses and picks up her phone. From the back seat Theo watches her scouring news sites, jotting down notes in a notebook.

Bored, Theo asks, "What are you working on?"

Piper glances back warily. She rightly assumes he might be goading her. Just a bit. "I'm preparing tomorrow's article."

"Are you still doing the 'Tense' article?"

"Yes, I'm still doing 'Today's Ten,'" Piper responds, unamused with the nickname. She seems more on edge than normal, which Theo unfortunately finds funny.

He holds up his hands in innocence, overreacting to Piper's response. "I'm not insinuating anything. Just asking."

Piper looks back at him. "It's one of the most popular articles in our national paper, OK? Several city papers have tried unsuccessfully to copy our concept. I'll eventually do other reporting, but for now I'm covering 'Tens' and some LA arts."

Theo looks out the window at the plains of East Texas. "OK no need to get defensive. Just asking."

Piper is on edge and Cam is silent, so Theo decides to give it a rest. He wonders, not for the first time, if Cam and Piper are more than friends, or working on it. It's clear to everyone that Piper would be open to it. And it would make sense why she's on this trip.

The landscape is flat for miles in every direction, but the desert brush has turned to green grass and some taller trees off the highway. Small towns pop up more frequently as well. Theo notices Cam's white knuckles and his repeated deep breathing. Despite the north Dallas morning traffic, they jumped back on I-30 rather quickly and are now headed east toward Little Rock.

Piper is uncharacteristically quiet throughout the morning and Theo's attempts to engage either of them in conversation go nowhere. *What kind of tense situation have I stumbled into?* He wishes he had brought a book along for the quiet stretches of the drive. But would rather catch up with his friend of 10 years. And Piper.

"So, what's the latest in LA?" Theo says to those in the front seat.

Cam doesn't seem to hear him. Theo sees Piper taking note of Cam's grip on the steering wheel and his leg bouncing rapidly.

"I don't know who all you met of my friends when you were out," Piper offers. "Madelyn and James got engaged a few months ago. They're getting married in June. Harrison and Jake are working out with a new trainer that everyone is raving about. They said they feel better than they have since college."

Theo doesn't respond to her updates and instead asks, "And you didn't have a chance to answer me before. Are you seeing anyone?"

Cam answers for Piper, maybe to make some peace between them, "No but she's giving insightful dating advice to everyone she knows."

Piper looks over at Cam and then looks out her side window. Theo watches them closely.

"So, no one on your radar Pipe?"

"Nope," Piper says and goes back to her work.

A half hour later Theo asks, "So what's the plan here? Work in Nashville I know, but any other stops along the way?"

"No," Cam says. "I need to make up lost time and head straight to Bucksport."

Piper shoots Cam a glance and her expression reads maybe a little hurt. Theo is not sure what happened before they got to Dallas, but he can tell something is up between these two.

Theo pulls up the Maps app on his phone. "Well, it's 28 hours from here through Nashville so if we push through, we could be in Maine Saturday night."

Cam doesn't respond and Piper doesn't fill the silence.

"What?" Theo asks.

"I don't know that I want to push it. We're in the middle of three big projects and some smaller ones. I owe Chelsea info on a couple. I promised I would make time during this trip to get the boss what she needs."

Theo lights up. "Oh yeah, how's Chelsea?"

"She's good. We would be lost without her. She takes care of everything at James. I could see Alison moving her into a casting role, out of the office manager work she's doing now. She reviewed some videos for me and has good instincts. She's also not mesmerized by the clients or the actors. Maybe it's growing up in LA, but Alison says that everyone she had on the team before Chelsea was there to meet celebrities, and of course Alison has no time for that."

Piper reflects, "Sounds like you three make a great team."

Cam misses the wistfulness in Piper's voice, but Theo hears it. "Not really sure which one holds the firm together because Alison and Chels are both incredibly competent."

"Sounds like it," Piper says softly.

Theo asks, "So Chelsea doesn't date actors then?"

Cam looks at Theo in the rearview mirror. "No. She hangs out with people outside of work mostly."

Theo nods once and glances out the window. "So, Piper, you're not going to fill me in on anything else?"

Cam looks at Theo in the mirror again but doesn't say anything.

Piper looks out her window and remains quiet. Cam pats Piper's leg and suggests she turn on the playlist she made.

"Oh, what playlist?" Theo asks, somewhat teasingly.

"That's OK. Theo can play what he wants. He'll think mine is a little too on the nose." She hands Theo the adapter equipment.

He starts flipping through his music apps. "Don't tell me. It's all songs about Road Trips."

Piper doesn't answer and Cam steps in again, showing her some support. "Yeah, songs about the states we've been through. Some really good stuff."

Theo charges ahead with a slightly scoffing tone, "Yeah, sounds like it."

Piper turns to Cam and asks, "Can we stop for a restroom break?"

Theo says, "Already? We're just two hours in."

"*Three* hours and I asked our driver."

Cam finds a service station that looks like they might have decent snacks and pulls into the fuel line. He's barely rolled to a stop when Piper opens her door and gets out. "Anyone need anything?" she asks.

"I'm going in after I fuel up," Cam tells her. She shuts the door before Theo has a chance to answer.

"Really?" Cam says to Theo as he gets out of the van.

"She is wound tighter than I've ever seen, and she is obviously pissed that I ruined her romantic road trip with you."

"No, she just needed a break from LA, and she doesn't want you annoying her."

"Right," Theo responds and walks toward the restrooms. Piper doesn't acknowledge him when he walks in. She pays for her water bottles and protein bars and heads back out.

Cam goes in, finding Theo in line with his own snacks. "Go easy on her. She didn't know you were coming."

"Because you didn't tell her."

"Oh, and what is your obsession with who is dating who?" Cam punches Theo playfully in the arm and goes to the restroom.

Back on I-30, Piper studies Google Maps and, seemingly less worried about Theo's reactions says, "Wow, I didn't know there was actually a town called Texarkana."

"You've never heard of Texarkana?" Theo asks flatly.

"Yes, I've heard of it, but I thought it was just the regional name. Not that it was a real town." She snaps a few photos outside the windshield. "You know I'm happy to drive anytime Cam."

Theo echoes her. "Yeah, me too. How do you normally switch off?"

Piper looks back to Theo and says, "Well Cam's driven the whole way so far. Never seems to need a break."

Theo counters, "Then why are you on the trip if not to help him out?" Piper glares at Theo and turns back around.

Cam doesn't respond after a few minutes. So, Theo asks again.

"This is a long drive. Maybe at the next break I can take a shift," Theo says, which for some reason irks Piper more. *Win-win.*

"Sure," Cam says, quietly.

Confused, Theo jumps right on it. "I don't have to - I just assumed you wouldn't want to drive this entire cross-country expedition."

Theo looks back and forth between the two in the front seat, clearly confused. He switches tactics. "How is your grandpa doing? Last time we talked your grandma was having times where she remembered him, but more frequently, she wasn't."

Piper looks at Cam and is about to say something but stops herself.

Theo, not backing down from whatever strange situation he's walked into, charges ahead. "I know he was still handling some probate and real estate law. Is he still doing that?"

"No, he's wrapped that up."

"OK. Is he enjoying his retirement a little bit? Has he been out to LA recently? I know he probably doesn't want to be away from your grandmother too much." Theo is not sure why Cam is hesitant to talk. *Is it because Piper is here?*

Cam remains silent and Theo has no idea what to say next.

Piper jumps in, "Theo is your family still in New Jersey?"

"My dad and brothers are," Theo responds.

"Oh, how old are your brothers?"

"Nathan is 27 and Marco is 21."

"What about your mom?" Piper continues her questions. Theo looks at Cam, unsure why he has again gone silent. Piper clearly doesn't give a rat's ass about his family but she's talking so Cam won't have to.

"Uh, they divorced 15 years. She's remarried. Why the sudden interest?" Theo asks her.

Piper ignores Theo's question and says, "Must be nice having brothers. You know I'm an only child."

"No, I didn't but I can see that," Theo says.

Piper ignores him again and says, "Remind me how you and Cam met. Was it at UCLA or before?"

"At college," Theo says. "And when did YOU meet Cam? Through your boyfriend?"

Piper smiles, refusing to get riled up again. "No, at a wedding. We were just reminiscing about that on our way past Palm Springs the other day. When was that, Cam? Was that Monday? Crap - it feels like a week ago."

"Crap?" Theo laughs.

"Fuck off," Piper amends, returning to her phone, smiling smugly like she won the match.

Theo tries again to talk to Cam about the family they'll be seeing in a couple of days. "It must be hard for your grandfather to see your grandmother slipping away like that. I'm sorry man."

Cam nods once but doesn't say anything. Piper looks over at him and then a pointed glance at Theo. Not anger or exasperation, just a knowing glance sent Theo's way.

Theo's cheeks turn a little red and he realizes there's more to the story. *I'll get it out of Cam later. Maybe over a beer tonight in Nashville. If we ever get there.* Theo looks out the windshield and sees more traffic than they had in Dallas. He pulls up Maps and notices there is a wreck about two miles up and no exits between here and there.

"Uh, not sure if your GPS has alerted you yet but it looks like a significant slowdown coming up. There's a wreck in a couple of miles."

Piper pulls up Google Maps and says, "I see three wrecks. Two after Little Rock, too."

"Yeah, but those should be cleaned up before we get there," Theo guesses.

Cam re-engages in the conversation. "Can we reroute?" He tries looking at Waze on his phone while navigating the traffic but gives up.

"There is no exit off I-30 before the wreck. Looks like we'll have a delay but can make it up the rest of the way," Piper tells him.

"I assume those other two wrecks will be cleaned up by the time we get to the other side of Little Rock but I'm showing lots of delays right now," Theo breaks the bad news.

"OH!" Piper exclaims, studying her phone. "I have an idea. Let's divert to Hot Springs National Park and go around I-30 past all the wrecks!"

Cam is quiet but clearly frustrated. "No, we're not going to Hot Springs," he says slowly.

Piper interrupts, "I'm looking here, and we could avoid the other two wrecks and get to see this little gem."

"This isn't a national parks tour."

"Yeah, I get it but if it will also help us avoid those other two wrecks..."

"No!" Cam says suddenly. Piper looks stunned. "I'm not going to take a side trip. I need to get to Maine. I've got work and a meeting in Nashville tomorrow and my aunt is wanting us to stop, and I have no idea if that is even on the way. I need to call my grandparents again too. Theo says those wrecks should be cleaned up by the time we get there so we don't need to go around."

Piper stares out her window at the green fields lining the highway and Theo says, "I think they will be Piper. I really do."

Piper sighs and returns to her phone. "Ready with that music yet, Theo?"

"Not now," Cam says, trying to control his voice. "I just want to focus on this traffic."

There is a long pause and then Piper suggests, "Hey Cam. It's at a standstill. How about you let me drive and you can answer those calls and texts I see coming in."

"I've got it," Cam says. Piper pats Cam's leg but he doesn't take his hands off the steering wheel. She pulls her hand away and looks back out the window.

ARKANSAS, THURSDAY
Piper

An hour later they take the loop around Little Rock, looking for I-40. Almost immediately they're at a standstill. Piper peeks over at Cam and sees that he is frustrated. She glances at Google Maps. "A new wreck has caused the traffic to stop. GPS is saying to follow this route."

"You don't think there's another way?" Cam asks, seemingly defeated.

"The parallel highway has construction and goes through a bunch of small towns," Theo tells Cam.

Cam looks at Waze on his phone. He can see what Piper and Theo are seeing – they are not going to make it to Nashville tonight until late. Piper knows he needs to get some work done. He's also got about 10 calls to respond to.

Cam asks, "Theo, did you tell Liv we were going through Memphis?"

Theo isn't surprised by the question. "No, since we probably wouldn't have time to see her."

"What about spending the night on the other side of Memphis so I can get some work done and see if she's available for dinner? I'd like to see her, and I don't think we're going to make it to Nashville at this rate," Cam suggests.

"Who's Liv?" Piper asks.

Cam doesn't respond and Theo says, "A friend. We met in college."

Piper looks over at Cam who doesn't offer any additional information.

Theo adds, "I don't think you've met her."

Of course, she hadn't. They all knew it.

"Let me give her a call and see if she's free tonight. It'll be great to see her," Theo repeats.

"Olivia, hey, it's Theo. I'm here with Cam and believe it or not, we are going to be in Memphis this evening. Wondering if we could get together for dinner. Sorry for the late notice. Would love to catch up. Give me a call any time."

The traffic inches forward and everyone remains quiet in the minivan. Cam seems to be more on edge than before.

"If I miss the Nashville meeting tomorrow then I won't be able to reschedule until Monday," Cam says aloud. "We should be in Maine before Monday so that won't work. God."

"If we spend the night in Memphis, we should make it tomorrow," Theo reassures him from the backseat.

"Have you given your grandpa an update?" Piper asks softly.

"No. I need to. And I've got some work to get to tonight. Let's just get to Memphis and we can figure this out."

Piper completes her article for Friday's edition and sends it off along with a quick text to her editor.

"Let me know if you want me to drive," Theo reminds him. Cam waves him off without any other response.

The traffic lets up a little and they get up to almost 60 mph before another slow down. Piper looks over at Cam who looks like he could blow, which she has never seen. She answers her remaining work emails and responds to multiple texts from her dad and a few friends.

She should call Carrie and talk through her issue but, looking at Cam, it's clear now is not the time for a baby shower-themed conversation. One of their friends, Mariah, is having a baby shower and Carrie, Piper, and many of their mutual friends have been invited. Half of them don't want to go and would rather just send a gift. It feels like a lame move to Piper but she's wondering if there are some underlying issues. Mariah was one of the first to get married after a short engagement and now she's having the first baby. Is there some misplaced jealousy that they're inadvertently taking out on their friend?

And then she sees a text from her mom from earlier in the day.

"Hey, I need to call my mom really quick," Piper says. "Is that OK?"

"Sure," Cam says and tries to smile at her, but his frustration at their situation is obvious.

"Hey, Mom, no I can't come over. I'm still on the trip with Cam. Remember? Can you send me screen captures of the issue you're seeing? You can take photos with your phone and text the photos or email them to me... I'll take a look and see what's going on.......Ok.............Yes, love you. Oh, and you've hung up."

"Liv's calling," Theo announces.

"Hey gorgeous. Screening me? You got my message. Yeah, we're going to be in town... A couple of hours, I think. There have been some delays on the interstate. Do you have time for dinner? I'm with Cam."

Piper shoots Theo a look which he ignores.

"We didn't think we were stopping in Memphis, but we've hit some serious traffic so we're going to stay the night and head to Nashville bright and early. Cam has a lunch meeting there... By 8 a.m.? OK...I looked earlier and there were no wrecks or construction on I-40 on that side of Memphis. But we hit it today. He's driving. Do you want me to put you on Speaker? OK you're on Speaker."

> A smooth voice says, "Hi Cam."
> "Olivia hey, small world."
> Piper notices Cam's eyes darting to the clock on the dashboard.
> "What's this about a road trip?"
> "Yeah, I'm heading to the east coast and Theo and Piper are going along as well."
> "Oh, is Piper with you now?"
> "Hi," Piper says and gives a little wave. She doesn't bother to look back at Theo who is undoubtedly rolling his eyes at her waving at the phone.
> "Oh hi. So why don't you stay at my place, and we can get dinner tonight? I've got room and I am off tomorrow, heading to Knoxville."
> "Oh, that's OK we'll just get a hotel," Cam automatically replies to her offer, eyes darting to the dashboard clock again.
> "Seriously, would love it if you stayed. I will be home in an hour or so. I just shot a location story and have a little clean up before I head out for a long weekend. I'll text Theo the address. OK?"
> Piper is certain Cam is going to say no again, but he surprises her, maybe looking slightly relieved. "Sure. Thanks."
> "Can't wait to see y'all. Bye."

Theo turns off the speaker and says, "OK sounds good. Yep, yep, it'll be good. Thanks."

"I'll set Maps to her address when it comes in and navigate us there," Theo says. "Man, it's going to be good to see her. How long has it been? Four years maybe?"

Piper is thrilled that his suave voice is turned off and he's back to normal, nerve-grating Theo. *So, Olivia is his ex, got it. Good for you, Theo.* She glances over at Cam who looks like he could use a dinner with friends. And maybe a beer.

Fellow Travelers – Odysseus Returns to Maine

"Arkansas Dave" by George Strait

"Arkansas Diamond" by Bill Kirchen

"Arkansas Heat" by Gossip

"Arkansas Killing Time" by The Pine Box Boys

"Arkansas Lovin' Man" by Johnny Cash

"Arkansas Traveler" by Jimmie Driftwood

"Arkansas" by Chris Stapleton

"Arkansas" by John Oates

"Going Back to Arkansas" by Big Bill Broonzy

"Mary Queen of Arkansas" by Bruce Springsteen

"The Lord God Bird" by Coach Kit

"Where the Arkansas River Leaves Oklahoma" by Don Williams

MEMPHIS, THURSDAY
Piper

When the traffic finally lets up, they cross the Mighty Mississippi and Piper holds up six fingers.

"Six," Cam says. Theo doesn't ask what game they're playing but types Olivia's address into his phone.

"How far do we have to go? Isn't she from somewhere near the west side of Memphis near the college where her mom taught?" Cam asks Theo.

"It looks like she lives in an area called Midtown."

They stop to fuel up for tomorrow and replenish the water and snacks, giving Liv plenty of time to get home. When the Odyssey pulls into her charming neighborhood, Piper can't help but admire the gorgeous homes on either side.

"Wow," Theo says. "Good for Liv."

As they drive up, Olivia steps out of her front door and laughs a happy laugh that perfectly fits the stunning woman in front of them. Between her mocha skin, gorgeous dark hair, and beaming smile, Piper immediately feels out of her league, and wonders how on Earth she could have dated Theo.

"Of all the vehicles I thought you'd pull up in, minivan is not on that list," she laughs again. Theo is out first, and Olivia walks over to hug him. "You've filled out," she teases him, poking his ribs. "Are you still playing?"

Theo grabs her fingers and kisses her lightly on the lips. "Yeah, a bit, not as much as I should be. And you've never ridden in Odysseus before? He's been around for a while."

"No, I think I'd remember." Liv walks over to Piper and extends her hand. Piper feels like a child in comparison, petite with a ponytail and the I've-been-on-the-road-for-4-days look. *Did they purposefully not tell me that Liv is gorgeous?* Piper says "Hello" in a soft voice.

Olivia smiles and steps around to give Cam a hug. They hold on a little longer and he whispers something in her ear, and she bursts out laughing.

"Come in, come in," she says. They walk inside carrying their bags and place them in the entry way.

"Hey, I'm starving," Olivia says. "Before we settle in - any way we could go to dinner? My treat. I'm rarely here so only keep the essentials in the kitchen."

"Coffee and ice cream?" Theo asks.

"Something like that," Olivia says while looking curiously at Cam.

Cam says, "I think I'll stay here and get some work done if that's OK. Maybe you can bring me something back. I've got a lot of work to catch up on."

Before Piper or Theo can step in, Olivia says, "Cam let's go out. I'd love to catch up. I won't keep you out late."

Cam rubs his palm over his face and agrees, which again surprises Piper. He and Olivia go way back to their college days, but Cam also looks like he's about to jump out of his skin with worry. Or exhaustion?

They freshen up quickly and Piper overhears Olivia asking Theo, "Is he OK?"

Theo must reassure her because they drop the subject. Everyone climbs into Olivia's black BMW. "Do you want to go downtown or somewhere close? Either one works. Beale Street isn't that far away," Olivia tells the group.

Theo and Piper are silent because they know Cam is on edge. Cam doesn't answer though.

"If it's close, I'd love to see Beale Street," Piper finally responds. "And there are restaurants there?"

"Yeah, good ones all around. We'll find something without a wait and then head back as soon as you're ready. OK Cam?" Cam just nods, looking out the window at the beautiful houses and mature trees lining the streets of her neighborhood.

On the drive south Olivia fills them in on the places they're passing. She and Theo share more than a few inside jokes. Cam is quiet and Piper decides to ignore any insecurities she feels around Olivia and be her true self. *Even if Cam ignores me and Theo gives me a hard time.*

"How did you all meet?" Piper asks brightly.

"In college," Theo answers.

Olivia looks over her shoulder at him in the backseat and says, "Short answer, OK." She continues to Piper, "Here's the long answer. Theo and I met playing PAC 12 volleyball. We would see each other at games and tourneys, and we started hanging out in the evenings. When I was at UCLA in my junior year and these two were seniors, I spent one crazy evening with them bar hopping and had the time of my life." Theo looks outside the window and smiles at the distant memory.

"Cam became a volleyball groupie, and we'd meet up whenever we were in each other's cities," Olivia says.

"Where did you go to school? Not UCLA?" Piper asks.

"UW. University of Washington."

"But your family is from Memphis?"

"Yes, I took the U-Dub scholarship because of their coach and because it was 2000 miles away."

Piper nods, and Cam says, "Kind of like Maine and LA I guess."

"It's worked for you, hasn't it?" Olivia asks him kindly. Cam grunts and leans his head back on the head rest. "So why are you going to Maine and why are you driving for God's sake?"

"My grandmother isn't doing well. My dad and I drove my grandparents' van out to LA in college. And then he left me there with the van. It was always the plan to get it back to them at some point."

Theo and Piper share a look in the back seat. *This is the most bitter tone Cam has ever used when talking about his dad.*

Piper repeats her questions from earlier. "Why would your grandfather want it back? Couldn't you have just sold it and sent him the money?"

Theo sighs heavily and says, "Who cares? He wants to give the Odyssey back."

Piper looks embarrassed that Theo is chiding her in front of Olivia. She feels like the bratty little sister tagging along.

Olivia must sense the tension between the three of them and changes the subject smoothly. "So, let's park at one end of Beale and walk down. We can head to the Rendezvous for BBQ after, or we can find a place on Beale. OK?" She drives them past the pyramid and points out the bridge they crossed a couple of hours ago, lit up and providing a different perspective of the river. Everyone is looking out their windows at the spectacular views of downtown Memphis.

"It's still early so Beale will be quiet but let's maybe check out some live music." They use an app to park and walk the length of Beale Street, stopping to check out the shops, the Orpheum theater, and the Elvis Presley statue. There are also several bars with music pouring outside. They decide on a restaurant that must serve food, but their real focus seems to be on large drinks in colorful plastic cups.

Piper loves the historical, yet touristy, part of the city. "There's almost a Mardi Gras vibe here, although I haven't been to New Orleans."

Olivia agrees, "Yeah, I can see that. I think the vibe is 'Blues, Drink, BBQ.'"

When they are seated, Cam immediately orders a beer for himself but everyone else takes a minute to look at the menu. The server returns with Cam's beer. He downs it while the others are ordering their drinks.

Piper mutters, "Good thing we're not driving any more tonight."

Olivia continues her catch up with friends. "So, Theo, where are you working these days? Are you back in California?"

"Not since college. I consult on the digital media side. I just finished a job in Austin."

Olivia nods, "Where next?"

Theo gestures his thumb toward Cam, "Shotgun for this guy." Cam doesn't seem to hear Theo. He takes the second beer from the server and starts on it.

"Can I get a Manhattan?" Cam says to the server.

She finishes putting their drinks down and says, "Sure, what can I get y'all to eat?" They take a quick look at the menu and order.

Olivia continues, "So Cam, catch me up. What's the deal with your cross-country trip?"

Cam looks for the server with his drink and answers, "My grandfather asked me to come back. I thought I'd drive the van back since I borrowed it and Piper and Theo wanted to come."

Theo and Piper glance at each other. *Did he even want us on this trip?*

Olivia notices the unspoken conversations happening. "When was the last time you were back?"

"Two, no three years ago, for Christmas. I think. I mean, with COVID I couldn't really, could I?"

Theo offers, "I met his grandfather Ben in LA when he came out for a visit. Good guy. I want to be him when I grow up."

"And when is that?" Cam asks Theo, clearly enjoying his buzz.

Olivia ignores him. "So, tell me about work Cam. Are you still doing voiceover work?"

Cam looks up at Olivia, confusion on his face. "No, I wasn't doing voiceovers. I was casting voiceover actors for commercials and TV mainly. I work for James Casting."

Piper notices how smooth Olivia is. She's dealt with Cam before and knows how to get him talking. "Oh wow, I've never known anyone in that business. Tell me about it."

"I work with producers and directors who are trying to hire actors, and then I work with talent agents representing actors to find a good fit. Where is our server?"

"And what about you Olivia?" Piper asks.

"I work in local news." ·

"Oh, are you an anchor?" Piper sits forward, fascinated.

"No, but that's the goal." She smiles and attempts to bring Cam's focus back to the table. "Cam, how's the rest of your family? Will they be in Maine when you get there?"

"I doubt it. My dad's been in Chicago for work, and he doesn't get back to Maine much. I don't think. I don't see his family when I'm there."

"So, this is your mom's family that you're going to visit?" she asks.

Theo jumps in and asks Olivia about her brother Damon.

Piper goes along with Theo's abrupt change in subject. "Wait, I've heard that name. Damon Carter? Is he in football maybe?"

"Yes, he plays at UT. I am heading over to Knoxville tomorrow for Saturday's game against Florida. How do you know Damon?"

"I read a lot of news articles for work. I must have come across his name at some point," Piper says, uncertain where she recognized his name.

"Yes, it's because our older brother was killed 10 years ago and Damon is an advocate for gun control, which makes him not so popular at times." They order a second round (is this the 4th round for Cam?) and Olivia hesitantly talks about her family.

"Look, this won't be used at your work, will it?" Olivia clarifies.

Piper looks surprised and says, "Oh God, no. I'm just curious. Sorry you don't have to talk about this," she backtracks as Theo shoots her a look.

"No, it's OK," Olivia reassures her. "My oldest brother was killed in a drive by. Wrong place, wrong time we think. The police haven't been able to find out who is responsible, so his case is still open, after all this time. It's easier to talk about now, but this is part of the reason I chose to go to Washington. I needed a break. It was tough."

"Oh Olivia, I can imagine."

Liv continues, "Because of the tragedy, and the fact that my father is a preacher at one of the largest churches downtown, everyone kept close eyes on Damon and me growing up. Damon was always getting into mild trouble. But I couldn't take the pressure and the constant attention. I had to get the hell out for a while. Damon was saved by football and our family could not be prouder of him. We go to as many games as we can."

Piper is rapt with Olivia's story, her tone, her modulation. Olivia smiles, "I have an idea. Any chance you've got room for me tomorrow? Maybe you could drop me in Knoxville? It looks like it's going to be on your drive from Nashville to Maine."

Cam returns to the conversation, his words slightly slurred. "No, we have to go to Nashville and then we've got to make good time after that."

Theo starts to speak, and Olivia stops him with a smile. "Sounds good. I understand."

"Plus, how would you get back?" Cam asks, confusion across his face, glassy eyes shining.

"I can ride back with family. Not a problem. Want to dance?" Liv suddenly asks Theo.

"Yeah," he says and jumps off his stool. They walk over to where another couple is on the makeshift dance floor dancing to 90s hip hop. Piper notices that Olivia is excellent, and Theo is not bad. *God, I give up. He makes me insane.*

Piper orders water for the table and chips and salsa. It appears Cam is barely aware of what's going on.

The server brings the chips right away and Piper smiles gratefully at her. "Hey, have some chips with me," she says to Cam.

"You don't have to mother me," Cam grumbles.

"Got it," Piper says. *I have never seen him drink this much. Or act this way, like a sullen child. Should I check out flights from Memphis to LA?* She glances back at Theo who's smiling at Olivia, and Piper checks her frustration. *I'm not going to give up. I said I was going to Maine and I'm not going to let Cam down.*

"Hey," Piper says, trying to engage Cam. "Are you going to feel like getting work done tonight?"

"Don't worry about it," Cam says quietly. No fight left in him. The dancers return to the table and Cam looks up, seemingly unaware that they have been gone.

"I've got to go to Nashville," Cam announces to the table.

"Let's get this food to go and we'll let Cam get his work done," Piper suggests.

Theo looks at his phone and says, "Liv I think you should ride with us. I'm looking at the map and Knoxville is on the way. We'll head north after we drop you off."

Piper says, "Yeah that sounds great!" when Olivia looks at her for her thoughts.

Cam just quietly says, "OK".

Olivia rubs Cam's arm "I'm really happy to see you, you know."

Cam downs his water, allows Theo to pick up the check and they head back to Midtown.

"Hey, where is Sun Studios?" Piper asks.

"About a mile from here. We'll drive by on our way back," Olivia tells her.

They stop at the historic studio and Theo jumps out for a quick photo. Piper doesn't mention that she wanted to do the same thing.

Olivia encourages Cam and Piper to get in the photo as well and the three of them pose together for the first time. Unfortunately, Piper glances up at Theo just as the photo is taken. She's going to be livid in two days when she sees that photo for the first time.

Back at her house, Olivia comes right out and asks, "OK no judgment, especially from me, but what sleeping arrangements are we after here?"

No one answers right away and finally Piper says, "We've had separate rooms." She quickly adds, "Cam has been working most evenings."

They glance at Cam on the couch, head in his hands, and realize that is not going to happen tonight.

Olivia pours four waters and says, "Piper why don't you stay with me. I've got a king and Theo you can take the guest bedroom. Cam can sleep there too, or he may just prefer the couch."

"I'm taking the couch," Theo says. "Let's get him some dinner, aspirin, and to bed."

Cam seems more alert now but in no mood to work so they agree to be up by 6:30 so Cam can get caught up, and they can be on the road by 8:00 at the latest.

Olivia gives Theo an extra-long hug goodnight while Piper averts her eyes.

Theo yells goodnight to Piper who grits her teeth and considers checking flights once again.

MEMPHIS, FRIDAY
Piper

Piper showers quickly and tiptoes to the kitchen to start coffee. She's surprised to see Cam on the couch, a little dazed, but not looking too bad considering.

She greets him cheerily but quietly, "Hey you're up. Do you want to take a shower and I'll make us some breakfast? I know you want to get on the road as soon as we can. I think Olivia is getting ready now. Have you seen Theo?"

Cam looks at Piper and says, "No."

Piper refills her water and Cam calls again from the living room. "You're cooking breakfast?"

"I don't know," she hesitates at his tone. "I just thought I'd get us ready to go. Coffee at least."

Cam snaps. "You don't have to make breakfast. I think we can take care of what we need." He walks into Olivia's room and calls out to her. "OK if Piper makes coffee?"

"Yes of course," Olivia responds. He takes his bag to the guest bathroom and turns the shower on. Piper decides not to take Cam's attitude to heart given the hangover he must be dealing with. She looks around for coffee supplies and maybe bread for toast.

Cam comes back out in running gear. "I'll be back in 20 minutes."

He takes off and Theo walks into the living area. "What's going on?"

"Olivia's getting ready, I've got the laundry almost done and Cam has left to walk or maybe run." Piper doesn't look at Theo. He walks into the kitchen, looks for mugs and puts four on the counter.

"How long have you been up?"

"Not long," Piper says. He notices her wet hair pulled back and her bags packed in the living room.

"Right," Theo says. "Thanks Mom." He pours coffee and walks toward the bathroom. He circles back and says, "Truce, OK? Sorry I was teasing you yesterday. Something is going on with him and I'm not sure what. I won't mess with you today."

"Truce," Piper breathes a sigh of relief. "I've never seen him like yesterday in the van or last night. I think he's just worried about his grandparents but it's odd, right?"

Twenty minutes later they've had toast, coffee, and packed up for the journey to Nashville. Just waiting for Cam.

Piper busies herself in the kitchen while Theo chats with Olivia about her work and friends from school, leaving Piper out of the conversation. She waits for a break and says, "I think one of us should drive since Cam didn't get any work done. I think he's got to make calls and do some work on his laptop before his meeting today."

"Yeah, I can drive, it's not a problem Pipe," Theo says, still focused on Olivia. Olivia looks from Piper to Theo.

"I know it's not a problem, I just wanted to mention that it would be nice."

Olivia loads her mug in the dishwasher. "Thanks for making the coffee and cleaning up. Let me get my stadium seat and lock up the garage. I'll be back in a minute."

"Truce, remember?" Piper whispers to Theo when Olivia is out of earshot.

"Yes, sorry, your planning every detail drives me crazy. I'll be nice." Theo walks out of the kitchen and packs his bag in the living room. He gets Cam's keys off the counter and begins loading the Honda.

Piper gathers her things as well and joins Theo outside. "Do you want to drive, or do you want me to? I'm happy either way. You can ride in the back with Olivia if you want."

Olivia and Cam come out and he walks to the driver's door. He's wearing his suit pants and dress shirt but no tie or jacket. Piper realizes she's staring and quickly looks away.

"I'm going to drive. I don't want to look at my email or answer any calls until this meeting is over."

Piper is concerned, "Cam are you sure? I can..."

He closes his eyes and says as patiently as he can, "Yes. Please just let me drive my vehicle." Piper goes to the passenger side and Cam sets Waze to downtown Nashville. "My meeting is near the Ryman," Cam says.

"We can walk around downtown and see the sights," Olivia tells the group. They take off for Nashville and Piper says a quick prayer to the traffic gods.

Olivia and Theo continue their catch up and Piper looks for articles due Sunday afternoon for Monday's "Today's Ten". Friday is a catch-up day for her at work since her standard weekday articles are done.

Piper attempts to talk to Cam several times and stops herself. She's tired of being snapped at, especially in front of Olivia. Cam does nothing to ease the tension and Piper wonders once again if she should just fly back to LA. She could leave Cam with Theo, but she can't bring herself to abandon him when he's clearly not himself.

An hour later, Piper switches to texts. She can't read one more controversial article. She answers all her friends' texts and decides to focus her attention on Olivia, who she could easily see as a close friend if she lived in LA.

"Olivia, tell me about your brother Damon," Piper turns slightly in her seat so she can face Olivia.

Olivia smiles broadly, "He's smart, charming, a good leader. He's grown up to be quite a good guy. I've always been his protector and have straightened him out a few times. I come from a long line of strong women, and we make sure Damon doesn't veer too far off the path. He's recently become involved in the conversation around assault rifle legislation which makes him unpopular at times in this state. But he's a killer running back so people let his activism slide."

Piper really appreciates how open Olivia is about her family. "So, he's using his powers for good?"

Liv laughs, "Exactly."

"And your mom is a professor?"

"She's an instructor at Lemoyne-Owen which is a predominantly African American college. My mom's sister too. My grandmother stayed at home and made sure her daughters put education first when they were growing up. Gran was very involved in my grandfather's church. He was the pastor at the largest black church in Memphis at the time. They've always kept a close eye on me and would not be happy to hear about some of the escapades I had with these two here."

Cam half smiles and Theo snorts. Liv continues.

"I was a good student and athlete and was involved in our church, but I had to blow off some steam growing up. It's hard being the kid of a beloved pastor. I learned to be discreet at a young age. What they don't know... I like being back near my family, but I don't plan to stay in Memphis my entire life. But don't tell my family that. Maybe I'll see where Damon ends up."

Piper nods, thinking the same about LA. Maybe they should swap for a week, a la *The Holiday*.

"So, what about you Piper? How did you become friends with Theo? And Cam?"

It's silent in the van and no one offers to correct Olivia. Piper decides to be delicate. "Cam and I met at a mutual friend's wedding a few years ago. I met Theo when he first came out to LA to visit Cam. When was that first time? Three or four years ago? He made quite an impression on our crowd. And here we are."

Liv laughs, "I bet you did." Theo stretches out his legs and intertwines them with Olivia's own long limbs, catching Piper's eye.

"And Piper is Cam's watchdog now. Well, she's everyone's fixer." Piper smirks at Theo.

"Maybe I'm just a good friend to my friends. No need to judge." Theo raises his eyebrows and lets it go.

Liv says. "So, Cam, who is this meeting with?"

"Two agents and seven of their clients, back for a second round of auditions. We're casting a new reality show based in rural Tennessee. We're hoping that three of these actors will be right. They're organizing lunch while I'm there, so I'll be ready after." Cam mutters "fuck me" as the traffic ahead comes into view.

Theo has Apple Maps up and says, "It looks like it's just a 10 minute slow down. We should be at the Ryman in two hours still, plenty of time before your meeting."

Piper notices Cam's grip on the steering wheel again, and it's concerning. "God I just need a break." No one offers again to drive. But Cam's cool is about gone.

They all silently agree on distraction and Piper offers to put the music back on which now includes Arkansas and Tennessee tunes. Theo groans and Liv punches him playfully and says, "Play nice." He kicks her foot and lays back to sleep.

Piper turns the music on low and she and Olivia continue talking about their jobs. Piper admits she's envious of upward opportunities in the TV medium. "I know I can do more than what I'm currently doing. The 'Tens' article is not the challenge it once was."

"Are you wanting to write more investigative articles? Or editorials?" Olivia asks.

"Well, this trip has renewed my interest in writing a book," Piper admits, appreciative of Olivia's interest.

"A travel book?" Liv asks.

"I don't know. I haven't figured that out just yet." Cam looks over at Piper but doesn't say anything. "But I want to hear all about your escapades with Cam and Theo. That sounds a lot more interesting than my job."

Theo opens his eyes and glances at Olivia who seems like she isn't quite sure where to start. "Well, let me tell you about one night."

Piper turns to face the back seat and eagerly anticipates the exploits of young Cam and friends.

"We met down in Berkeley one weekend after our season was over. I was a junior and they were both seniors, I think. A bunch of the volleyball players I knew were going there so Cam and Theo drove up.

"We hung out with the group for a couple of hours, hitting bars in the area. But I wanted to dance and most of our friends were more into talking at this English style pub. So, the three of us took off.

"We found a pretty good dance club and danced for hours. Closed the place down. We pooled our remaining cash and got In-n-Out and a hotel in a not-so-great part of town. We had one of the most fun nights of my life. These two are part of my favorite college memories."

Cam looks up in the rearview mirror and smiles and Liv rubs his shoulder. Theo keeps his eyes closed but reaches out for Olivia's hand and caresses it while he settles back to get some sleep.

Piper smiles at Olivia and thinks there might be more to the story there. But her big question is, *Did Olivia date Theo or Cam?* It's really not clear.

WESTERN TENNESSEE, FRIDAY
Piper

Finally, the traffic lets up and the van crosses the Tennessee River on what turns out to be a beautiful Friday morning. They notice more and more vehicles with orange license plates, flags, and stickers.

"Wow," remarks Theo. "A lot of people are going to the game."

"Yeah," Liv says. "The Tennessee stadium holds over 100,000 and since this is a Southeastern Conference game and a rivalry, chances are it'll be close to full."

"Wow, I never went to a college football game. Did you Cam?" Piper asks him.

"Yeah," Cam tells her.

"Yes, we went to games Piper," Theo repeats.

"Great." Piper rolls her eyes at his sarcasm and shakes her head at Olivia.

Olivia squeezes Theo's knee in solidarity with Piper and it makes him jump. "I wish I could introduce you to my family in Knoxville but it's probably OK that I don't," she laughs. "I think I'd rather keep you two a secret," Liv says tapping Cam's shoulder.

"What? Why?" Piper asks.

"In my family's eyes, the only things I did in Seattle were study and play volleyball. No need to mess with that."

Outside Nashville the traffic starts to pick up and Cam mutters under his breath. With over an hour until his meeting, it's not clear why he's so concerned.

"Looks like we'll be there in 20 minutes," Theo assures him. Olivia watches Cam and must be concerned. She looks at Piper and raises her eyebrows, silently asking if Cam's OK. Piper gives her a little smile and a small shrug of her shoulders.

They all remain quiet, watching Nashville come into view. Theo turns on Johnny and June Cash at a low volume. It seems to calm Cam a little. Liv looks at Theo, raises her brows, and nods her head at Cam. Theo shrugs his shoulders. Piper resumes her leg bouncing as they get closer to downtown, the skyline in full view now.

"Piper, have you been to Nashville before?" Olivia asks.

"No!" Piper exclaims. "Wow, it's much larger than I expected. I guess I assumed it was a main street filled with cafes and music studios." Behind her Theo must roll his eyes because Olivia smacks his leg quietly.

The traffic suddenly slows as I-65 and I-40 merge, and Cam grows tense again. But, minutes later they easily find parking near the Ryman Auditorium.

"OK, I'll text you when I'm done." He pockets the van keys.

"Yeah, we'll be fine. Good luck. Don't worry about us." Piper reassures him, giving him a somewhat awkward hug.

Olivia follows, giving him a longer one. "You look great," she tells him. He looks at her, smiles a little, and walks off in the direction of his meeting. Piper can't help but wonder again what the history is with these three. She shakes off her curiosity and turns to catch up with Theo and Olivia.

"What do you want to see?" Olivia asks. "Broadway is probably not quite open just yet but later tonight it'll be filled with party buses and live music. The Country Music Hall of Fame and the Johnny Cash Hall of Fame are right over here. There's the Cumberland over this way and there's one of those murals with wings over at Biscuit Love," she says, looking at Piper.

"Do you come to Nashville a lot?" Piper asks.

"I have some family here, and I've come with girlfriends several times, and a few times for work. Yeah, I guess I come here quite a bit."

"Do we have time for the Country Music Hall of Fame?" Theo asks.

"It's really big - we could hustle through but the Johnny Cash one may be better. Then lunch?"

"I wouldn't mind seeing the mural you mentioned," Piper says hopefully.

"Of course, you would," Theo mutters loud enough for everyone to hear. Liv elbows him and Piper thanks her.

The Johnny Cash Museum is open, so they leisurely walk through looking at the displays and videos of his life.

"So, you're a fan?" Olivia asks Theo.

"Wow, he had a longer career than I realized. I didn't grow up listening to him. My parents didn't listen to any country. Growing up in Jersey, I didn't know anything about country music really. But I've come to appreciate the older stuff in the last few years."

They agree the kitschy museum is worth the admission and leave, making their way to Biscuit Love Gulch. Theo is evidently hungry and orders a large plate of biscuits and gravy. Piper watches with amazement as he devours it. *We're not in LA anymore,* she thinks to herself. The coffee is good, and they stop at the wings mural for a photo of Piper. Theo shows admirable restraint, even taking a photo himself, and they make their way to Broadway. They eventually walk over to the Country Music Hall of Fame and enter the lobby.

"Wow, you were right," Piper says. "This is much larger than I was expecting. Has anyone heard from Cam?" Olivia and Theo both check their phones but no word yet.

Theo purchases three tickets and meets the ladies coming out of the restroom a few minutes later. "Let's see what we can, and Cam can pick us up when he's ready," he suggests, handing them their tickets.

They take their time going through the massive rooms chronologically displaying the history of country music in the United States. So many names Piper has never heard. Theo takes photos of a few plaques and Olivia asks about the photos. "I'm going to look up their music later," he says. She takes his arm, and they continue their slow walk around the museum.

An hour later they meet in the lobby, surprised they still haven't heard from Cam. "Would you be interested in going next door to the Museum of African American music?"

Theo responds, "It feels like the perfect follow up." They walk across the street and Liv purchases the tickets, even though Piper offers.

"Please let me do this," Liv smiles at her. They walk through the museum, Olivia pointing out singers she grew up listening to, many of them with roots in gospel. Piper is embarrassed that once again she has not heard of many of these artists. They finish up and Piper vows to add some musicians from these three museums to her Maine trip playlist.

Piper opens her arms wide in the sunshine and says, "God, I feel like I have more energy than I have had in several days. I needed this break from the drive. I guess I didn't realize that." *And maybe I needed a short break from Cam? Something's going on with him and I'm just hoping I'm not the issue.*

Still no word from Cam so they walk toward the Cumberland River and spot a pedestrian bridge and the Glen Campbell Museum. They opt for the bridge, everyone checking their phones frequently for a call from Cam. Finally, Theo gets a text.

Can you meet me at Jason Aldean's on Broadway? I'm heading over there now.

Piper finishes up photos on the bridge and they walk back to Broadway. They enter Jason Aldean's restaurant where Cam is waiting for them at the bar, half of a large beer in front of him.

"I guess it went well," Theo says, pulling up next to him.

"Yeah, good meetings. I needed this and the office said the food was good here."

Piper asks for a table, and they order water and a couple of appetizers to share. Cam orders a burger and fries and finishes his beer. "I'll just have a Coke," he says to the server. "I've got a drive ahead of me."

"Have whatever you want," Theo says. "I'm going to drive us to Knoxville."

Cam looks up a bit confused and then remembers they are on their way to Knoxville next for Olivia to meet up with her family and go to Damon's game. "OK right yeah." He hands his Coke to Theo and orders a beer when the server returns.

They finish their food and load up the Odyssey with Theo in the driver's seat, playing driver, navigator, and DJ with his music on the makeshift stereo. Piper finds herself in the front seat with him. Cam has his head leaning toward Olivia, looking utterly exhausted in the next row. They follow signs to Knoxville, getting through Nashville traffic as quickly as possible.

Liv and Piper notice Cam's phone going off, on silent, with 'Ben Young' on the screen. Cam doesn't notice it or is ignoring the call. They decide not to mention it. *He can call Grandpa Ben back when he's had time to rest.*

Everyone seems to be enjoying the peaceful ride past small towns and hills that are getting taller and taller. "How long does it take to get to Knoxville?" Piper asks quietly.

Olivia answers her before Piper looks it up on GPS. "Less than three hours if there is no traffic on I-40."

"Hope is like the sun," Cam mutters.

"*Star Wars*?" Theo asks, looking at Cam in the rearview mirror.

"Yep," Cam says.

Piper spends the drive checking her email, reading a few articles she bookmarked, and making notes for Sunday's delivery of the Monday column. Olivia works through a couple of work texts and emails as well and Theo hums to his music playing softly in the background.

Cam wakes up around Kingston and they make a quick pit stop. Piper refreshes their waters and protein bars and notices that the glove box is full of the last ones she picked up. This has not turned out to be the breakneck-don't-eat-just-grab-a-bar sort of trip she was expecting. She also notes that Cam should look more relaxed but still seems like something is really bothering him. *Maybe he's not looking forward to saying goodbye to Olivia?*

Although she seems just as close to Theo as she is to Cam. *Hmmmm.*

Piper is the first one back in the van, so she checks her hair and teeth before Theo comes back and has a chance to comment. Cam gets in the driver's seat and Theo doesn't seem to mind. They pull out and Theo asks where in Knoxville they are going so he can set it up on Waze.

"I have an idea," Olivia starts. "Cam, what do you say about going to the game with me tomorrow? I have two tickets and I think it would do you good to have a day off. We can have a great time in Knoxville after the game. All the bars will be open. Do you think your grandpa would mind?"

Piper is about to speak up and explain that Cam really needs to get to Maine, when Cam interrupts her. "Yeah, let's do that," he says, stunning the rest of the passengers. Piper glances back at Theo before she realizes what she is doing. He looks just as surprised as she is with Cam's agreement.

Olivia continues, "We should be able to find two more tickets for you two. Is this OK?" She looks apologetically at Piper with an expression that reads *Sorry I sprung this on you without OK'ing it with you first.*

Piper reassures her and bounces in her seat. "Ooh! I'd love to spend some time in a true college town. Let's do it!"

Olivia looks relieved. "Why don't we look around for a hotel and let Cam get a good night's sleep tonight?"

Theo starts looking for a hotel near the game. "Where do you usually stay?" he asks Liv.

"Oh, I'm not staying with my family. Not this weekend. Let's just stay anywhere we can find a decent rate. Game weekends are ridiculous."

"Here's one. Um, how many rooms do we need?" Theo asks but no one answers. "Let's get two," Theo decides. "They're not cheap and I'm sure we don't mind sharing. OK?"

Piper assumes, somewhat cautiously, that she won't get stuck with Theo tonight. He reserves the rooms and sets up his maps app.

As Odysseus enters the Knoxville area, they watch the gentle slopes of the countryside turn much steeper. "We're not in Texas anymore," Piper tells Cam.

Once in Knoxville they check in to their high-rise hotel and set a plan to meet up at 7:00 to walk to dinner. Theo made a reservation at a restaurant on the river.

Piper and Olivia check into their room and get ready for dinner. They both wear light jackets and walk to the elevators going to the lobby. "OK, what is up with Cam? I'm worried about him," Liv starts.

Piper shrugs and says, "He's been quiet like normal, but for the last few days he's been really tense. I am just trying not to make it worse."

"It's got to be work," Liv says.

"It could be," Piper agrees. "I think it's a great idea to take a break tonight and tomorrow. I could use it too. I'm really surprised he agreed to stay for the night. I think it's been somewhat hard for him to let someone else make a decision on this trip. But I think he needs a day off. Hopefully he's had a chance to call his Grandpa Ben back."

"Oh, is that who was calling in the minivan? His grandpa?" Liv puts two and two together.

"Yes, Cam hasn't said much about what is going on in Maine, but I think he's feeling a little guilty about not getting back to see his grandparents the past couple of years. And he thinks he has to return their minivan. They are kind of his only family."

"Yeah, but he has you. And Theo."

"I'm not sure Cam sees it that way, but you are absolutely right. And he has you."

After dinner on the river, Piper walks back to the hotel and settles into her queen bed with a large bottle of water and *10 Things I Hate About You* on the TV. She has no idea where Cam, Theo, and Olivia ended up, but she needed to give them some time to catch up. And a break from Cam's silence and Theo's teasing sounded like a good idea.

At 3:30 a.m. Piper wakes up with the TV still on. She turns it off and notices Olivia has not made it back yet. *Are they maybe all in the other room down the hall? Should I go check? Text Cam and make sure they are OK?*

She checks her phone and sees there are no missed calls or texts. She rolls over in bed, deciding her sleep is more important than her curiosity at the moment.

Fellow Travelers – Odysseus Returns to Maine

"Back to Tennessee" by Billy Ray Cyrus
   "Back Where I Come From" by Kenny Chesney
   "Copperhead Road" by Steve Earle
   "Crazy Town" by Jason Aldean
   "Dixie Chicken" by Little Feat
   "Dixieland Delight" by Alabama
   "Down in Tennessee" by John Anderson
   "Girl Named Tennessee" by NEEDTOBREATHE
   "Just to See You Smile" by Tim McGraw
   "Maybe It Was Memphis" by Pam Tillis
   "Memphis Tennessee" by Elvis Presley
   "Murder on Music Row" by George Strait, Alan Jackson
   "My Tennessee Mountain Home" by Dolly Parton
   "Nashville Blues" by The Everly Brothers
   "Nashville" by Noah Gundersen
   "Nashville Without You" by Tim McGraw
   "Rocky Top" by The Osborne Brothers
   "Smoky Mountain Rain" by Ronnie Milsap
   "Southern Comfort Zone" by Brad Paisley
   "Tennessee River Run" by Darryl Worley
   "Tennessee Christmas" by Amy Grant
   "Tennessee Homesick Blues" by Dolly Parton
   "Tennessee Jed" by Grateful Dead
   "Tennessee Mountain Girl" by The Rubber Knife Gang
   "Tennessee Mountain Top" by Kid Rock
   "Tennessee River" by Alabama
   "Tennessee Rock N' Roll" by Bobby Helms
   "Tennessee Rose" by Emmylou Harris

"Tennessee Song" by Margo Price

"Tennessee Stud" by Johnny Cash

"Tennessee Waltz" by Elvis Presley

"Tennessee Whiskey" by Chris Stapleton

"Tennessee" by Arrested Development

"Tennessee" by Conner Smith

"Tennessee" by Sugarland

"That's How I Got to Memphis" by Tom T. Hall

"This Ain't Tennessee and She Ain't You" by Tom Jones

"Walking in Memphis" by Marc Cohn

"Wrong Side of Memphis" by Trisha Yearwood

"A beloved, honored friend, but it's been so long, your visits much too rare. Tell me what's on your mind. I'm eager to do it, whatever I can do...whatever can be done."

~ Calypso to Hermes in Homer's *The Odyssey*

KNOXVILLE, SATURDAY
Piper

Showered and downstairs by 8:30, Piper realizes she hasn't felt this rested in days. She orders coffee and oatmeal in the hotel restaurant and scrolls social media and her email, responding to everything needing her attention. There are *Heralds* out, so she grabs one and reads her own newspaper over a second cup.

She's finishing the Arts section when Theo shows up and drops into a chair in front of her, hair wet and long sleeve tee pulled up to his elbows. "What are we doing today?"

"We?" Piper asks, returning to her paper.

"Yeah, are we going to the game or doing something else?"

"Where are Cam and Olivia?" Piper looks around the hotel lobby.

"They're getting ready I think." Theo thanks the server for the cup of coffee. "She's got their tickets - her dad dropped them off last night at the front desk. We just need to get ours or make other plans."

"What do *you* want to do?" Piper hesitantly asks. "I'm surprised you would want to spend the day with me unless you have to, trapped in the van."

"Um," he starts. "I'd like to hear what *you* want to do, like I asked you two minutes ago."

Olivia walks up looking beautiful in jeans and a UT T-shirt with a white denim jacket over her arm. "We missed you last night Piper. Did you have a good night?"

"I did! I needed a good night's sleep, and I got it. I hope you did too. Sorry - did you not have a key to our room?"

Olivia orders a cup of coffee and fruit. "Oh, I did. I didn't want to wake you."

Piper looks confused but Theo interrupts. "We were just talking about what we are going to do today."

Olivia sips her coffee and goes over the day's events. "The game is at 1:00 and we are tailgating ahead of time. You two are invited of course. I'm sorry I couldn't get more tickets for you - my entire family has come in for this one. I gave my aunt and uncle the better seats and Cam and I will take the ones up higher."

"No problem," Piper says, "really." After a pause she asks, "Olivia, would you be offended if I didn't go to the game today? I don't know much about football, and I'd really like to explore the area if that's OK. Maybe we could meet up after the game?"

"Oh, that's fine! Don't worry about it! I wouldn't be here if it wasn't for Damon playing."

Theo looks over at Piper. "What did you have in mind?"

Cam walks up, looking tired again, grabs a chair and says "Hey" in Piper's direction.

"Hey," she whispers back. *Screw this* she thinks. *He doesn't need me right now*. Piper sits up straight. "Cam, would you mind if I borrowed Odysseus today? I'd like to explore this area. I'll fill it up and have it ready for our trip tomorrow. And I promise I'll take good care of it."

"Yeah sure," he says, reaching into his pocket for the keys. He orders an omelet and coffee, and Piper pays her bill.

"OK! Do you need a ride to the game? I can drop all of you off first."

"No, that's OK," Olivia tells her. "We can walk from here. You sure you don't want to tailgate with us before you take off? It'll start up about 10 or 11."

"No, that's OK. But I'll be ready to celebrate the win tonight if you guys make plans. I'll be back by 5:00 or so, does that work?" She looks at Cam who barely registers what she's saying. *Screw this* she thinks again. She puts on a big smile, excited for her day.

Olivia answers for the group, "Yeah, that's great! The game will be over around 5:30 and we'll text you where we're headed next. Have a fun day - almost wish I could join you!"

Piper waves goodbye and locates the elevator down to the parking garage. She's so excited to explore. She should explore more in LA. Why doesn't she? Maybe because she has lived there all her life? The thought of a day visiting somewhere new fills her with true happiness.

Theo drops cash on the table. "Mind if I take off as well?"

Cam looks up. "Sure, see you later tonight?"

"Yeah, I think so. Can you text me?" He bends down to give Liv a quick kiss and takes off for the elevator, intercepting Piper just in time.

"Hey, what's the plan?" he asks, without a trace of testiness.

"Well, I'm going to Great Smoky Mountains National Park." Piper loads snacks and essentials into the back seat of the van. Theo notices instead of her normal skirt and tank top she is wearing jeans and a sweater, holding her jacket. She glances at him because he hasn't said anything and walks to the driver's door. "It's an hour away and is supposed to be beautiful. It's the most visited National Park in the country and I might not get a chance to see it again."

Theo puts his hand on her arm. "I'd like to join you if that's OK."

Piper looks up and sees Theo's serious expression, dark eyes and heavy brows looking more solemn than normal. "You want to spend the day with me in the Smoky Mountains?"

"Yes," he assures her. He looks down at his clothes and must decide jeans, boots, and a long sleeve T-shirt will be OK for the park.

"Um, OK. Can I drive?" Piper's tone is more of a statement than a question and Theo hesitates.

"Yes, I mean great that you are going to drive." he responds, moving to the passenger's side. "But can we clean out this van first please?" Plastic bottles, wrappers, and hotel receipts all get recycled and then Theo gets in. "I hate clutter," he admits.

Wow, thinks Piper, *something we finally agree on.*

KNOXVILLE, SATURDAY
Cam

Cam spends the morning getting work caught up and sends Chelsea a quick update via email. At 11:00 he meets up with Olivia in the hotel lobby and they walk to the stadium along with many other Tennessee fans. They've crossed a couple of busy streets and are strolling companionably, enjoying the sunshine when Olivia finally says, "Spill it." Cam doesn't say anything, and Liv nudges him. "It's just us. I know something is going on and I have no idea what it is."

"Nothing you can fix," Cam says.

"I'm not asking to fix it. And maybe don't snap at Piper just because she's trying to take care of you - it's clearly just who she is."

Cam looks at Olivia, perplexed, but he pushes through. "I'm OK, I guess just tired of the drive. And we're still only in Tennessee. We're probably only halfway there. When my dad and I did this trip four or five years ago we did it in four days straight. Only essential stops. Spent the night in Buffalo, Des Moines, and Cisco."

"Cisco?" Olivia asks as they cross another busy street.

"Utah. We moved all my things from Maine out to LA when I got my first apartment. I thought he might move to California one day, but he hasn't yet. Work has kept him in the Midwest for the last several years."

"You know, I know very little about your family or where you grew up. You were kind of quiet about yourself in college."

"Yeah, I've been told that before," Cam says.

"I don't think I've ever heard you mention your dad. What's he like?"

"Laid back. He's good at what he does. He's done a lot of different things in his career. It was great to spend that time with him on the trip. I don't see him much. He left Maine after my mom died."

"I'm so sorry, Cam. So, your grandparents loaned you the van to move your things and now you're returning it?"

"Yeah, my dad was going to take it back, but he bought a motorcycle instead and went back to Pittsburgh. He travels a lot and said he'd always dreamed of a cross-country motorcycle trip."

"That's fucked up," Olivia whistles.

Cam looks at his friend. "Not really. That's my dad. He's the cool one in our family. Spontaneous, adventurous."

"So, he left you in LA with a minivan that belongs in Maine? Not sure I'd call it cool. And how was it four or five years ago? Didn't you graduate about six years ago?"

"Yeah, I guess so. I'm 28, I'd have to do the math. I'm terrible with dates. I got my apartment after I turned 21. Maybe seven years ago. Is that right?"

"Did he make it to your graduation?"

"No, I can't remember why but he couldn't be there. My Grandpa Ben flew out though and spent the week with me. We traveled up the coast and did some deep-sea fishing. It was great."

They continue their walk in silence, Olivia obviously still trying to fit the pieces together. Cam smiles at her.

"So, your grandfather wanted the van back and he called and asked you to bring it?"

Cam hesitates. "Not really. I don't think he cares about the Odyssey. My grandmother bought it when I was in high school, and she hadn't driven it in a few years. We used it to move my stuff." Another long pause as Olivia lets Cam have the time he needs.

"My grandfather called last weekend to let me know Granny has cancer. He asked me to come home and I decided to drive the van." Cam pauses again and Olivia lets the silence hang between them.

"Look, my dad's a good guy, but it was kind of hard when he left LA that day. I haven't seen him since. I call him every few weeks or so but we're not close like Piper is with her dad. I'm a lot like him though, and we are good. We just don't need relationships like other people seem to. But I feel bad for basically leaving my grandparents by themselves in Maine. I should have gone back more often. I shouldn't have kept their van this long. They are the closest family I have and they're getting older."

"Oh, Cam, I'm so sorry. No wonder you're upset. I thought it might have to do with work."

"Work? No that's the one thing in my life that is going great. I thought it would be temporary and I'd move into a different side of production or even digital media like Theo is doing. I landed at James for an internship between my junior and senior years and they made me an offer after I graduated. I've learned a ton, I'm good at it. I don't really want to leave at this point. And besides my grandparents, James is all I have that's long-lasting, you know?"

"I'm sure your grandparents are really proud of you. And I'm sure they understand why you didn't move back to the east coast."

"Yeah, I'm not sure. I mean, work and family are all I've got, and I'm going to have less family soon. I guess it's why I spend so much time focusing on work. Like my dad."

"And you said you are working for a woman? Is casting a female-dominated profession?"

"Definitely not. But Alison is considered one of the best for a reason."

"How long has she been doing this?"

"Her entire career, I think. She started in talent management and moved to a big casting agency and then went out on her own eight years ago."

"Oh wow - how old is she?"

"No idea," Cam says. "She doesn't share that information and I've never asked. 40 maybe? 45?"

"Oh OK." Olivia says, looking at Cam curiously. "So, it's not work - just family then?"

Cam stops on the sidewalk letting fans behind them pass. "Yeah, they raised me after my mom died. And my grandpa has had to watch Granny decline with dementia over the years. I'm worried about him, and I think he's having a harder time than I first thought. But work is good."

"Come on, the light turned, let's cross the street. I mean you have me. And Piper. And Theo."

"Well yeah but I mean family, you know, long-term people in your life."

"Are you saying you don't see friendships and girlfriends as long-term?"

"I think friendships and girlfriends come and go for the most part. You can't count on them. And I wouldn't put that burden on them."

"Cam, what are you talking about? OK, why did you move to LA for school if your grandparents are on the east coast?"

"Well, UCLA has one of the best film schools."

"No, I know. I mean there are good film schools on the east coast aren't there?"

Cam feels himself getting defensive. "Not sure it would have mattered if I was in New York or California. I still wouldn't have been there for them."

"Yeah, OK," Olivia says softly.

Cam stops again and says, "I wasn't trying to get away like you were. I got into UCLA and didn't want to pass up the chance."

"No, I get it. Did you apply to other schools?"

"No just UCLA," Cam admits. They continue to the tailgating area outside the stadium.

"You know I wouldn't say I was trying to get away. I would say that I was offered a few chances to play and get help with tuition and Seattle sounded great. I wasn't running away from my family, it was just a happy coincidence that it was that far away," she bumps her hip with his.

"Didn't you get an offer from Memphis too?"

"Alright let's change the subject," Olivia smiles good-naturedly and Cam laughs.

"And what about you and Piper? Let me ask quick before my entire family sees us coming."

"There's nothing going on with Piper," Cam says plainly. "Hey, let's stop over here. I want to buy a UT shirt before I meet the Carters."

They walk to a vendor and purchase the loudest orange shirt available. Cam slips it on over his gray tee.

Olivia nods approvingly. "Yeah, looks great, gorgeous. Alright we'll come back to Piper, but first, you've got to meet my frightening family."

After a ton of "hellos" and "sit down here let me make you a plate" greetings, Cam looks to Olivia for some help. Her family is almost as talkative and cheerful as Piper. They spend the morning asking a barrage of personal questions of their guest. Olivia answers most of them but Cam gets in a few words, too.

"Damn this food is good," he whispers to Liv when he gets a chance. He sees several other tailgates have different set ups but one thing they have in common is chicken. *Does every tailgate in the south have a bucket of KFC?*

"Reverend Carter, thank you for including me in your tailgate," Cam says, picking out another piece from the bucket.

"You're welcome any time, Cam. Get you some more of that chicken before the game starts. Fried chicken is perfect tailgating food, and no one does it better than the Colonel. Unless you count Popeye."

"I think I've tried everything here, and it was delicious. I thought tailgating was chips and salsa."

"Not in the south, baby." Olivia's mom hugs him goodbye. He joins Olivia and her cousin Tiffany as they walk toward the other side of the stadium where their seats are. Tiffany is a teacher outside Nashville and she and Olivia are close. When they part ways, Tiffany gives Cam a hug and tells him she hopes they can catch up later after the game.

"What's the plan, Liv?" Tiffany asks.

"No plan yet. Maybe go out for a drink after? I'll text you."

She and Cam walk a mile up to get to their seats. Cam stops and takes it all in, a bit overwhelmed at the number of people in and around the stadium. He stops for a beer and popcorn because it feels like a football game thing to do. The sun is bright, but it isn't exactly warm yet. He's glad he's got his long sleeve t-shirt on.

"Your family is great, Liv."

"Yeah, I know I'm pretty lucky. You did well because I know they're a lot."

"I was proud of myself. I don't have much experience with big families."

"I bet you will one day. Let's get back to Piper. Nothing there?"

"No, I wouldn't date Piper because she's a friend. I wouldn't want to lose her when it ends."

"Who says it has to end? Friends to lovers is a pretty common thing you know."

"Not for me. They always end and I don't want to ruin a friendship. Plus, I don't date a lot. I don't think most relationships last, or I'm not built for them. Better for me to focus on work."

"Yeah, I get that. But I bet you'd be great as a long-term boyfriend," Olivia laughs at Cam's expression. "Your face, Cam! Was it the term boyfriend? Or long-term that freaked you out?"

"Funny. Aren't we here for a football game?"

"Ok, I'll drop it, but I promise you, you can be in a romantic relationship that lasts longer than a week, Cam. You're one of the good ones."

EASTERN TENNESSEE, SATURDAY
Theo

Piper sets the cruise control once they're on Hwy 441 outside of Knoxville. Her left leg is bouncing, and she is sitting up straight, watching the landscape change.

"It's gorgeous here. Mountainous even."

Theo looks up from his phone and watches her for a moment. Her pale skin and big blue eyes. He shakes his head. Her enthusiasm and need for order are typically exhausting but today he finds he's just amused. He looks back at his phone. "It's a big park. What do you want to do? We should arrive by 11:00."

Piper glances at him and hesitates before she says, "Laurel Falls. There's a hike, and I know it's really popular and it'll likely be crowded with tourists, but I'd like to see it. And I want to go to North Carolina just to see that side of the park."

Theo returns to his map, tapping in new information. He notices Piper glancing over at him, probably surprised he didn't immediately disagree with her. He moves back and forth between websites and Apple Maps.

"Do I need to get off this road at any point?" Piper asks.

He flips back to the map. "No, you're going to stay on this basically until Laurel Falls. What about going to Clingman's Dome after the Falls? It's another half hour or so. They have an overlook and then a hike to a lookout."

"Is that the strenuous one? I'm not really dressed for it."

"Oh, come on. You work out, I'm sure you could do it. We've got to do some hiking while we're there."

Piper sighs. "What are you talking about? I'm not talking about *not hiking*. I'm saying I read that one of the popular trails is really strenuous and I'm asking not to do that one. You're on *my* trip you know."

Theo laughs. "These aren't strenuous - they say 'Easy'. Come on. It'll be fun to go to the lookout at Clingman's Dome and that's technically inside North Carolina."

"OK, and we can make it back tonight easy enough?"

"Yeah, based on this traffic we shouldn't have any problems. Everyone seems to be going *to* Knoxville today," Theo says, pointing at the other side of the highway. "We should be going against traffic this afternoon, too."

Piper sits back with a huge smile.

"What are you smiling about?" Theo asks her.

"Although you're here and I pray you don't ruin the day somehow, I'm just really excited. I haven't felt this happy in a while. I love exploring new places. Don't you?"

Theo watches her bouncing leg and shakes his head again. He pulls out two waters, places one in Piper's cup holder and returns to his phone.

"Yeah, I don't do enough of this. And hopefully you won't ruin *my* day," he teases her.

"So, what's new with you?" Piper asks, not taking the bait. "You're done in Austin?"

"Yep."

"So where are you going next?"

"I haven't agreed to any contracts yet. I've got a couple possible projects, but I'm taking a break before starting anything new."

"So where is all your stuff? Is it still at your apartment in Austin and you'll just move it when you get reassigned or are you staying in Austin?"

"I won't stay in Austin. Just not sure where to next."

"So how long will you be on this break?"

"I don't know Piper, OK? Just taking a break, helping out a friend who's visiting his grandparents. I don't have my next assignment planned out yet. Does that drive you crazy?"

"No," Piper says. "It kind of sounds awesome. I was just asking. Making chit chat. Being polite."

"Got it," Theo says. "Not much to report. Let's talk about you instead." Piper gives him a pointed look. "Why aren't you seeing anyone, Piper?"

"Why do you care?"

"Why won't you tell me?"

"Why should I?"

"Is it a problem that I'm curious?"

"Why would it be a problem?"

"Why do you avoid this subject?"

"Why do you keep bringing it up?"

"Why didn't you want to go to the football game?"

"Why wouldn't I want to see a national park?"

"Why would you want to leave Cam's side?"

"Why wouldn't I if he has Olivia?"

"Why do you think Cam has Olivia?"

"What do you mean?"

"Why wouldn't you want to go to the game?"

"Why would you ask me that again?"

"Why are you on this trip?"

"Why are you?"

They stop the game and glance at each other. Piper doesn't immediately turn away like she normally does. He knows she doesn't like him, but it's never been clear why. And he's not about to ask.

"Tell you what. You spill your next assignment plans and tell me why you're on this trip and I'll tell you who I'm dating and why I chose the Smoky Mountains over college football."

Theo grins and lets it drop. "OK - we're getting close to the first trail in the park."

"What, really?" He shows Piper the Maps app, and she sees their little blue dot entering the green area. "Is that really it? Oh wow."

They follow the signs to Laurel Falls, find a parking spot, grab their waters, and fall in line behind people walking toward the trailhead.

"This is supposed to take two hours or maybe a little more," Theo says. "So, we should get going."

"Wait, you mean two hours there and back, right, not one way?" Piper glances at her watch.

"Yeah, there and back, two or longer."

"I don't know where you saw Easy. This map says Moderate," Piper says pointing to the trailhead map. She takes off, respectfully passing people with walking sticks, families with kids in backpacks, an older gentleman with a bright UT hat, and two women with dogs. Theo keeps up easily with her - his long legs up to the task - but Piper seems like a woman on a mission. She stops suddenly to look at a beautiful old tree covered in moss on one side. She reaches over to touch it, making sure no one can see her, and then starts back up the path.

"Hey, slow down," Theo says. "We've got time."

"I know but this is my only day here, I want to see as much as I can." They power on in silence, Theo taking photos as they go. Piper's back will show up in many of them, but he doesn't care. This is the most peaceful place he's been in a while. They keep going, up steep climbs that flatten and curve. Passing people as they go, Piper not losing any momentum.

"How much further?" she asks.

"About an hour or so."

"Not likely," Piper mutters.

"I'm going to stop for a second." Theo takes a couple of photos of the woods and drop offs and drinks half his water bottle. They start up again. "Do you want to take any photos? Want me to take one of you?" he offers.

"When we get to the Falls," Piper says, resuming her speed walk without touching her water.

Twenty minutes later Theo checks his app because damn, they are at the falls. "Are you a runner?" Theo asks.

"What?" Piper asks. "Oh my God, look!" The series of falls is gorgeous, but Piper's face is what catches Theo's attention. He snaps a photo of her happy profile before she can stop him. "What are you doing? Theo look."

He stands next to her, and they listen to the beautiful falls. There are only four others at the falls and there is a quiet reverence for the place - whispers and water is all he can hear. He closes his eyes for a minute and takes it all in. When he opens his eyes, he sees Piper putting her phone down. *Did she just take a photo of me?*

"Would you like me to take your picture?" an older woman with a golden retriever on a leash asks.

"That would be great," Theo says, handing her his phone and turning around to pose in front of the falls. Piper steps away and Theo grabs her arm and pulls her back. He puts his arm around her shoulder, and they smile for the camera.

"Thank you," Theo says to the woman. "Here, let me take one of you and your beautiful dog. What's his name?"

"Her name is Dolly," the woman says.

"Oh sorry," Theo laughs.

"Well, it's hard to tell from your height," the woman grins at him. She steps to the falls and Theo swears both she and the dog smile at the same time.

Piper takes a photo of them too and says goodbye, petting Dolly before they leave.

"Oh my gosh, this is the most beautiful place I've ever seen."

Theo looks at Piper and says, "You live in California, and this is the most beautiful place?"

Piper doesn't respond but asks him if he is ready to head back. She takes a few more snaps of the falls and a selfie with a huge smile on her face and they start back to the minivan against the scattered walking traffic. Finally, she speaks. "I love SoCal but there's no break from the sun. I used to love the beach, but I've seen so many friends have melanomas removed from their chests, shoulders, faces. And I've never seen a waterfall before."

"What?"

"Not in person," Piper says. "I've hardly left California. I've never been to a national park outside of Southern California. My family did Mexico or Europe for vacations growing up." They walk in silence and rather quickly back to the van. Piper asks Theo if he wants to drive, and he jumps at the chance. He shows her where they're headed next, and they follow the signs to Clingman's Dome.

"So, it's a mountain," Piper realizes. "Clingman's Dome." Theo starts to answer when Piper squeals, "Oh my God!" and grabs his arm. He almost slams on the brakes before he realizes what she's seen. A sign for the Appalachian Trail.

"Is that really part of the trail?" she asks.

"God, you scared me. Yes. It cuts through the Smokies and Blue Ridge Mountains. I think it goes through something like 10 states?"

Piper is already on Wikipedia reading out all the basic facts. "2200 miles! Georgia to Maine! 25% of the thru hikers each year succeed. Can you imagine walking 2200 miles in one year?"

"I think there are only certain months that it can be done. A lot of people start in the spring in Georgia so they can get to Maine before the winter weather makes it impossible to finish."

"Would you ever do it?" Theo continues to be surprised at her interest in his thoughts.

"I'm not a big camping guy," Theo says. "I wouldn't mind doing some day hikes though."

A sign tells them they've entered North Carolina and Piper says "seven" quietly.

"Seven what?" he asks.

"Seven states. On this trip."

"Oh OK, got it. Now you'll have to add North Carolina to your playlist."

"You laugh but it's been fun."

"I'm not laughing," Theo says.

GREAT SMOKY MOUNTAINS NATIONAL PARK, SATURDAY
Piper

Theo and Piper pull into the parking lot at the end of Clingman's Dome Road and park for the half mile hike straight up to the lookout. On the long drive to the summit, they passed several overlooks. They stopped at each one that had safe parking and now Piper is anxious to get to the top.

Mindful of the time, they get new water bottles from the backseat and start the hike. Piper hurries past those taking their time and Theo follows her, matching her determined strides easily. Finally, they reach the summit and Piper turns around, beaming. "Look at the fall colors just starting!"

Theo pulls out his phone and takes her water. "Let me take your photo." She puts her arms up in the air and smiles wide. She offers to take his, but he snaps a quick selfie instead and then they both take ample photos of the views of Tennessee, Georgia, and North Carolina.

"This was awesome, but we probably need to go." Piper picks up her water bottle and starts back down the trail.

"Hang on. I've got two things I want to do before we go back to Knoxville," Theo says as he jogs to catch up.

"What?" Piper asks, somewhat warily.

"Let me show you."

They walk side by side down the path and then Theo points out a hidden tunnel off the main trail. "This is so cool," Piper says quietly. They go through the tunnel and take photos out the other side.

"One more thing up ahead," Theo points.

Piper locks into her yoga breathing, taking in the pines, the fresh autumn air, nature itself. "God, I love this. I don't know when I've ever felt this relaxed."

She assumes he has a biting comeback about her normally always being on her phone. Piper braces for it but Theo agrees, "Yeah, me too."

She speeds up a bit and Theo moves to catch up with her. "Here," he says, pointing to a trail. "This is a part of the AT. Let's hike it for a mile or two."

Her face lights up and she nods "Yes" enthusiastically. She doesn't consult the time and they set off on the path, walking companionably and quietly for almost 20 minutes.

"Do you hike a lot?" Theo finally breaks the silence.

"No, not really. Well, I've done some with friends in the hills in LA, but this is very different. I want to start doing more."

"Do you run with Cam?"

She gives Theo a confused look. "No, we're not joined at the hip you know. He's a quiet guy, mostly focusing on work or whoever he's seeing that month. I have been doing yoga and Pilates almost daily for years. I stick to those."

"Don't you spend a lot of time with Cam though?"

"Why would you think that?"

"Are we playing this game again?"

"I don't know, are we?"

Theo faces Piper. "I guess I thought you two were maybe seeing each other. Or maybe had in the past. Or maybe that is what this trip is about."

Piper notices they've stopped walking, so she starts again. "Cam and I aren't together. I know he's dated quite a bit in LA, but I don't really know those women. He is hard to read, and I do most of the reaching out in our friendship."

Theo doesn't say anything, so Piper continues.

"Have you been to his apartment?"

"No," Theo answers. "When I went to LA the last couple of times, I stayed closer to campus to catch up with friends."

"Well, he lives in a great area of LA and rents from an older man who appreciates someone occupying his guest house. Cam is doing well in his career, but you would not know it from the way he lives. At first, I thought maybe he was saving money to send back to his family, but that doesn't seem to be the case. My impression is that he is almost waiting for a part of his life to begin. I'd like to be a part of his life. I introduce him to people, try to get him to open up some. Except for work, he seems kind of alone."

"And maybe you need to let the man figure it out for himself. He's going to be 30 soon. He knows what he's doing." Theo softens his tone.

Piper looks up at him, "When was the last time you saw him?"

He doesn't answer.

"I'm not trying to be a fixer. He lives a pretty non-existent life part of the time. I picked him up for lunch one day when the van was getting some work done. His apartment was dark, lifeless, and felt like it was not lived in. I suggested we open the curtains up and let some light in and he looked at the windows like he hadn't even noticed them."

They're quiet for a while. "I'm probably making too much of this. I know he's an adult who can manage himself. I just like spending time with him, and I hope that he knows I'm there for him if he needs anything."

It's clear Theo is thinking about what Piper has said. "I think I was the only reason he did anything more than go to classes at school. All his college friends he met through me. It looks like you've filled that role lately. I guess it never occurred to me that he needed help, though."

"And maybe he doesn't," Piper acknowledges. "But I want to be there for him if he does. If he'll let me." They reach a clearing and view the ridges and peaks for miles around.

Theo sighs, "Hate to say it but we need to head back to civilization." Piper nods and they start a light jog back to the Odyssey. Piper hands Theo a protein bar and he sets the GPS for their hotel.

"I always thought of you as a SoCal girl, but now I think you might thrive on the east coast."

"I'm glad you came with me," Piper relents.

Five minutes later Theo says, "Thanks for letting me tag along."

KNOXVILLE, SATURDAY
Olivia

Olivia waits in the lobby while Piper gets ready in their hotel room. Piper emerges from the elevator in slim fitting jeans, a tank and a light jacket. Olivia is eager to catch up on their days.

"Have you seen Cam?" Olivia asks her.

"No not yet. I can tell from the crowds that Knoxville won!" Piper exclaims.

"Yeah, *Tennessee* won!" Olivia subtly corrects her. "And we got to see Damon for a minute. He'll be with his team tonight and my family is at the hotel where they always stay. So, I'm going to join them after we hang out tonight."

"OK great. I saw your bag in our room. Do you want me to go get it now?" Piper looks around the sea of excited fans for Cam. Or Theo.

"No, I'll swing back by here and pick it up later."

"Great! What did you want to do?"

"Well, we need to get some food in Cam. He's already had two beers here at the bar before he went upstairs to get ready to go out. Does he always drink this much?"

"Not in LA," Piper responds. "In fact, I don't think I've ever seen him have more than one drink at a party. But most of my friends are not big drinkers. You know - we take our calories very seriously in Southern California."

Olivia laughs, "Yeah, I've heard that. Well, I know he's worried about his grandparents. And just really quick, before the guys get here. He told me about his dad," Olivia confides.

Piper looks confused. "What do you mean?"

"Cam told me about his dad leaving the van in California. It made me mad to hear the story. I would have felt abandoned if my dad pulled that on me. Will Cam see him in Maine?"

"Oh, I don't know. He lives in Chicago. I don't think they talk much. I always got the impression that his dad had a serious career that took him away a lot, so Cam was raised by his grandparents."

Olivia ponders this. "I'm not sure his dad is that involved in Cam's life. Or ever has been. I think since his mom died his grandparents are the only people Cam can really count on."

"He never talks about anyone but his Grandpa Ben to me. Theo might know more than I do."

Olivia laughs again. "I doubt it. They were great friends in college, but I get the sense they haven't talked much in the last several years. Cam isn't great at reaching out. And Theo probably doesn't think to."

"Yeah, if Theo hadn't called him last weekend, I don't think Cam would have let him know about his grandmother's health. And he wouldn't be on this trip," Piper tells her.

"I know you're keeping an eye on him and that's great." Olivia slides a business card to Piper. "I hope you will text me and let me know how the guys are doing. I doubt I'll hear from them again anytime soon."

Piper starts to ask something but seems to change her mind. "I'm so glad I got to meet you."

"Me too! I was just thinking that. I want to hear about your day."

Theo walks in, says "Hi" to Piper and puts his arm around Olivia. "How was the game?"

"Great! Damon had a great game. I'm heading to their hotel later tonight. Can we go get some dinner before the restaurants fill up?"

"Cam was on the phone with Grandpa Ben. He said to text him where we're going, and he'll meet us there."

They find a table at a restaurant on the river and get a good spot near the windows. Drinks and an appetizer arrive along with Cam. Piper thinks he looks more relaxed than he has in days.

"Hey," he says to the table in general and orders a beer before he even sits down. "You missed a great game."

"We heard," Theo tells him. "How is your grandfather?"

"Um good. I feel bad that I'm not there, but he knows we're on our way. He's kind of hard-headed so I don't think he's telling me everything. I'm worried about him. And of course, my grandmother. Can we not talk about it tonight?"

Everyone nods and Cam changes the subject. "So, Liv, what are we doing tonight?"

"Well, there are two bars I think we should check out. One has great live music, and one has karaoke. They will be packed later tonight but if we go quickly, we should be able to snag a table."

"You singing tonight?" Cam asks Theo.

Theo shakes his head grimly. "There's not enough beer."

"No seriously, I remember a couple of times in school when you were the first one up to karaoke."

Now Olivia is stunned. She leans over to Theo. "What, really?"

"I don't remember," shrugging her off.

While Theo and Olivia reminisce, Piper takes a moment to check in with Cam. "I know you don't want to talk about it but everything OK in Maine?" Piper asks.

Cam's face softens a little, and he confides, "Yeah, he's OK. But he's really focused on getting legal paperwork done. I'll be happy when we get there so I can help. Speaking of - I need to stop at my aunt's tomorrow in Virginia. She's got a place for us to stay. I realize this trip is a lot longer than you thought so I can take you to an airport tomorrow. I'm sure we'll pass several."

Olivia notices that Piper doesn't respond to Cam's offer. And she doesn't look surprised by the suggestion.

Theo interjects, "I think I'm good to Maine."

"You don't have any work you need to get to?" Olivia asks.

"No, I have time."

Dinner is less awkward than the last few days. They discuss recent concerts they've attended and Cam's work, which seems to be his favorite subject.

"So, I want to hear about any new trends in LA that I should be aware of," Olivia nudges Piper.

"None that I can think of," Piper says, racking her brain.

"That's because it comes naturally to you," Olivia says. "You look so put together."

Piper starts to speak and stops, looks down and blushes. Olivia continues, "Oh, come on. You are effortlessly gorgeous. Guys help me out here."

"Don't embarrass her," Cam tells Liv. "Piper doesn't like to talk about herself – she's always focused on everyone around her. But yes, she's gorgeous," he says and smiles at her.

Why does Cam think he can't date Piper? Olivia asks herself again. They would be perfect together. *Cam clearly needs a Piper in his life.*

"Thanks," Piper says quietly. Theo doesn't weigh in but doesn't disagree either.

Piper awkwardly changes the subject. "So, tell me about karaoke, guys."

Cam lights up, "I saw Theo sing twice back in college. 'Livin' on a Prayer' of course."

"Of course," everyone says.

"And what was the other one?"

"I can't remember," Theo says.

"Fuck," Cam says. "What was it? We were in San Fran with the volleyball team and a big group from school made the drive up. What was that song?"

"'Sandman', Metallica," Theo says and Cam bursts out laughing.

"Yes!! That was awesome!"

"I don't know it," Olivia tells them.

Cam recovers from his laughter. "I'll play it for you when we get outside where it's not so loud."

Olivia looks outside and says, "Not sure it'll be any quieter. Look at the crowds."

They finish their meal quickly, Theo picks up the check, even though Piper insists on paying. Theo says, "No, I got it" and hands the server his card.

"Then first round's on me," she declares.

Olivia notices Cam is walking straight enough but seems way more animated than she's used to seeing him. Lots of talking with his hands. The crowds have picked up, a sea of orange everywhere you look.

"Where are we going?" Piper asks Olivia.

"We've got a few more blocks until we get to the bars. Let's see where we can get a table because I don't want to stand all night."

They finally settle on a karaoke bar and order a round of beers for the guys and gin and tonics for Olivia and Piper. The music on the sound system is loud enough that they have to yell over it.

"I don't drink a lot," Piper tells Olivia, "So I usually choose something that will take me all of dinner to get through. This one, though, is going down smoothly," she laughs.

Piper puts her hand on Cam's arm and leans into him, "Is work OK?"

"Yeah," he looks at her puzzled. "I'll get some done tonight and we don't need to leave tomorrow until 10 or 11 to make it to my aunt's by 4:00. Why?"

"Just asking to be nice," Cam gives her a half smile and Theo asks Olivia about Damon.

"He's a senior, right?"

"Yes, he's studying political science. Not sure what he's going to do next. I don't think Law School or grad school, but I don't really know."

"Think he'll stay in Knoxville?"

"I think he'll go wherever he gets a job. I don't think either one of us wants to live in Tennessee forever."

"Why?" Cam asks.

"It's a big world out there. Lots of opportunities. We both like to travel, not that we had a lot of chances to growing up. Our friends have tended to stay in Memphis, but Damon and I have talked about making a change at some point. We'll see."

A man dressed in jeans and UT orange with a clipboard runs onto the small stage and announces karaoke starting. There's a loud cheer and Cam starts to say something to Theo about choosing a song, but it doesn't look like they'll have a chance for a while. A long line forms in front of the stage for sign-ups.

"So, Cam, you sing?" Olivia asks him.

"Not like Theo," Cam says. Before he can answer any other questions, he puts his head in his hands and says so only their table can hear, "If I never hear this fucking song again..."

Four very happy and inebriated students launch into their song which immediately brings a deafening wave of cheers from the crowd. They sing the Tennessee state song that is played over and over at the UT game. Olivia laughs at Cam and sings along with "Rocky Top" at the top of her lungs.

Piper looks around amused. Cam is shaking his head, staring at the table. Theo almost falls off his stool cracking up. By the time the chorus hits, the entire bar has joined in. "Rocky Top, Tennessee". The four guys take their bows and exit the stage, somehow without falling off, and the cheers finally start to die down.

Next a group of young ladies runs up in their orange and white dresses, jeans and cute tops and shout the opening three words. The place goes wild again, this time with female voices screaming. *Ah, Shania.*

It's hard not to join in when you're talking about going totally crazy. Piper sings along, and Olivia shakes her head, smiling at her. Cam and Theo are laughing in Piper's direction. Piper shoots them a look that says *screw you* and Olivia laughs again.

The bar gets steadily louder and more crowded and Piper is clearly having a blast. "My LA friends don't let their hair down like this really. I wonder where the karaoke crowd is in California."

"You think Chelsea would karaoke?" Theo asks Cam. Piper turns so quickly to look at Theo that she slides off her bar stool and into Cam's lap.

"Whoa," Cam catches her.

"I forgot," Piper yells, getting back onto her seat. "You know Chelsea."

Theo looks at Piper and raises his eyebrows, his dark eyes reflecting the lights in the bar. "Yeah, I met her last time I was in LA."

"Right. I forgot about that. Do you stay in touch?" Piper watches Theo intently. She stage whispers to Olivia, "We all met up at a party when Theo flew out to LA. I saw Theo hitting on Chelsea for part of the night, and then they left together. I don't think he knows that I know. Ha!"

Olivia smiles at her, pretty sure Theo could hear her, even with the raucous crowds.

"Hey, why is my drink so full?" Piper asks.

"That's your third," Cam tells her. "The server just brought it."

"Third? I've only had one."

"You've had two."

"Oh wow," Piper says. "I want to sing."

"Really?" Olivia asks her. "Just making sure you know I'm not going up there with you."

"That's OK - I'm going to do it. I've never been to karaoke before, and no one here knows me. I'm going to do it." She takes off to join the line, immediately starting a conversation with a young co-ed who looks like she is on the fence about signing up to sing. Olivia watches the guys as the guys watch Piper.

"Who's Chelsea?" she asks.

"I work with Chelsea - she's Alison James' right hand. We're good friends. I think Piper thinks you two hooked up, Theo."

"I didn't hook up with Chelsea," Theo tells Cam.

"Yeah, but she knows you left pretty early with someone that night and I'm pretty sure she thinks it was Chelsea."

"I wouldn't do that to you," Theo says and smiles at Cam.

Cam looks confused. "What are you talking about?"

"You and Chelsea. Nothing going on?"

"No," Cam says, emphatically.

"OK. I guess I was wrong on that one."

Cam shakes his head at Theo and returns to watching Piper who is next in line, talking with a group of young ladies behind her.

Olivia watches Piper too. "She is the most adorable woman I've ever met. I can't believe neither of you has gone out with her. Oh wait, or have you?"

They both turn back to Olivia and say "No" at the same time.

Cam keeps an eye on Piper while Theo launches into the story of the first time he met her and her friends.

"She asked me a whole series of personal questions, spent most of the night dragging Cam to introduce him to all the people she knew or met at the party, and then planned our entire next day. And the whole night she spent going from group to group talking excitedly with everyone there."

Olivia says, "What's wrong with any of that?"

"She's just annoying. She annoys the hell out of me," Theo says, probably louder than he meant.

"Why?" Olivia asks, trying her hardest to hold back a grin.

"Are you kidding? She's just all over the place, organizing everything, constantly talking. If she isn't helping someone solve a problem, she's making plans. I wish she would just calm the fuck down," he mutters.

Cam looks at Theo calmly. "None of that bothers me. I wouldn't know anyone but Chelsea in LA if it wasn't for Piper."

"And don't you think it's time to cut her loose?" Theo asks.

"What are you talking about?" Cam asks. Piper comes racing back to the table.

"OK so first I'm going to sing with that group of Phi Mus which is great because I've never done this before, and then, I picked a *Dolly* song and I'm going to sing it all by myself. It'll probably be another hour or so until it's my turn but, oh my gosh, you guys. This is the best night of my life."

Cam reaches over and tugs her close to him. "I'm glad you're here," he says, close to her ear. "I'm sorry I'm such an asshole."

Piper's cheeks heat up. She turns her face away from Theo and Olivia and she brazenly whispers to him, "But you don't want to go out with me, do you?" Cam shakes his head "no" very subtly and she leans against him, still looking away from the table.

"I don't have friends, Piper. You're it. I can't lose you when I screw it up. And I know I would."

"You wouldn't lose me. How could you think that? But I get it. Don't tell the guys, OK? I'm just going to go to the restroom." She sniffs and speeds off toward the line to the ladies' room.

"What was that all about?" Theo asks, standing suddenly.

"Nothing. She's had a little too much to drink. She's OK though. I'm going to get her a Diet Coke."

Cam leaves for the bar and Olivia and Theo share a look. "She'll be OK," Olivia says.

"What's going on?"

"He let her down gently and Piper gets it. Now's not a good time for Cam. He's not able to think about anyone but his grandparents right now. He has it in his head that relationships don't last, and everyone leaves him."

"Woah, that's a lot. You talked about Piper at the game?"

"No, not really." Olivia turns back to the stage and cheers for the lady who butchered Adele's "Someone Like You". *Also, read the room, girlfriend. This is not an Adele crowd.*

The "Rocky Top" group of guys returns, and Cam's face goes red, "Oh no." The announcer reminds everyone that "Rocky Top" can only be sung once an hour, so the guys shift to "Ring of Fire", doing a decent job for four drunk football fanatics.

"What's this?" Piper asks, returning to the table.

"I got you a Rum and Coke - drink up," Cam says.

"Oh yay!" Piper says. Theo looks at him and Cam shakes his head.

"You know what I want next? A margarita. With salt!"

"Got it. After you karaoke. Let's stick with this for now."

Olivia watches the drunkest of Knoxville having the time of their lives. When a guy she recognizes (*maybe one of Damon's friends?*) starts singing Nas's "The World is Yours", she's impressed. He's good. She cheers louder than she has all night and decides she is just about over this. She considers letting everyone know it's time she says goodbye, but then the Phi Mus are called up and Piper throws back her "Rum and" Coke and squeals as she heads to the stage. Theo stares at her, shaking his head.

Olivia punches him in the arm. "Don't be an asshole to her. I mean it."

Cam screams, "Piper!" And the ladies launch into impressive choreography for seven women who are each about two drinks over-served at this point. A cute blonde in the middle starts in with the Carl Carlton classic and the room erupts. Two more Phi Mus join in the first verse, and by the chorus they're all dancing in sync and singing about an "Everlasting Love".

Theo pulls out his phone. He zooms in and catches the rest of the performance. "Why aren't we recording this?" he yells.

The bar goes wild when they do a synchronized bow and then the Phi Mus step back. The microphone is handed to Piper.

"I have never seen her that red," Cam yells, looking back to make sure Theo is still recording. Olivia stands up to try to see over the crowd between their table and the stage.

The Phi Mus dance in the background and a sweet, shaky voice begins one of Dolly's best about waltzing in a door with dreamy eyes.

Olivia screams and the crowd goes crazy. Who doesn't love Dolly, especially fans from Tennessee? Piper's voice is less shaky now, singing to the crowd. Theo keeps his phone on Piper and looks around the bar at everyone singing along. "How does everyone know the words?"

During the instrumental break the background dancers take it up a notch then step back again for Piper's big finish to "Here You Come Again". And it's *strong*. Piper's new best friends join her for the very end and the crowd goes wild with applause. Piper hugs everyone and runs back to her table, and straight to Cam who picks her up, spins her and kisses her on the cheek.

"You were amazing!" Olivia yells. "How does it feel?"

"I've never felt anything like this. Oh My God. I'll be right back." She runs over to the Phi Mu table, and they pull out their phones for selfies with their new LA bestie. Cam orders the smallest margarita with salt the bartender will make, another round of beers, and returns to the table.

Theo hasn't said a word, but Olivia and Piper don't seem to notice. They enjoy one last drink together. Several people pass their table and tell Piper she was awesome. "I love Knoxville!" she yells and smiles for photos with everyone.

Olivia asks, "Guys, are you karaoke'ing? I assume you don't want to follow that."

"Nope, not me," Cam says.

"Then I think I'm going to say goodnight when we get back to the hotel and meet up with my family. Piper, are you good on your own tonight?"

"Yes, of course but I'm going to miss you!" Piper looks genuinely sad to be saying goodbye. She reaches out tentatively for a hug and Olivia hugs her tight and whispers "you're awesome".

Piper smiles at Olivia and then stifles a yawn. "God I'm exhausted. About ready to go?"

"Yeah," they say in unison. Theo goes to the bar to settle up and they walk out into the brisk night.

"Glad we stayed?" Piper asks Cam.

"Yeah definitely. I guess I didn't realize how tough the last week has been. I've got some work to tackle tomorrow morning. Can we leave at 11:00?"

Theo agrees, "A late morning sounds great. I've got a few things to do, too."

They take the elevator to Piper and Olivia's room so Olivia can get her bags. She says goodbye to Cam and Theo, giving them both quick kisses and extra-long hugs.

"Come out to LA one of these days," Cam whispers to her.

"I'd love that. Be safe on your way north. Thanks for calling me. And you," Olivia says, hugging Piper one last time, "take care of these two."

Fellow Travelers – Odysseus Returns to Maine

"Livin' on a Prayer" by Bon Jovi
    "Sandman" by Metallica
    "Man! I Feel Like a Woman!" by Shania Twain
    "Ring of Fire" by Johnny Cash
    "Someone Like You" by Adele
    "The World Is Yours" by Nas
    "Everlasting Love" by Carl Carlton
    "Here You Come Again" by Dolly Parton

KNOXVILLE, SUNDAY
Cam

Cam makes a cup of coffee and opens his email to find one from Chelsea titled, "Woody I have a question."

"I have all the questions," the email reads. "Where are your recs from the Nashville meeting? How was the Nashville meeting? Are you still alive? In Maine yet? Might want to send what you have asap. Help me Obi-Wan. You're my only hope."

Cam sends his recommendations and a recap of his Nashville meeting to Chelsea. He signs off with "I'll see you down the road," pretty sure she will never place it as a *Nomadland* quote. Too new a movie.

He cleans up his other emails, sends a thank you to the two agents and the hosting team in Nashville, copying Alison, and then decides it would be good to reach out to Alison directly. Too early to call so he starts a new email.

"I'm in Tennessee, I'm alive, and I'm caught up. Sorry if I worried you. Should be in Maine in a couple of days. Thanks again, Cam."

He's not happy with the way he left things with Grandpa Ben yesterday but doesn't really need to call him back. As he closes his laptop, Theo returns to the room.

"Gym?" Cam assumes. He was in the shower when Theo took off this morning.

"Yeah," Theo says. "I'll shower and pack so you can finish up work."

"Already have," Cam says. "Did you see Piper downstairs?"

"No," Theo says and goes to the shower.

"Hey, I was thinking about walking over to the river - do you want to go?"

"I'm going to pass but I think Piper would want to see it too."

"I hate to wake her up this early. I need to get outside before we're in the Odyssey all day again. See you downstairs at 11:00."

Cam enjoys walking around Knoxville and stops for biscuits and gravy before returning to the hotel. Piper meets them in the lobby a little before 11:00. They load the Odyssey and set the GPS for Charlottesville.

Cam notices she is happy but somewhat subdued. Or maybe she's just relaxed. Piper takes the back seat, stretches her legs out, and gets back on her phone. "Did you get caught up on James, Cam?"

"Yeah, Chelsea isn't going to let me fall too far behind."

"Theo, you never told me - do you and Chelsea stay in contact?"

He glances at Cam. "No. I haven't talked to her since that night last year. Why?"

"Just curious," Piper studies her phone.

"Obviously but why?"

Cam interrupts the inane back and forth. "Hey when do we get off I-40? I think it was less than an hour outside Knoxville."

Theo pulls up GPS on his own phone and realizes it's just a few miles away. "Yeah, we'll get on US 81. I-40 is about to turn south, and we don't want that."

"Nope. Going north from now on."

"We'll be on 81 for almost the entire rest of the drive today. There are no accidents or closures so I'm shutting off Maps. Have you updated your playlist?" Theo raises his voice toward the back seat.

Does Cam note a hint of hostility back? *I thought their day together would have taken care of some of that.*

"Yes, it's all caught up," Piper responds. Theo hands her the adapter and the first song starts - "Rocky Top". Theo busts out laughing and Cam groans. Piper smiles and changes the song. "Walking in Memphis" starts, and their quiet Sunday morning relaxes into hills and highway, as they pass small town after small town, with national forests on their right.

A few minutes later "Smoky Mountain Rain" starts, and Piper sits straight up in her seat. She resets the song, and it starts up again. She gasps at the lyrics talking about a trip from LA to Knoxville. Theo turns around in his seat and gives her a little smile.

"Oh my God," Piper says. "I didn't know this song when I added it to the playlist." She starts the song again and lets it play out.

"Wow," Piper says when the song ends. "Have you heard this song before?"

"Yeah," Cam and Theo both say.

"Wow," Piper says again and marks it as a favorite.

***

"So, tell me about your aunt, Cam." They stop for snacks and water and Piper finally pitches the rest of the healthy snacks from Whole Foods.

"I guess she's my great aunt. She married Grandpa Ben's brother. He died several years ago."

"Oh no," Piper says. "How is she?"

"Um, I don't really know. We used to drive to Virginia in the summers, and I know they came up to visit my grandpa and Granny and Aunt Ginny's family in Maine. I don't think I've seen her since his funeral. Or that may not be right. She's a nurse and I think her mother lived with them. But she's gone too. I know she plays Bridge. She tried to teach me once."

Piper asks, "It's a card game, right? I hear about southern ladies playing Bridge but I'm not actually sure if it's cards or like dominoes or something."

"Old southern men play dominoes. Southern women play Bridge," Theo says. "Or that's what I've seen in Texas."

Cam doesn't offer any more memories and the group goes back to singing along to Piper's playlist. On the other side of Bristol Cam announces "Seven". Theo looks back at Piper who's intent on her phone and making notes in her sturdy notebook.

Piper looks up at Theo's expression and asks, "What? Oh, we're not going through North Carolina today? That was my seven yesterday. We hiked the Appalachian Trail in North Carolina!"

Cam is surprised. "What? What did you do yesterday? You went all the way to North Carolina?"

Piper explains, "The park is in Tennessee and North Carolina, and I really wanted to see North Carolina so we crossed the state line for a hike up Clingman's Dome. It was spectacular. I was hoping we'd drive through North Carolina today, but I didn't study the map. I feel like we're in a different country at times and we've only been through seven or eight states. I've been thinking about the hike all morning. We did part of the Appalachian Trail too! And the views, oh the views!"

Cam is quiet, not sure what to make of this information. *Why should I care that Piper and Theo saw an extra state yesterday? Would I have preferred hiking to the football game? Or time with these two over the crowds of the SEC? Or maybe I just like spending time with Piper and Theo.* Turning off the questions in his mind, he enjoys the open road with surprisingly little traffic.

"I guess the UT crowds aren't heading home to Virginia."

"No, I'm guessing they're not driving north like us," Theo offers.

"How much time do we have before we get to your aunt's house?" Piper asks.

"About four hours," Theo updates his GPS again.

"OK, I'm going to try to get this done in the next hour or so and send it off. For some reason I'm struggling on five of Monday's 'Ten'."

"Maybe you just need a break. How long have you been responsible for this article?" Cam asks.

"Four years, I think. Yeah, maybe, but it's a great gig. Maybe my heart's just not in it today." Piper puts in her earbuds and Cam and Theo lapse back into silence.

A few minutes later "Sweet Virginia" by the Rolling Stones comes on and Cam looks back at Piper in the review mirror. She doesn't look up but can feel him looking at her. "Yes, I know," she says loudly over her earbuds. "Thought I'd start with the songs before I tackle work." Cam grins.

"Man, we are passing so much history," Theo says as the Odyssey drives past signs for Roanoke and Lynchburg. "I would love to spend some time in this area. OK I'm going to stop googling Virginia history now."

"You sound like Piper and her National Park selfies," Cam whispers.

Piper speaks up from the backseat. "I'm going to take a call from Amy, OK?"

"Sure," Cam says.

"Hey, tell me what's going on. Are you going to brunch? Who's going? I saw that you're going to The Vine. Enjoy a bellini for me. Great, all is good. Yes, he's OK. Amy says hi."

Cam gives a little shrug when Theo looks at him with raised brows. "No idea," he whispers.

"OK so what happened with your mom? Uh huh. Uh huh... Did you tell her you couldn't take her? Can't her sister take her? Boundaries Ame. I know...I struggle with it too, especially with my mom who always has an emergency. I know. Kisses to everyone today. I miss you all... I don't know. A few more days maybe? We're in Virginia. Yes, it's been good though...I hiked in the Smoky Mountains yesterday! OK, I'm looking at what you sent... I love your style - send me a photo when you have it pulled together but I'm sure it'll be great... Bye."

Piper sighs, probably not realizing it, and shoots Theo a look when he glances back at her with raised brows. Cam watches his friends continue their annoyed, but thankfully silent, communications. Piper goes back to her work.

"Done," she announces an hour later when she finishes her article and sends it off to her editor. She sits up between the two front seats, leaning as far forward as the Odyssey will allow. "Beautiful state," she murmurs.

Cam nods in agreement. "Yeah, I don't think I've been in this area before. One year we went to the beach - it was a few hours from their house. And Aunt Ginny took me to Williamsburg one time. I don't think anyone else was with us."

"I'd love to see Richmond," Theo says. "Not sure what all is there but I hear it's a great little city on a river."

"The James River," Piper adds and Cam glances again in the mirror. "I know that from Patricia Cornwell novels that I read like crazy in high school." They leave US 81 and take I-64.

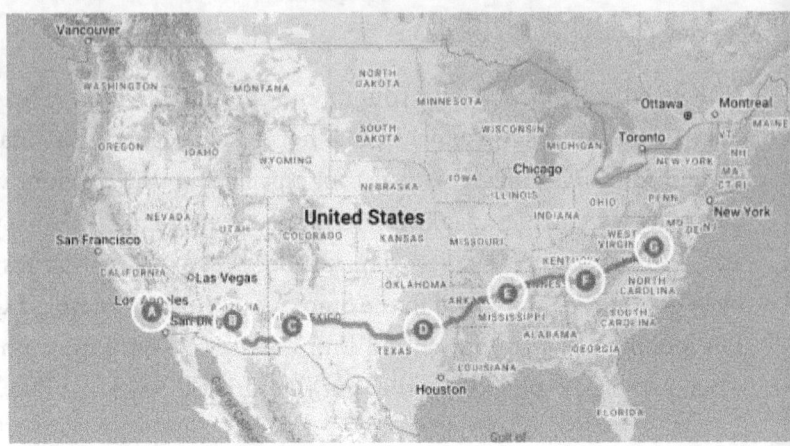

NORTHERN VIRGINIA, SUNDAY
Cam

Cam calls Aunt Ginny to get an exact address. He has her on Speaker. "Hi Aunt Ginny, it's Cam."

"Hello! Are you on your way?"

"Yes, I'm just getting on I-64." Ginny gives Cam the directions and Theo jots them down in his phone.

"How are you doing Cam?"

"I'm good. Looking forward to seeing you."

"Yes, me too! It's been so long. I can't wait to hear all about California. I'm leaving my book club now. See you when you get to the house. Love you."

They hang up and Piper asks, "Does she know we're coming Cam? Theo and me?"

"Well, I didn't mention it when I called her this week. She won't care."

Piper looks taken aback.

"OK. Do you want us to take off for a little while so you can spend time with her?" Theo asks.

Cam looks surprised. "No, she's feeding us. She'll be happy to meet you."

"But is she cooking for two?" Piper asks.

"I'm sure it'll be fine," Cam assures them.

Piper snaps her fingers. "Wait a minute. You didn't think I'd still be on this trip when you got to Virginia, did you?"

"What?" Cam asks. "I didn't really think about it." Cam follows Theo's directions, and they arrive at a beautiful colonial house with hydrangeas tucked in close all around the wide porch.

Cam watches Piper's expression as she looks out the Odyssey window. "I imagine lots of great family celebrations here, a garden out back, and maybe a sun porch. How many kids do Ginny and her husband have?" Piper asks, still staring at the beautiful facade.

"None," Cam tells her. "I'm the only grandchild on the Young side."

A striking woman with silver hair, dressed in tan linen pants, a pin-striped linen top and wearing a chunky necklace steps out onto the front porch. The only thing out of place are her bright orange Crocs. "Well Cam, you've brought me some new friends!"

Cam is taking his time getting out of the van, so Theo and Piper step up and introduce themselves. "And who are you exactly?" Aunt Ginny asks them in a kind, but surprised, voice.

"Friends of Cam's who are along on the drive to Maine. I'm a friend from Los Angeles," Piper clarifies.

Theo starts to explain that they are college friends when Cam comes up and gives Aunt Ginny a hug.

"Oh Cam, you've turned into a man in the years since I've seen you. OK, OK, that's enough from me. Come inside and we'll get caught up."

Theo and Piper share a look behind Ginny and Cam and follow them inside. Once everyone has had a chance to freshen up from the day's drive, they meet on the sun porch (Piper called that one) for iced tea along with crackers and a cheese ball.

"Cam, I can't believe how grown up you are. 28, right?"

"That's right," Cam says. "Sorry I didn't mention Piper and Theo - it's been a busy week. I haven't been thinking straight I guess."

"And how has the drive been?"

No one says anything and Aunt Ginny laughs.

"No," Piper says, when she realizes Cam isn't going to say anything. "It's been good. We've been through seven states now. An unexpected extra night in New Mexico due to the alternator going out. We also spent two nights in Knoxville, TN to visit Cam and Theo's friend. It's been a good trip overall."

"It's been a long trip," Aunt Ginny says, eyeing Cam.

"Yes, it has," Piper agrees but then changes the subject. "I see you have a garden. I realize it's fall but could I take a look?" Piper asks, making eye contact with Theo.

"Yes of course. I was just out there," Aunt Ginny says, pointing to her Crocs. "I've picked just about everything but there are some pumpkins on the vines, and the flowers are still thriving since we haven't had a frost yet. I'm making pasta and salad for dinner. I hope you'll join us."

"We'd love that." Cam watches Piper and Theo go out into the garden and look at the pumpkins. Piper sits on a little bench and admires the garden, probably trying to give Cam and Aunt Ginny a few moments alone.

"It's so good to see you. How is your grandpa?" Aunt Ginny takes a sip of tea.

"I think he's OK, but have you talked to him lately?"

"Not in the last couple of weeks. I left him a voicemail yesterday when you let me know you were coming. I haven't heard back." She reaches for her cell phone to double check.

"Um, I'm not sure if you know or if I should be the one telling you, but Granny has been diagnosed with pancreatic cancer."

Ginny's hand goes to her heart. "What? No, I didn't know that. When?"

"He called me last weekend. Piper and I left LA on Monday."

"And how are you, hon? This has got to be hard."

"Well, I kind of feel like I lost her a while ago. I haven't facetimed with her in a long time."

"Or visited?" Aunt Ginny asks gently.

"No, I was going to before the pandemic, but I guess time goes by and I don't even notice how long it's been. Grandpa Ben came out to LA a couple of years ago but that's the last time I saw him. I am ready to get there and spend time with both of them."

"Did he say anything about treatments? I assume they are not going that route."

"I don't really know for sure," Cam responds. "I think they've decided against it. He asked me to come out and I thought I would drive the van back."

"What do you mean?" Ginny asks.

"It's Granny's minivan. She got it when I was in high school. Dad and I drove it to LA after I moved into an apartment. We moved the rest of my things from Granny's house. He was going to drive it back but decided to buy a motorcycle and drive to Pittsburgh where he was working then."

"And where is your dad now?"

"The last I heard was Chicago. We haven't talked lately. I guess I should let him know about Granny."

"Yes, you should. When was the last time you saw your dad?"

"When we moved my things to LA."

"And when was that?"

"I don't know exactly. I was in college."

"So, tell me about your friends. I'm glad you've had some company on this drive."

"I know Theo from school, and I know Piper from LA."

"You've known her a long time?"

"For the last few years. We met through friends."

Ginny raises her eyebrows.

"We're not dating. She's from LA and knows everyone. She loves introducing me to people. She's the reason I do anything except work."

"You've been in California almost 10 years Cam." He looks alarmed. "Well, I guess at least 9. You've made it your home. I hope work isn't the only reason you're there."

Cam sits back and thinks about it. *Has it really been 9 or 10 years? Yeah, I guess it has.*

"And what about Theodore?"

Cam chuckles at the proper name. "We went to film school together in LA."

"And does he live in California too?"

"No, he moves around for work, and we don't do the same kind of work. I don't see him much. He stays in touch, though."

Theo walks through the front door and asks Cam for the van keys. He returns with Piper in tow.

"What time were you planning on dinner, Aunt Ginny?" Theo asks in a more formal voice than Cam has ever heard. "Piper and I were thinking about driving to Monticello but only if it doesn't interfere with your plans."

"Oh, it's only a half hour from here but I think it might be closed for tours of the interior by the time you get there. Go enjoy and we'll see you when you get back."

Cam looks surprised. "Really? Monticello?"

"Are you OK if we do that? We'll be gone an hour and a half, and we'll fill up."

"No, go ahead," Cam says.

"Thanks," Theo and Piper say in unison and head toward Thomas Jefferson's home.

Cam calls Grandpa Ben and leaves a voicemail. "I'm here at Aunt Ginny's. Staying at the Shenandoah cabin tonight and New York City tomorrow night. I'll be in Maine by Tuesday night, I think. Can you call us back? OK hope you're doing OK."

Aunt Ginny waves him into the kitchen and places a cold beer in front of him. "So why don't you catch me up," she says.

"I think I just did," he says, pointing to the sunroom.

"Tell me about your work."

Cam's face lights up and he dives into James Casting, how he started as an intern and immediately loved the independent feel of the company. He talks about Chelsea and how he started casting voiceover actors and thought that would be his niche. But then Alison started involving him in extras work, which is quite different since these actors will be seen but not heard typically. He stayed with James after he graduated because he was offered a full-time position and is now an associate casting director. He manages relationships with several talent agents on the West Coast and now Chelsea has set up a meeting with a talent agent he hasn't met before in NYC tomorrow evening.

Aunt Ginny notices the change in Cam's enthusiasm when he talks about his job. "How many casting companies are there?"

"Several. There are some very large ones, but I really like the small agency where I can learn all the work. Alison did the same. She left a large firm where she moved up quickly and started her own agency several years ago."

"Would you want to do the same? Start your own agency?"

"No, I like where I am. I feel like I belong there, you know? And how about you? What is going on? Do you ever think about returning to Maine?"

"No, just to see family from time to time, but less now. It's hard to travel by yourself when you're as old as I am, Cam. After all these years I couldn't take the winters and so many of my distant relatives have left Maine or have died there. If you feel like you grew up with a small family, imagine it at 84 with no younger generation behind you. No complaints from me though. I am very busy with church, Bridge, golf from time to time, gardening, and I started taking water aerobics at my club. Can you believe it? I haven't played tennis since Warren was with us but I'm 84! So, water aerobics is my new thing."

Cam rinses out his glass, puts it in the dishwasher and gives his sweet aunt a hug. "Love you," he says.

"You too, sweetheart. Has your grandpa called back?"

"No, not yet. I know he's been busy with Granny and the doctors. Plus, he said he had some legal things to take care of."

Aunt Ginny's head tilts up to him. "What do you mean?"

"I don't know really. He wanted to talk to me about it a couple nights ago and wouldn't let it go. I guess there's just a lot to take care of when someone is sick."

She looks at him with narrowed eyes and decides not to press. "Well, let me put this dessert together and we can put on some football and relax." She leaves the kitchen and Cam searches for a glass for water. He hasn't been here in so long he's forgotten where everything is.

"Aunt Ginny, would you mind if I changed and headed out for a run? I wouldn't mind seeing the neighborhood and park again."

"Of course, hon, but you can take my car if you'd rather not jog."

"I think I could use the exercise," he says.

Ginny starts to ask how he can run after drinking a beer but remembers the perks of being 28 and lets it drop.

Cam heads to "his" bedroom, the one he always stayed in when he visited. A lot has changed, including the linens. And this paint color he doesn't remember. He changes, stretches, and goes out the front door, first walking and then jogging through vaguely familiar streets in the general direction of a park. After half an hour or so he winds his way back to Aunt Ginny's house and a long hot shower before dinner and their next stop.

CHARLOTTESVILLE, SUNDAY
Piper

Theo follows Piper's directions, and they pull into a beautifully wooded parking lot. He drops Piper at the front desk to check on tour tickets, parks and walks up the stairs to meet her.

"The last tour is over, but we can walk around the grounds, and the grave is a 15-minute walk from here. There's also the visitors center. I got a map."

They walk in silence through the grounds and end up at the Hemmings cabin which looks to be part of the Slavery Tour. They walk back to the van and then drive to see if they can park near the gravesite.

Piper realizes they've barely talked, but she did not fill the silence with questions about Theo's life or observations on the grounds. In fact, she realizes she's enjoying the peace again, walking in this historic, if somewhat eerie, space. She's had to rethink her awe of Thomas Jefferson given all that she learned about him in US History. Especially his complicated relationship to slavery and the founding of the country. She says this out loud to Theo and regrets it almost immediately.

"Yeah, I get that," Theo says, surprising Piper. He didn't look at her with incredulous eyebrows raised that seem to say, 'did you really just say that?'.

Instead, he shares his own thoughts. "I've read three founding fathers' biographies in the last few years, and I think it comes down to having immense respect for all they did to create our nation, but not agreeing with all of their choices, or the way they built or maintained their wealth." Piper nods and they return to the van.

"Would you mind driving back? I want to check out the scenery, maybe take some photos," Theo asks.

Piper smiles and exclaims, "Sure!", happy to be trusted with the task and adjusts the seat and mirrors before they take off. She had never driven the van before yesterday. *It's a lot bigger than my Prius, but it drives smoothly.* Theo turns the car radio to NPR, and they listen to classical music with the volume low on their way back to Aunt Ginny's.

Piper looks over at Theo, who is studying the landscape out his window, and smiles. Theo turns back and snaps a photo of her, which she doesn't seem to mind.

Piper, eyes on the road, asks, "So what are the options for your next work project? Is there one you're hoping to do? How does that work?"

"None of them are anything new. Maybe that's why I haven't signed a contract yet. I would like to see what else is out there."

"And where could the next project be?"

"It could be anywhere." Piper looks at him incredulously. He laughs, "I travel light. And I've had a chance to work in some cool places - Austin, Syracuse, Boston, Vancouver... Just not sure what I want to do next."

"It sounds great."

"What about you Pipe? You seem a little more Piper than normal."

"What does that mean?" she tries to laugh it off.

"You're always super organized, you've got Cam going out, you've answered multiple distress calls and probably 10 times that many texts. But you don't seem that happy with work."

"I'm bored," she says quietly. "I love LA. I love my friends and my family. But I haven't gone anywhere. I want to hike the Smoky Mountains and visit Mt. Vernon. I work from home, even before COVID, so I make sure to stay connected with people outside of work. I go to classes even though I can work out at home. I don't know. I have nothing to complain about really." She smiles wide, as if she's just being silly. "I guess I'm just a little bored with my job, but honestly I'm so grateful for it."

"What do you want to do - you studied journalism right?"

"Journalism and English," she says, surprised that he knows that. "Honestly, I'd love to travel and write about it," she admits, somewhat sheepishly.

"And that's why you're on the trip? To write this story?"

"What? No! It just sounded so romantic - and not in the way you think. Driving cross country sounded like the fun I needed. And I wanted to be there for Cam. Tease me all you want but I'm not going to apologize for taking care of the people I love. I'm good at it and it doesn't stress me. I want good things for all the people around me."

There is a long pause in their conversation as they enter Aunt Ginny's neighborhood. "Even me?" Theo finally asks.

Piper puts the van in Park. She opens her door and says, "Yes, Theo, even you."

****

Dinner is fantastic. Aunt Ginny seems happy to be entertaining young people. And Piper, especially, absolutely adores Cam's aunt. She asks a litany of questions about her marriage to Warren, her time as a nurse, how the transition was to Virginia from Maine, and all about her friends in Charlottesville.

Cam and Theo load the dishwasher and wash the pots and pans while Aunt Ginny and Piper serve up dessert. Apple crisp and vanilla bean ice cream with coffee before they head to Aunt Ginny's cabin to spend the night.

"The good news is, it's on the way to Maine so you can get another ninety minutes in on your way to New York tomorrow. I'd love to have you spend the night here or stay here for a week or more! But I know you've got places to be."

"What's in New York?" Theo asks.

"Oh, I'll fill you in on the way," Cam tells him.

Piper gives Aunt Ginny a big hug. "Here is my phone number. It was just amazing meeting you." Piper looks genuinely disappointed to be leaving.

Theo thanks Ginny for the dinner and her hospitality. She reaches up for a hug. "You need to come back when you've got time to do some real sightseeing." He smiles, excited at the prospect, and tells her goodbye.

They walk to the Odyssey and Aunt Ginny hugs Cam tightly. "After you see your grandfather and find out how he's doing, will you give me a call? I'm a little concerned about him as well. I left him another voicemail when you went out for a run. Give them both my love."

"Yes, I didn't mean to worry you. I'll call you then."

"And I hope you will come back to see me real soon. Your room is always ready here."

"OK," Cam says quietly into her shoulder.

"I love you, Cam." Cam hugs her again and walks to the van.

Grandpa Ben never called.

EDINBURG, SUNDAY
Theo

The Odyssey pulls up to the quiet cabin at 9:30 p.m. Cam brings in firewood and they open the flue to start a fire. There are two bedrooms but five beds, so they each choose their spaces and dress for bed, meeting back in the living room where it's toastier. There is central heat, but it hasn't warmed up yet and the mountain air is chilly.

"Did you come here a lot when you were younger?" Theo asks Cam.

"No, I've never been here. We always went to Charlottesville. I don't know when they bought the cabin."

Piper tells him, "Your Aunt Ginny said about 15 years ago once your uncle retired from the university. They had more time to enjoy the area then. I can't wait to see it in the daylight tomorrow. So, you said something about New York City?"

"Oh, I forgot to tell you, but Chelsea set up a meeting for tomorrow night. Dinner. I think it's five or six hours away so I told her it would work. We can make it to Bucksport the next day. We'd have to find a mid-way point tomorrow anyway."

"NYC tomorrow night?" Piper asks. "Yes! Sounds great to me! I have friends in Manhattan and Queens. I'll see what they are up to. Where do you want to stay?"

"Chelsea made a reservation for me in Lower Manhattan. I asked her to make a reservation for a second room."

"Great," Piper says, putting her phone away, "I love your Aunt Ginny, by the way."

Theo agrees, "My great aunts are nothing like her. She's pretty amazing."

"Yeah, she told me she's 84," Cam says. "I've never known how old she was. Or maybe I never thought to ask or try to do the math. It's kind of like Alison. She doesn't share her age."

"How old do you think she is?" Theo asks.

"45 maybe? Why, what do you think?"

"I don't know. I've never met her."

"Oh, that's right. You met Chelsea at that party, but Alison wasn't there."

Piper looks at Theo with a blank expression. *She wants to ask me about that night.*

"I don't think she's even 40, Cam," Piper tells him.

"Really?"

"I think she's really well put together, tough, and demands a seat at the table, but I don't think she's very old. I think she wants to be taken seriously so she might give off the impression she's older than she is. I would guess 34 or 35. And just a tip, I would never tell her you thought she was 45. OK, heading to bed. What time do you want to leave tomorrow?"

"8:00 OK?" Cam asks. "In case we hit traffic."

Piper nods and walks down the hall. Theo looks at his phone. "If we take I-95 we'll go through or around D.C., Baltimore, Philly, and Trenton on a Monday. Take a look at 81 and 78, Cam. It might be better." He gets a glass of water and heads to bed as well.

Cam grabs a couple of blankets from the chest near the end of the couch and stretches out in front of the fire. *Two more days,* he thinks, and he drifts off.

***

At 2:00 a.m. Theo wakes up and notices a light in the hall. He goes to the bathroom and then follows the light to Piper's room. He lightly taps on the door and walks in. She's on her phone tucked up to her chin with blankets.

"Cold?" he asks.

"Yeah. What are you doing up?"

"I woke up and saw your light. Not sure where Cam is."

"He's on the couch asleep," Piper whispers. "I got some water and saw him. The fire has gone out."

"It's fucking freezing in here," Theo says.

"Yeah, I know. I've got all the blankets I could find."

Theo leaves to adjust the thermostat in the living room. He returns to Piper's room. She's got a small lamp on, and her phone is put away. He walks over to her, looks down at her face barely visible against the pillows and blankets. He takes a tentative seat on the edge of the bed.

"Turns out you're a fun travel buddy."

She scowls at him. "I'm fun all the time."

Theo reaches over and touches her face. She doesn't move a muscle. He turns off the light, kisses her lightly on the lips, then stands up and walks out of the room.

Fellow Travelers – Odysseus Returns to Maine

"East Virginia" by Joan Baez
  "Green Rolling Hills" by Emmylou Harris
  "I Went Down to Virginia" by Frank Sinatra
  "James River Blues" by Old Crow Medicine Show
  "Leave Virginia Alone" by Rod Stewart
  "My Blue Ridge Mountain Boy" by Dolly Parton
  "My Old Virginia Home" by The Carter Family
  "Night Train" by James Brown
  "Our Great Virginia" by Mike Greenly
  "Sweet Virginia Breeze" by Robbin Thompson
  "Sweet Virginia" by The Rolling Stones
  "Virginia (Wind in The Night)" by The Head and the Heart
  "Virginia is for Lovers" by Jordin Sparks
  "Virginia Moon" by Foo Fighters
  "Virginia Plain" by Roxy Music
  "Virginia" by Tori Amos
  "Virginia" by Whiskey Myers
  "Wagon Wheel" by Old Crow Medicine Show

EDINBURG, MONDAY
Piper

Piper and Cam load the van. "Did you sleep OK?" Piper asks him.

"Yeah, I was freezing but I really like the cabin."

"This morning it wasn't as bad. I think it just takes a while to heat up."

Theo asks if they have everything, and he locks the front door following Ginny's instructions.

"Want to ride up front?" Theo asks.

Piper assumes he's talking to her, so she says sure and goes to the passenger side. Cam loads Waze, they cue up Piper's playlist, and hit the road. Everyone is quiet as they drive by Shenandoah National Park and get back on 81 north.

"God it's beautiful," Theo says.

Cam looks over his shoulder, surprised. "Trees, highway, yeah it's pretty."

"Have you ever taken the Blue Ridge Parkway?" he asks Cam.

"I don't know, we may have on a drive here years ago. I don't remember anyone pointing it out. Can you check your app? How long to New York City?"

"Five and a half hours or so. Hopefully no traffic."

"Hey, I'm going to take a call from Wintner, OK?" Piper asks.

"Sure," Cam answers.

"Stephen, how are you? Yes, all caught up and just started working on tomorrow's article. It's early for you! Oh, OK that makes sense. How are you? How's Millie? Yes, on a trip, handling everything through email. Yes, OK sure definitely. I think she's leaving for maternity soon. I'll take it. Yes, thank you. Please let me know if you need anything else. No specific timeframe. A few days. Uh, leaving Virginia and entering Pennsylvania in a few minutes. Thank you, Stephen. Have a good trip. See you next week."

"What's going on?" Cam asks.

"New assignment. We have a relationship with the Getty group and their foundation. He asked about some work I did on them in the past. I'm going to forward my notes to him. I'll take on that work starting next week when there is time to pull a meeting together. Dr. Chase from the foundation knows my dad so it works out well."

She sees Cam frowning. Piper lays her hand on his arm, "What's wrong?"

"I guess I thought if it was important enough for him to call that it would be about something more important than Getty publicity. And isn't it 4:00 in the morning there?"

"Hey, this works for me. I like what I do, I get to traipse around the country with you, and I get to work for this rag I love. And they love me. It works, Cam. Until I figure out a bigger goal, it works. Don't worry about me. And he's in Florida visiting family. How is your grandpa?"

"Nice change of subject. I don't know," Cam says. "I called him at Aunt Ginny's, but he hasn't called back. When we stop later, I'll try again. He seems really focused on getting things done so maybe he's just busy."

"Want me to call him?" Piper asks.

Cam glances at her, "Really?"

"Um, yeah, sure!"

"Go ahead." Piper pulls up the recent calls in Cam's phone and presses call on Ben Young's number. No answer.

"Hi this is Piper Nelson-Keller, a friend of Cam's. Everything is fine! We just wanted to check in with you and Cam is driving. We hope you and Mrs. Young are OK. Can't wait to see you! Give us a call!"

"Chipper as hell," Theo says from the backseat. Cam cracks up.

Piper says, "What? He doesn't remember me, I'm sure. I only met him at lunch when he was in LA the last time. I want him to know we're thinking about him." They continue laughing.

"Fuck you," she mumbles to them both and turns up the playlist. A little later Cam says, "Eight" and Piper says "Nine" back on speaking terms with the guys. She switches from the Mongolian trade rabbit hole she was just in the middle of, to songs about Pennsylvania, and then on to articles on the reprise of Southern Rock despite the return to 90s fashion. She is determined to get her Tuesday's "Ten" turned in before they get to NYC. And she's got Getty to research too.

Half an hour later as the lyrics start up, Theo sits up straight and sings along with his favorite TV show theme song growing up.

And then Cam joins in, singing about a Prince of Bel-Air.

When Theo runs out of lyrics he knows, Piper glances over her shoulder and says, "You karaoke after all."

"Sometimes," he grins. Piper turns back before she catches his eye. She has blocked their late-night conversation out of her mind.

Outside Allentown they stop for a much-needed stretch break. Theo fuels the van while Cam and Piper go inside the service station for the restroom and something to eat. They didn't want to break into Aunt Ginny's canned rations at the cabin.

Piper notices Theo doesn't walk into the store with her but waits a few minutes. *He's obviously avoiding me too after last night.* Piper asks for the backseat, so they move their things and switch.

"How much longer until we arrive?" she asks.

"About two hours," Cam says when Theo doesn't respond.

Is he ignoring me? Piper thinks. *There is no way he's mad at me.* "Hey Cam, what's the plan for this afternoon and tonight?"

"Uh nothing. I have a dinner meeting. I need to figure out which hotel Chelsea put us up in. Could you call her Theo?"

"Sure," Theo says.

Ooooh, this is good, Piper thinks.

Cam says "Call Chelsea" into his phone and hands it to Theo.

"Uh, hi, Chelsea, I have no idea what you're talking about. This is Theo. Uh Theo Harris, Cam's friend. God no he's fine. He's just driving. Good, you? Yeah, just finished in Austin. Not sure yet but I'm working on it. How's LA? Yeah? I should. We're two hours out. Yeah, I think that's all he has planned tonight."

He glances over at Cam who nods.

"Yeah, that's it. OK. Ironwood. Got it. What time? 7:30. OK yeah, I'll tell him. Got it - can you tell us which hotel though? Battery Inn. OK. No problem. OK. Great talking to you too. Yep. See you soon."

"What did she open with?" Cam laughs.

"'Good morning, Vietnam.'"

"Well, it is pretty early there."

"Yeah right. So, you're having dinner at Ironwood at 7:30 and we're staying at the Battery Inn. Two rooms - one with two doubles and one with a queen."

"Because I'm a queen," Piper says. No response from the front.

"Who are you meeting with Cam?" Piper asks.

"An agent who's based in New York. I don't know him, but he represents a lot of stage talent and several people who are looking to move from commercials to movies and TV. I have not filled any commercial spots, but it'll be good to learn a little about stage."

Theo is curious. "Do you ever work with directors, DPs, cinematographers...? Does James ever get asked to help find other staff or just talent?"

"I'm not sure. Alison may handle that, but I don't. I don't think she's helped cast much Broadway either. It's still a young firm but you wouldn't know it in California."

"Ten," Cam says as they enter New Jersey.

"Eleven," from the backseat Piper says. She sends off her Tuesday "Ten" and rolls her head from side to side, so ready for a break.

"Sure you don't want us to drive, Cam? I am kind of tired of being a passenger."

"I'm OK. Have you driven in NYC before?"

"No, but I got my license driving in LA, so I think I'm good."

"I wonder if the hotel has parking," Theo says.

"Surely Chelsea would have looked into that. Can you call her back?" Theo calls and taps the speaker button so Cam can talk with her.

"Hey Chels - is there parking at this hotel?"

"I already checked, just in cases."

"I know that one! *Love Actually*!" Piper yells from the back.

Chelsea laughs. "Hi Piper! There's a parking garage next door."

"Thanks darlin'. Talk to you later." Theo hangs up the phone.

***

"Want me to leave you in New Jersey so you can visit your family?" Cam asks Theo an hour later.

"No, I won't even let them know we drove through. I haven't seen my dad and brothers in a while though. I should make some time to get out here, maybe before my next project."

Piper checks Google Maps. *OK. Less than 2 hours, I can make it. God, I need to work out.*

"What is the name of our hotel again?" She looks up directions to the Battery Inn and says, "Are we really driving this interstate all the way into Manhattan? I guess I didn't realize there were interstates on the island. There is a yoga studio six blocks from the Inn. I'm going to set up a class this afternoon. Guys want to join me?"

"Going to pass," Cam says.

Theo says, "Pass".

Piper spends the time adding New Jersey and New York to her playlist. She hits "Start Spreading the News" as they enter the Holland Tunnel.

"Oh yeah," Theo says.

The parking garage has tight turns and is clearly not meant for minivans, but they eventually park and walk to the hotel.

"OK, have a good meeting Cam. What time do you want to leave tomorrow?"

"9:00 would be good. It's about eight hours to Maine. Hey this could be our last night on the road," Cam says.

"9:00 is good," Piper tells him. "See you guys." Piper checks in and changes into something that will work for the hot yoga class she signed up for. As she leaves the hotel, she sees Theo at the bar and gives him a little wave in case he's looking in her direction. She doesn't wait to see if he waves back.

Fellow Travelers – Odysseus Returns to Maine

"Anywhere With You" by Jake Owen
    "Charleston Girl" by Tyler Childers
    "Chicken Fried" by Zac Brown Band
    "Down in West Virginia" by Viper Central
    "Hills of West Virginia" by Phil Ochs
    "Leaving West Virginia" by Kathy Mattea
    "Take Me Home, Country Roads" by John Denver
    "The Girl from West Virginia" by Doyle Lawson & Quicksilver
    "The West Virginia Hills" by Rick Pickren
    "Universal Sound" by Tyler Childers
    "West Virginia My Home" by Hazel Dickens
    "When I Get Where I'm Going" by Brad Paisley, Dolly Parton
"Allentown" by Bill Joel
"Bandstand Boogie" by Barry Manilow
"Clampdown" by The Clash
"Dancing in the Street" by Martha Reeves & The Vandellas
"Fall in Philadelphia" by Daryl Hall & John Oates
"I'm in a Philly Mood" by Daryl Hall
"I-76" by G Love & Special Sauce
"Motownphilly" by Boyz II Men
"New Sensations" by Lou Reed
"Ode to Pittsburgh" by Loudon Wainwright III
"Pennsylvania Is..." by Everclear
"Pennsylvania Polka" by Frankie Yankov And His Yanks
"Philadelphia Freedom" by Elton John
"Philadelphia" by Neil Young, Richard Stoltzman
"Philly Thing" by The Bacon Brothers
"Philly, Philly" by Eve, Beanie Sigel

"Pittsburgh Sound" by Wiz Khalifa
"Pittsburgh Town" by Pete Seeger
"Pittsburgh" by The Lemonheads
"Pittsburgh" by They Might Be Giants
"Punk Rock Girl" by The Dead Milkmen
"Sailing to Philadelphia" by Mark Knopfler
"South Street" by The Orions
"Streets of Philadelphia" by Bruce Springsteen
"Summertime" by DJ Jazzy Jeff & The Fresh Prince
"The Range War" by Todd Rundgren

"4th of July, Asbury Park" by Bruce Springsteen
"America" by Simon & Garfunkel
"Atlantic City" by The Band
"Bad At Love" by Halsey
"Big Casino" by Jimmy Eat World
"Garden State Stomp" by Dave Van Ronk
"Hackensack" by Fountains of Wayne
"I Like Jersey Best" by John Pizzarelli
"I'm From New Jersey" by John Gorke
"If I Never Get Back to Hackensack" by Tom Rush
"Jersey Bounce" by Ella Fitzgerald
"Jersey Boy" by Eddie Rabbitt
"Jersey City" by Bobby Long
"Jersey Girl" by Tom Waits
"Night Falls on Hoboken" by Yo La Tengo
"Palisades Park" by Freddy Cannon
"So Jersey" by The Bouncing Souls
"Tweeter And The Monkey Man" by Traveling Wilburys
"Walk Through the Bottomland" by Lyle Lovett
"Who Says You Can't Go Home" by Bon Jovi
"Wildwood Days" by Bobby Rydell
"Woke Up This Morning" by Alabama 3

"You Vandal" by Saves the Day

"You Can't Catch Me" by Chuck Berry

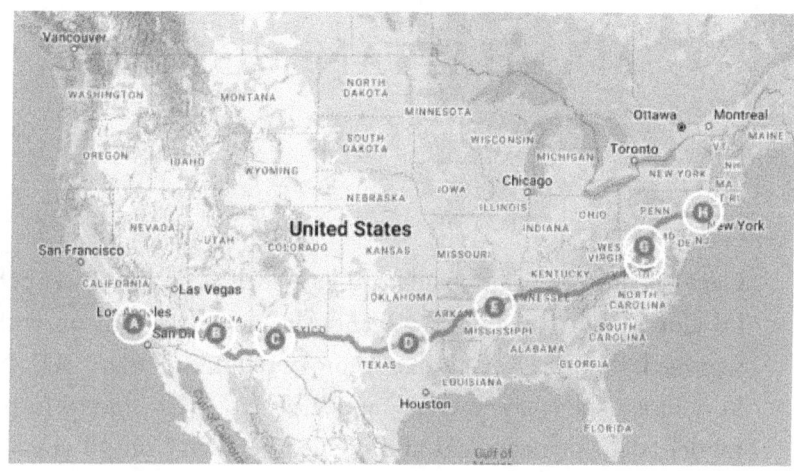

"There is a time for making speeches, and a time for going to bed."
~ Odysseus to the Greek God Alcinous in Homer's *The Odyssey*

MANHATTAN, MONDAY
Cam

Cam has time for some emails, a call to Chelsea, and a shower before he Ubers to Ironwood. The agent Alison has set him up with is seasoned. Simon Kaplan has represented more than 400 New York-based stage, commercial, and TV actors. He started in print model talent management and opened his own firm 30 years ago. They hit it off immediately.

"How long have you worked for James?"

"More than five years now. First as part of my film school internship and then hired on full time when I graduated. I've focused on voiceover, animation, and now assisting on TV and movies."

"Are you from Los Angeles?"

"No, Maine. Heading back there tomorrow. And you?"

"I'm from New Jersey but have been based in the city for over 40 years. So why LA? New York is in some ways a smaller pond. Are you thinking about going out on your own?"

"No," Cam says, "I like where I am. I have friends in LA, I've been out there quite a while. I plan to make it my home base for now."

"You should spend some time in New York, though. Two different worlds. Would help your firm if you knew the New York talent and markets."

"Yeah, sounds like it," Cam says, engrossed in their conversation.

"Do you have family in Maine still then?"

"Some. My grandparents."

"Both your mom and dad from Maine?"

"Yes, but I don't see my dad's family much." *Why am I sharing family history with this man I've just met. Maybe the whiskey is stronger at the Ironwood.*

"Yeah, I didn't grow up with a father either."

Cam bristles at the implication that his dad was not around. "Yeah, my dad traveled quite a bit for work. I just wasn't as close to his family as I am to my mom's. But it's all good."

"Where is your dad now?" Simon asks.

"He's in Chicago. He's currently in health care administration."

Simon nods. "So, you made a pit stop in NYC to meet with me. Are you flying out to Portland tomorrow?"

Cam rubs the back of his neck. "Actually, no, long story but I'm driving tomorrow."

"I like a long story," Simon says and orders another round with their steaks.

****

Cam and Simon finally call it a night and Cam picks up the bill. "I know James organized this dinner and is picking up the check, but I feel like I personally owe you for your time. This was a masterclass in the talent world."

"Well, it's my world and I know it well. In New York at least. I hope I see you again in Manhattan soon. If I were in your shoes, knowing what I know, I would not specialize. There's a world of opportunities in various cities including Los Angeles. Take advantage of all of it. Get out of the silos that naturally pop up in this industry."

Cam nods vigorously. "That's what I like about James - the vision to do things differently." He sees his Uber coming down the street, so he turns to shake Simon's hand.

"I hope you enjoy your time with your family, Cam. I know it's not easy for them with you across the country. Take care of those you love, OK?"

"My 90-year-old neighbor told me the same thing. Is that from a movie I don't know?"

"No," says Simon. "It's just advice from old men who know a thing or two."

A few minutes later Cam walks into the hotel lobby and stops at the front desk, pulling out his driver's license. To the beautiful woman behind the counter he says, "I have no idea what room I'm in. I've been on the road and have stayed in several hotels recently. There should be two rooms under my name. I'm wondering about the one with the two double beds."

"812," Kelly says. Cam smiles at her and makes his way to his room. When he gets there Theo is out, so he uses the time to go through his texts and emails. One notable miss is Grandpa Ben. Still no response.

Cam calls and Grandpa answers. "I owe you a call I know. Where are you now?"

Cam pauses. Grandpa's voice sounds much frailer than a week ago. "Uh, Manhattan. I had a work meeting. We should be in Bucksport tomorrow evening."

Grandpa seems distracted. "How is she?" Cam asks.

"The good news is, she's not in any pain. We've now got round-the-clock care. The house is being taken care of too, which she would want. I sit with her as much as I can, and we have music playing. She seems as peaceful as when she wasn't dealing with dementia and cancer."

Cam chuckles softly. "I've never seen her ruffled. Is serene the right word?" Cam asks.

Grandpa laughs. "The Honda doing OK for you two?"

"Actually, I picked up a friend in Dallas who I went to college with. I think you met Theo," Cam says.

"The volleyball player?"

"Yes. He was finishing a project in Texas, so he asked to tag along. We had that one issue with the Odyssey but nothing since. I think he'll make it back to Maine in good shape."

"OK I'll get rooms set up for your friends too. How long will they be staying?" Grandpa asks.

"Um, I don't really know. I guess they'll want to see you and Granny. I can take them to the airport when they get flights out, I guess."

"Sounds like they have the same flexibility that you have. That sounds like a good thing."

Cam senses that his grandpa is going to end their call soon, so he asks the question he's been dwelling on for days. "I just want to make sure you're OK. I feel bad that I haven't been helping you more with all of this."

"Oh yeah, I'm fine, fine. Don't worry. Looking forward to seeing you. I need to go. Thanks for calling back. See you tomorrow." Grandpa Ben hangs up and Cam finds himself still sitting on the edge of the bed 10 minutes later. *Grandpa sounded tired and distracted.* Cam tucks away his fears and makes the call he probably should have made several days ago.

"Camden, is this really you?"

Cam laughs and says, "Hey Alison. Sorry I haven't called. I met with Simon Kaplan tonight. I picked up dinner because he was full of great advice for me, and for the firm."

"I've got a Zoom starting in 3 minutes, but I want to hear more about that. How are your grandparents?"

"Oh, they're great," Cam says, somewhat automatically.

"Really?" Alison sounds doubtful.

"Yeah, I just talked to my grandfather, and he said she's comfortable and peaceful. Hey, I don't know how long I'm going to be in Maine. I haven't talked with my grandfather about that. And you and I haven't really talked about it either."

"You focus on your family. Chelsea has kept me up to date on all the work you're doing. I also want to hear about Nashville. But you've got big family concerns in front of you. Get your head straight on that. I've gotta run. Drive safe."

Alison hangs up and Cam feels relieved that he finally made the call. He doesn't want to dump his workload on Chelsea, and he really doesn't want Alison to regret letting him make this trip. He's more energized about work than before, and he's always energized about work. But this talk with Simon... Cam has some new ideas and he'll need time to think them through before he's ready to talk with Alison about them.

Cam also knows they have more than work to talk about, but now is not the time.

MANHATTAN, MONDAY
Piper

Piper returns from yoga and enjoys a long cool shower. She dresses in the hotel robe and slippers and dries her hair using the products she brought but hasn't used yet. She pampers her skin and stretches out on the king-sized bed (upgraded by Mark at the front desk) and starts to think about dinner. She texts Theo.

"Are you still in the bar?"

"Near the bar," he responds.

What is "near the bar". Oh, never mind. "Have you eaten?"

"No, want to get a table here in the hotel?"

"No, let's walk." She gets dressed in comfy jeans, a V-neck tee, and a light jacket. She swipes on a little mascara and lip gloss. She's enjoyed not wearing makeup much this entire trip - and no one has seemed to notice. Normally she does a good 15-minute face, even if she's working from home.

Piper sees Theo walking out of the lobby restroom. He pauses when he sees her. *What is this look on his face?* Piper thinks, nervously.

"Maybe I need to try yoga," Theo says, instead of hello. He's not smiling and seems annoyed with her, yet again. *But that was a compliment, wasn't it?*

"So, what is 'near the bar'?" Piper asks, matching his gruffness.

He points to a row of comfortable chairs. "I've been reading. It's depressing sitting in a hotel room this early at night."

"Agreed," Piper says. "Ready?" Outside they walk east, with no plan. They pass groups of New Yorkers heading to the subway, some walking purposefully with bags probably on their way home, and a lady with six dogs crossing the street to a small park.

They turn randomly down sidewalk lined streets until Piper decides to fill the silence. "I hope Cam has a good meeting tonight. It's great that he has been able to work this whole time and didn't have to take time off to see his family. I think Alison really depends on him."

Theo grunts, and Piper can't read his mood. She doesn't know what else to say, so she tries a different tact. "We're so close to your family. It's too bad you won't have time to see them."

"I was home last year and I'm going to see them in the next few months. They're OK - it's a couple hours out of our way, anyway."

"And you have a brother, right?"

"Two," Theo tells her.

"Are they younger or older?"

"They're younger. Marco is the baby, and he is still with my dad and stepmom. Nathan works for my dad but has his own place."

"And your dad played football?"

"Yes, he played in the NFL— "

"Oh wow - I didn't know that," Piper interrupts.

"He was retired by the time we came along."

"And what about your mom?" Piper asks.

"She's still in Argentina."

"Argentina? Traveling?"

Theo looks at her. "No, my mom is from Argentina. She was in the States when she and my dad met, and they got married. But they divorced a long time ago, and she is now remarried and living there."

Piper must look shocked. "They're all very happy," he reassures her.

"But when do you see your mom?"

"When I visit her. She doesn't come back to the states much. She came back my senior year of UCLA to see me play in a tournament and then for my graduation. She gets me a ticket there every year and I take her up on it. Have you been to Argentina?" Theo realizes he's rambling, but Piper looks almost sad.

"No, I've never been anywhere really. I didn't grow up traveling much. Well, I've been to Cabo a lot. And I went to London with my dad and his girlfriend at the time when I was in high school. And I did a trip to Italy with girlfriends three years ago."

They stop in front of a bistro with twinkling lights in the windows and candles on the tables. "Oh my God, it's straight out of *You've Got Mail* or some other New York City RomCom," Piper looks around.

Theo walks up to the hostess stand. "Excuse me, we don't have a reservation."

"Table for two?" the server asks. "Follow me."

Piper doesn't miss a beat after ordering water and hot tea. "When did you last see your mom?"

"Last February. I took a week off before the Austin job and went down. It's summer there in February so it's a great time to visit. She lives in the mountains, so it gets cold in the winter. What about your parents? They're in LA right?"

"Yes, my dad hasn't remarried but he has dated some nice women over the years. My parents divorced when I was 12 and I lived mainly with my dad, so I didn't have to switch schools. My mom is also alone. Well, I guess I mean she's also not remarried. She's not too far from my condo. I'm her person, you know? She calls me daily about something. She's rather helpless without my dad, or a man around the house. She seems to have no interest in seeing anyone or starting a hobby. She lives very comfortably though. I shouldn't say all of that. She's happy and she's got me."

"And let me guess, you're an only child. "

Piper looks down so she doesn't show the hurt on her face. She takes a sip of her tea. They covered this topic of family and siblings before but maybe Theo doesn't remember. "I am. Is it obvious?"

"Maybe a little. And why hot tea?"

"I like to hydrate and eat healthy, especially after a hot yoga class. Something about the pores and my blood vessels. But screw it. Hi!" she says to a passing server. "Can I get a whiskey sour? How much whiskey does it have in it?"

"Do you want a double?" the server asks.

"Oh no," Piper says. "A regular is great."

Theo attempts to cover his smile and orders a second beer for himself. They sit with the lull, having exhausted conversation about family and Cam. Piper is pretty sure Theo doesn't want to talk about 2 a.m., but she decides not to fill the silence for him. *Make him squirm just a bit.*

"So, tell me about this book," Theo says.

Piper looks up. "Yeah, I figured you'd have something to say about that. I don't know. It's an idea. Part of me is content at *The Herald*. I've been given some great opportunities and, because we have millions of online subscribers, the readers I connect with are typically younger and more liberal in their views and I really relate to them. I know I connect with people well, but I've always dreamed of writing a book."

"'All readers dream of writing,'" Theo says.

"Vonnegut?" Piper asks.

"No, me. Let me guess, you grew up reading any chance you could get. You have read everything from Jane Austen to Nora Roberts, along with a good dose of John Grisham."

Piper looks at him coolly.

"You fell in love with Joan Didion and Margaret Atwood and Eudora Welty in college."

"Why does everything you say to me sound mocking? Yet, you're a normal human with Cam. Oh, and Olivia."

Theo continues, "You read everything Judy Bloom ever wrote when you were growing up and you have a favorite Bronte sister."

"You done?" Piper asks.

"So, what's your book about?"

"Like I would tell you," Piper says sweetly.

The dinners arrive and the food is delicious. Theo finishes his steak and creamed spinach and watches Piper moving the filet around her plate.

"You really don't eat much, do you?"

"I eat when I'm hungry. Does your room have a fridge?" Piper asks.

"I didn't pay any attention to the room," Theo responds. Piper cuts another bite of steak and eats it with sautéed mushrooms.

"If you're not going to finish it, I'll help you."

She cuts off a large portion and slides it onto his plate. "Where do you put it?" she asks.

"Growing boy," he answers. Theo picks up the check. Piper starts to protest, and he looks at her.

"I guess you do owe me," she says.

They walk back in the general direction of the hotel. It's gotten chilly and Theo is glad he brought a light jacket with him.

"Have you talked with Cam about your book?"

"Not really," Piper says. "It's just an idea at this point and I don't know why *you and I* are talking about it so much. What about you - what's next? You keep saying nothing yet. Are you worried about that? Not having something lined up? It sounds really romantic going from city to city working with different organizations. Is it as great as I'm picturing?"

Theo suddenly stops. "Want to grab dessert?" he asks in front of a small cafe.

"Is this open?" Piper asks. "Yeah, I wouldn't mind a tea."

They walk in and note they're the only ones there. They order at the counter and Theo leads them to a table near the back. The owner comes over with their coffee and tea and two slices of caramel cake. Piper immediately digs in.

"So, you're hungry after all?"

"Just for cake," Piper smiles.

Theo moves his dessert to the side and says, "How much do you know about James Casting?"

"Um, a little. Basically, I know Cam is doing well there. He and Chelsea seem to be a good team, too. Why?"

"I am considering talking with them about a position."

"I don't understand," Piper says. "You want to do casting?"

"I want to be a part of something good. I've got some experience that I think they could use, to expand. I've looked into them. They currently cast talent but not production. I could help with that."

"And you want to live in LA?" Theo watches her face. She stares down at her tea, using the cup more to warm her hands than to drink from.

"I don't know," Theo says. "It's a long shot and there's probably no better way to kill a friendship than to become co-workers. Why are you upset?"

"I'm not," Piper says looking at him. She plasters on a big smile and says, "It can't hurt to talk to Cam about it right? And you know Chelsea really well - maybe she would have some insight."

"I wouldn't say I know Chelsea really well. We hung out the night we met a couple of years ago but that's it. I haven't talked to her since. I like her though. And I wouldn't mind working with her."

"Yeah," Piper says. "It sounds great. I think you should talk to Cam. Are you ready to head back?"

Theo takes a couple of bites of his cake, finishes his coffee and they thank the owner. She immediately turns the Open sign to Closed and draws the cafe curtains.

"So why are you upset?" Theo asks her. "I can never tell with you."

Piper doesn't respond. Theo touches her arm and stops her. "Just tell me what the problem is. No need for the moodiness, Piper."

"*My* moodiness?" she asks, not bothering to keep her tone light. "Are you kidding me? *You* are the one who is moody. I never know if you're going to be in a good mood or if you're going to make fun of everything I say."

Theo snaps back. "My mood is the same. But sometimes you set me off with how you boss Cam around and always have to organize everything. Just let him lead his life."

"What are you talking about? I'm Cam's friend. He's a lost boy, and you would see that if you lived near him. He's also a lot of fun to be with and why am I defending myself to you?" Piper feels her face getting flushed.

"And he's too afraid to tell you you're wasting your time. He is not going to marry you."

"Marry me? What the hell are you talking about? This is between Cam and me and we're good. Cam doesn't want to date me, I'm cool with that, we're friends, and nothing has really changed. You're the one who has problems with how I help my friends, what I'm doing with my life, and the essence of my personality. It's just *me* you don't like. Is that it?"

Theo walks ahead and then turns back. "I have no idea how we got to this point. I am considering a change and I thought you might be the right person to talk to about it. I haven't talked to anyone about this - not Cam, my family, friends I work with. No one. I didn't mean to upset you."

What the hell has happened? Piper is completely confused. *Am I upset that Theo might move to California?*

"Are you worried I'll take Cam away from you?" Theo asks in a calmer voice.

"What? No! From what I can tell, you two aren't even that close. When was the last time you saw him? Or even spoke to him? I see Cam every week. And Cam is free to pick and choose what he wants to do. What is your problem, Theo?"

"Oh wait," Theo realizes, "Is it Chelsea?"

Piper stops and turns around.

"You got weird when we talked about Chelsea."

Piper takes a deep breath and begins walking back toward the hotel, glancing down the next street to see if she can see it. "I don't care what you do Theo. Or who you did it with."

"I thought you liked Chelsea," Theo says.

"I have no idea what's going on. Where is the hotel?" Piper asks.

Theo pulls out his phone, looks at the map and steers her across the street.

"I'm getting cold and I'm tired of talking about this," Piper says. "I said I think you should talk to Cam. I don't care if you move to LA. I like Chelsea. Can we just stop talking about this?"

Theo is quiet. *Well at least he didn't bring up kissing me last night*, Piper thinks to herself.

They finally reach the front doors to the hotel and step inside. Piper shrugs off her jacket and turns to Theo. He waits for her to say something, but she just stands there. She's silent in the busy lobby. She feels tired, and maybe a little sad.

"I know why I grate on your nerves," Piper starts. "But it's not my problem. Cam is a good friend, I don't care what you think about any of my friendships, and I am OK with your not liking my job or my hobbies. I probably won't see you after Maine. Good night."

Theo stops her. "Wait, Piper, can we talk?" Piper turns to face him again. Theo seems to be gathering his thoughts. "I'm a great listener, countless women have told me this."

She gives him a withering look.

He attempts a smile, "I have no idea how this conversation has gone so far off-course."

He walks to stand in front of Piper, a few feet away, giving her space. "Can we talk for just a minute before you go upstairs?" She follows Theo to the comfortable chairs he said he was reading in earlier.

"Near the bar." Piper looks at him, waiting for him to talk.

"I said something that upset you and I'm not sure what that is." Piper shakes her head and Theo keeps going. "I'm not used to asking people for career advice, or really advice on anything. Maybe I didn't handle this well. I honestly don't know. Maybe you just don't like *me*," he chuckles.

Piper says nothing.

"Thanks for listening to me. And thanks for not saying anything to Cam until I find the right time to bring it up. He's got enough on his plate right now."

Piper looks over his shoulder toward the groups of people talking in the bustling hotel lobby. She takes a deep breath and says, "It feels a little inappropriate for you to pursue this given your relationship with Chelsea. It might put her in an awkward position."

"Why?"

"She's young, she's in her first professional position, and she's really protective of Cam and Alison James from what I've seen. Don't do anything that could risk her success there."

"How would I do that?" Theo asks, maybe taking a little offense. "I like Chelsea. I work well with women. I think you're the one who doesn't think very much of *me*," Theo says.

Piper stands up and resists the urge to walk away without responding. She smiles softly at him. "I'm not used to having people not like me. Sue me. I'm a people pleaser, I guess. But I'm not going to change my personality so that my friend's friend will like me. Good night. See you at 9:00."

MANHATTAN, MONDAY
Theo

Back in their hotel room, Theo finds Cam working on his laptop with barely a glance in his direction.

"How was dinner?" he asks his obviously preoccupied friend.

Cam brightens and tells him about the dinner with Simon. Theo is restless and walks around the room to the window. As he listens to Cam's ideas Theo realizes he is envious, and it is making him insane. He wants to do innovative work where he can make a real difference. He'd like to work on multiple projects at one time, and he'd like to live near friends. He ruled out returning to New Jersey to live near family a long time ago. But he is missing out on building professional and personal relationships and he's almost 30. He's ready and he thinks James might be the key. *Is now the time to bring it up?*

"I also talked to Grandpa Ben. He'll be ready for us tomorrow night. He didn't know you were with me, but he remembered meeting you."

Theo unpacks his bag and looks over at Cam. "You like surprising people, don't you?"

"What? What are you talking about?"

"You didn't tell your aunt that we were with you. You didn't tell me that Piper was with you."

"I talked to you before Piper decided to go," Cam reminds him.

"Yeah, I know, you've told me that. Not even a text though?"

"What's up?" Cam asks, going back to his work.

"Nothing," Theo says, going to the bathroom to brush his teeth.

"Aren't you a little short for a stormtrooper?" Cam asks and Theo looks back at him as if he's lost his mind. Then he sees Cam on the phone. *Gotta be Chelsea*, he realizes.

"Yeah, I talked to Alison. Yeah, I know I know. Theo's here. Chelsea says hi."

"Hi to Chelsea," Theo says.

"Was the date a date? I told you. I just finished emails and I didn't see it," Cam says opening his email. "OK, you just sent it so give me a break. When do you need them? We're trying to get to Maine tomorrow. No don't worry about it. I'll work on it now. I've got time. I'll send you what I finish tonight."

He ends the call and looks up at Theo who goes to his bag and pulls out shorts and a t-shirt. "I'm going to check out the bar, hit the gym, or maybe read. Take your time with your work."

Cam looks a little guilty. "Sorry, I just didn't want Alison to have to look at these when I can do it and make recommendations. Trying to make sure she knows I'm indispensable."

"Honestly, I need to get out of the room," Theo says. "I need a break."

He stops before opening the door to the hall. "Hey, I know you said there's nothing between you and Chelsea but is it something you're interested in?"

Cam, focused on his laptop, says, "No, she's not really looking for anything."

"Well, you aren't either," Theo retorts.

"No, I mean Chelsea sees her dating life as a chance to meet all different types. Saturday was a guy from her Ralph's who asked her out kind of as a joke and she took him up on it. She is exploring the world, you know? Not jealous, are you?"

Theo laughs, "Why?"

Cam says, "I know you left with that girl from USC that night. Wishing you had stuck it out with Chelsea?"

"Ha, no. Chelsea is really sharp. I like her but I got the feeling that you two might be exploring options there."

"Nope. Hey, 9 still work for tomorrow?" Cam is completely distracted.

"Yes, I'm flexible. I do have a couple of things I want to talk to you about though. Some life advice."

"You should ask Piper. That's her domain." Cam is now completely absorbed in work so Theo takes off.

He has no idea where to go. He decides to take the stairs to the lobby. Too cold for a walk outside and he really doesn't feel like hitting the treadmill. He opts for the bar to read his book, but in the stairwell, he stops on Floor 4. *God, what was the room number?* His phone is back in Cam's room, charging. He's also without his wallet. *What was the number? 412? No, we're in 812. 419,* Theo remembers. He taps on the door and Piper answers.

"Theo?"

"Yeah," he says.

MANHATTAN, MONDAY
Piper

Piper opens the door and realizes she must look unhappy based on the concern in Theo's face. He steps toward her, and she takes a step back. He steps forward again, and she backs up again, a small smile forming on her face.

"Do you want to come in?"

"Oh yeah, sure, thanks," Theo says with his own small smile. "Damn, you got the good room."

"Mark liked me," Piper says. Theo looks at her with his eyebrows raised. "He checked us in. Actually, everyone likes me. Except you. Why is that?"

Theo says nothing but continues looking around the room. "Your room looks like you've been here for days. Where's all your stuff?" he asks.

"Put in its place," Piper answers him. "Is that mockable?" Theo walks to her bathroom and notices colorful little tubes and jars lined up on the counter.

"You have plants in your apartment, don't you?"

"Yes," Piper says. She has stopped rolling onto the balls of her feet over and over. She stands still and watches Theo walk around her hotel room.

"And you have decorative pillows on your couch."

"My sofa, yes," she corrects him. "I'm not an animal, Theo."

"And you have dated a lot of Ken-like guys who surf, hike, and have a car they're really proud of."

"You just described every guy I grew up with so yes."

"And you secretly wish you had a sister, don't you?"

"Every only child fantasizes about having a sibling. Did you work out?"

"Not yet. Cam's got some work he's got to get done so I took off, without much of a plan. Or my phone or my wallet. Somehow, I ended up here."

"Strange," Piper says.

"Yeah," Theo concedes. "I figured out why you've been so moody," he says, probably ready for her to push back. Instead, she looks at him coolly, refusing to take the bait. "You think I slept with Chelsea the night of the pool party."

"I know you did," Piper says. "And I think it's pretty insensitive to consider working with her after never talking to her again."

"I just talked to her tonight," he says, stretching the truth just a bit. He takes a risk and walks one step toward her. She doesn't back up. He takes another step. She stands her ground.

"The gym is on the 1st floor," Piper says. Theo stands right in front of her.

"The only thing I can't figure out is why you would care if I slept with Chelsea or not." Piper says nothing but looks up and directly in Theo's eyes.

What is happening here? "I don't really care, except that you seem to treat the many women you date much like you treat Cam – you don't seem to care all that much. Cam doesn't have many people and you don't make much of an effort. I don't like that about you."

"I'm here. On my way to Maine," Theo says.

Piper takes a couple of steps back and leans against the desk. "The last time you were in LA you said I steamroll him. Maybe I do and maybe I could handle that better. But you don't see him in LA. He worries me. Outside of work he doesn't have much. And I care about him. My friendship is good for him. Are you good for him? Or are you here because you want to explore a job change?"

Theo is quiet for a minute. "I can't believe you remember that. I said you steamroll him because from what I see you plan his social life, and he goes along with it instead of pushing back. I'm with him because I thought it would be good to spend some time with him one on one. Until you pulled up at the restaurant," he smiles. He reaches for her hand and Piper notices his is large and warm and surrounds hers. "I'm here because I want to kiss you again."

"Why?" Piper asks. Theo stops and laughs. "Honestly, I have no idea. I know I like it when you bounce your knee in the van. And I like it when you look super happy on the top of a mountain. And I really, really like it when you sing Dolly Parton."

"You do?" Piper asks quietly.

"And I know you don't like much about me just yet, but my guess is we can change that," Theo continues.

"Doubtful," Piper says sweetly.

"Wanna bet?" Theo asks her, moving his hand to her cheek. She leans slightly into him and shivers, as goosebumps crawl up her arms. "Oh, that's my new favorite thing about you," Theo says. He leans down and kisses Piper very gently on the lips.

"This OK?" he asks. She nods and returns the sweet kiss. His hand moves to the back of her head, playing with her hair. Piper deepens the kiss and smiles when Theo places his other hand around her waist and moves it to the small of her back.

He pulls back a little and Piper whispers, "I have no idea what you're doing."

"You want me to stop?" he asks.

She stands on her tiptoes and says "No" a little too quickly. Theo makes the smart decision not to tease her. He pulls her tight against him and kisses her again. Piper tentatively moves her hands up his chest and to his shoulders. Theo's made no secret what he thinks about her, and he's also got that infuriating confidence that comes with experience. She sets her doubts aside and lets him take the lead. She can kick him out if he annoys her. So far though, it's just nice.

Theo runs his fingers down her spine and his lips move to her ear. "You OK?" he whispers.

"Yep," she says back, feigning cool. *What is happening??? And where is this going???* Again, she sets aside her natural tendency to think ahead and chooses to focus instead on Theo's lips. And his hands on her waist and cradling the back of her head. Her knees buckle just a bit, and he pulls back, grips her around the waist and places her on the desk.

She opens her legs, letting the hotel robe fall apart just a little more, and Theo steps in between, returning to her lips. *Oh God this is so good. Do I want this to be good with Theo? Thoughts aside, focus on this moment.* Piper releases a big exhale and plunges straight in. Her hands are in Theo's thick dark hair, pulling gently. She eases a little closer to him, spreading her legs a little more, allowing her robe to loosen a little.

Theo runs his finger down the inside of the lapel from her collarbone to where the two sides of the robe meet above her breasts. Piper sucks in a deep breath and leans into his fingers, inviting more. Theo removes one side of the robe. He traces his fingers across her soft skin. She arches her back, allowing him to touch her more. He loosens the other side of her robe, exposing her completely to him. He cups and caresses her with one hand, the other on the small of Piper's back, holding her in place.

Theo must feel how he's driving her crazy, but he hasn't said a word. He watches her responding to his lazy touch. He continues the kisses while his hands roam. Unhurried, taking his time.

Piper isn't sure how much longer she can take this, but she also doesn't want it to stop. "God," she says. Theo smiles and continues his exploration. She feels herself trying to get closer and closer to him. She moves to the edge of the desk and wraps her legs around his, kissing Theo with more enthusiasm than she has anyone in the last year at least. Maybe years.

What is this? Is on the tip of her tongue but she refuses to say anything. She lets out a quiet moan and Theo responds by moving his lips back to her neck and ear, his hands roughly teasing her.

Touch me she almost blurts out, but she bites it back. She also resists reaching for him. She can feel him there, obviously as turned on as she is. But she's letting him take the lead.

Piper's a little embarrassed by how needy she feels but she decides *Screw it*, almost saying it out loud. If he didn't want her to be this turned on, then he shouldn't have kissed her neck, or loosened her robe, or sat her on the desk. This is his doing.

"I like your little moans." Theo kisses her neck again and she involuntarily lets out another which makes him chuckle.

"I like your swollen lips too," he says, kissing them again.

Piper gasps as he runs his fingers up her arms and goosebumps appear. He steps back just a bit and Piper moves to follow but he stops her with his hands on her shoulders and their foreheads pressed together. "There are several reasons why this might not be a good idea," he says.

A tiny whimper of complaint escapes her throat. She leans up to kiss him and he doesn't stop her. He takes her hands and places them on the desk beside her hips and holds her wrists in place. "I need you to tell me what you want," he says into her kisses. Piper shrugs her shoulders and continues kissing him, trying to move her hands but Theo holds them securely.

"It might make sense to stop while we're ahead," he says, giving her a chance to think about this logically, and regretfully agree with him. Instead, she plunges her tongue into his mouth, squirming to get even closer to him. He grips her wrists more tightly and says, "Piper if I sleep with you, are you going to destroy me?"

She looks up to meet his eyes but he's not meeting hers. He's looking down at her open robe and it's clear he's trying to give her space. Or himself. "No," she says quietly. He finally meets her eyes. They stay locked as they both try to figure out how they got to this point.

He lowers his forehead to hers and says quietly, "I don't have a condom."

She gasps and says in a voice that should be reserved for true tragedies, "Neither do I."

The pout in her voice is about all he can take. He scoots her off the desk and walks her to the bed, kissing her the entire way. Piper falls back and props herself up on her elbows. She watches as Theo undresses down to his briefs and lowers himself on the bed beside her. Why hadn't she paid attention to how good-looking he was until just now? *And maybe even a little nervous?* She reaches up to reassure him, but he smiles at her and resumes taking the lead.

"Just let me play, OK?" he whispers into her ear, and she nods OK. He traces her arms again, watching her draw in deep breaths. "I don't want you to worry about me, OK? I know it's not normal for you to let someone else take care of you. Let me worry about you tonight?" Piper looks at him in surprise and shakes her head yes.

"Say yes, Piper."

"Yes, Piper." Theo gently pinches her waist, and she gasps and laughs at the same time.

"That's the sound I'm getting addicted to," Theo tells her. "We have 10 hours so let's just take our time, OK?" he looks at the clock by the bed. "No hurry," he murmurs, and she moans again at his feather-like touch.

"God, you're gorgeous," Theo chuckles, probably surprised it slipped out. "Let's play a game. Let's see how long you can go without gasping or moaning." Piper looks at him and starts to say something biting, but he stops her. "Don't move." Theo gets up, opens the curtains to let in the beautiful city lights, and turns off the overhead lights in the room. Piper watches him and feels a surge of happiness at this turn of events. *Why have I never thought of Theo in this way?*

He climbs next to her and says, "I bet you can't go three minutes."

Piper says, "You're on," and kisses him. One minute later she regrets ever believing she could control her body given what Theo has shown her so far. Her conscience says she needs to play a more active role here, so she moves to sit up.

Perched on an elbow, Theo must see the mild guilt across her face. He kisses her and says, "You don't have to take care of me, OK?"

Piper nods again. *I like compliant Piper* she thinks to herself.

"If you don't like something, just tell me."

She nods again and thinks to herself: *In charge Theo is working for me.* And then she stops thinking for a little while.

She doesn't focus on the fact that he doesn't live in LA when he makes her laugh. She doesn't worry about his presumably exhaustive experience with women when he moves the covers, and they climb inside them. She doesn't dwell on the times he teased her on multiple occasions, which made her feel belittled. And she definitely doesn't think about the first time she met Theo. When he walked into her favorite restaurant with Cam that first night and Piper thought to herself, *Oh my God. Who is that?*

And only one word escapes her lips tonight, "Theo".

****

Theo leaves her room a little later with a goodbye kiss, but no conversation about tomorrow. Piper stretches across the bed, ready for a long sleep before tomorrow's long drive.

Theo returns to his room, trying not to wake Cam. He isn't sure if he's successful, but he falls asleep immediately, not even a moment to relive the most surprising night of his life.

Fellow Travelers – Odysseus Returns to Maine

"52nd Street" by Billy Joel

"53rd & 3rd" by Ramones

"A New York Christmas" by Rob Thomas

"Angel of Harlem" by U2

"Autumn in New York" by Ella Fitgerald, Louis Armstrong

"Brooklyn Baby" by Lana Del Rey

"Downtown Train" by Tom Waits

"Empire State of Mind" by JAY-Z, Alicia Keys

"Englishman in New York" by Sting

"Ever Since New York" by Harry Styles

"Fairytale of New York" by The Pogues, Kirsty MacColl

"Harlem Blues" by Nat King Cole

"I Guess the Lord Must Be in New York City" by Harry Nilsson

"Leaving New York" by R.E.M.

"N.Y. State of Mind" by Nas

"New York at Night" by Old Dominion

"New York City Cops" by The Strokes

"New York City Serenade" by Bruce Springsteen

"New York State of Mind" by Billy Joel

"New York, I Love You But You're Bringing Me Down" by LCD Soundsystem

"New York" by St. Vincent

"Rockaway Beach" by Ramones

"Subway Train" by New York Dolls

"Talkin' New York" by Bob Dylan

"The Only Living Boy in New York" by Simon & Garfunkel

"Theme From New York, New York" by Frank Sinatra

"Welcome to New York" by Taylor Swift

MANHATTAN, TUESDAY
Theo

Cam is up by 7:30 and goes for a run in the gym. The guys take the elevator down a little before 9:00 and aren't surprised to see Piper already in the lobby with a coffee. But they are alarmed by how tired she looks.

"Did you sleep much?" Cam asks.

"No, not really. I'm fine though. About ready to go?" she fakes a smile.

Theo notices she is avoiding his eyes and looks more tired than he does. *What is going on?*

""Is it work?" Cam asks.

"No nothing. I guess I woke up early this morning just worried about a couple of things. I'll take a nap in the Odyssey. Do you want to walk over to the parking garage?"

"Give me just a second," Cam says and gets himself a coffee for the road.

Theo steps closer to Piper and stops himself from putting an arm around her. "Are you OK?" he whispers.

"Yep," Piper says, avoiding eye contact.

Oh shit, he mumbles to himself. *What happened?*

Theo looks at Cam who shrugs and says, "Want to grab a coffee?"

"No, I'm OK."

Piper loudly asks if she can have the backseat and the guys both say sure. Theo turns to Piper but can't catch her eye. *What happened after I left?* he thinks. Cam unlocks the back so they can put their bags in, and Theo pulls Piper aside. "What's wrong?" he asks her roughly.

"Nothing," she says and pulls her arm away gently. She chooses to sit behind Theo which means he can't easily look over his shoulder and see her. Theo sets his GPS, and they leave Manhattan at the tail end of rush hour. It's still a nightmare, but they're crossing the Williamsburg Bridge and going north on 278 in pretty good time.

They merge on to I-95 and Piper still has not said a word. A few minutes later Cam sees a sign and says, "Hey Piper – Larchmont."

She looks up from her phone and says, "What?"

"Larchmont, New York," he tells her, "Coming up." Theo looks confused at Cam who doesn't notice.

"I live in Larchmont Village in LA," Piper says.

"Oh," Theo says, sensing an opening. He turns to look back at Piper. "Um, sorry you didn't sleep well." Cam looks at Theo with raised brows and Theo sits back in his seat.

They didn't talk about Cam last night, but the unspoken agreement is that they're not going to mention it to him today. Actually, Theo has no idea what the plan is. But he's pretty concerned that he did something wrong.

Half an hour later or so Cam says, "I've lost count. What state am I on?"

Piper looks up from the articles on her phone and says, "Are we in Connecticut yet?"

"Yes," Theo says.

"That's 12 for you Cam, 13 for me."

"Is that all?" Cam asks. "It feels like we should have crossed close to 20 states by now."

"California, Arizona, New Mexico, Texas, Arkansas, Tennessee, Virginia, West Virginia, Pennsylvania, New Jersey, New York, Connecticut."

"And 10 for me," Theo says. He looks in his side mirror and sees Piper behind him, clearly lost in thought. She puts in her earbuds and pulls out her notebook, focusing on work. Theo sets up some music for the front seat and turns his discussion to Cam.

"How was your grandfather when you talked to him last?"

Cam thinks about it. "Worried, distracted. But I guess he's OK."

"I don't want to be in the way so I can fly out whenever it makes sense."

"Yeah," says Cam, noncommittally.

"Do you want me to start looking for flights out tomorrow? Or I could do some errands for you and your grandfather over the next couple of days," Theo suggests, realizing he's become the planner, much like Piper.

"Nah, don't worry about it," Cam says. "We'll figure it out."

"OK," Theo says. He starts to bring up James and stops himself. It doesn't feel like the right time. It feels self-centered to talk about job prospects when Cam's grandmother is dying. *Maybe I should just call Chelsea? Or maybe just leave it?*

He knows he needs to ask though. This could be a great opportunity for their firm to branch out into other spaces of casting crew in addition to talent. And it might be the change he's been needing. Not the right time, though. No idea when that will be.

Theo reflects that he hasn't been alone with Cam much on this trip. *What the hell? Of course, I have. We've stayed in the same hotel rooms.* It just never seemed like the right time even though they had plenty of time. "Hey Piper," Theo tries again to engage her in conversation.

"Yes," she answers.

"Did you count Maryland?"

"Wait, what? I didn't know we went through Maryland!" She pulls up Google Maps. "Oh, wow, we just barely went through Maryland. I had no idea. Ok, I'll add to our playlist."

"I think we're going to stop again for gas," Cam lets them know.

"Great," Piper responds.

They pull into a large rest stop outside New Haven and Piper steps away from the van to make a call. Theo is looking for a good time to figure out what is going on with her, but she makes that difficult without alerting Cam that something is up between the two of them.

Should he broach James with Cam now? He's standing at the gas pump and Piper has headed inside. It feels wrong to bring it up right this moment. *What is with his timing? Fuck,* he thinks. When was the last time he was this frustrated about his feelings? He shakes it off and goes inside.

He doesn't see Piper, so he hits the restroom and snags some snacks for the remainder of the trip. *About six or so hours to go,* he guesses. When he leaves the rest stop, he looks toward the Odyssey and sees Piper and Cam engaged in a serious conversation. Piper reaches up on her tiptoes and hugs him. He says something to her, and she nods OK. She glances at Theo and returns to the backseat, putting her earbuds back in.

"Everything OK?" he quietly asks Cam.

"Yep." Cam gets back in the driver's seat and starts messing with Waze. "Six hours," he says. "Let me know when you want to stop again."

Piper says, "I've updated the music if you want to play it."

"Sure," says Theo in an embarrassing bid to show how agreeable he is. Cam glances at him and Theo connects Piper's playlist to the adapter as Cam takes the exit for I-91 North. "Connecticut is the place for me to be...." During the instrumental break Theo asks, "Dean Martin?"

"Bing Crosby and Judy Garland," Piper answers.

When Bing starts back up, he says, "Yeah, OK, that makes sense. So, what are you working on?"

"I just finished up my article for Wednesday's edition and I sent some notes on the Getty foundation to Mr. Wintner." Theo feels Cam's questioning look, but he doesn't look over. *At least she's talking to me.*

A few minutes later when Vampire Weekend starts singing about Walcott, Cape Cod, and Mystic, Theo discreetly checks his phone and notices they haven't made it to Massachusetts. Yet she's updated the playlist.

Piper seems to read his mind because she says, "I've added our last states to the playlist and made it public. It's called Fellow Travelers. And I'm caught up on work so if you want me to drive, lemme know. Or if you want to switch, Theo, we can."

"Up to you," Theo says. They watch early fall New England colors from the interstate and enjoy the music for a while. The green hills of the northeast are vivid on this sunny day.

Quietly Piper says, "California is great, but New England is pretty awesome too." "Thirteen," she says when they cross into Massachusetts. Theo resists the urge to look back at her and smile.

Everyone is lost in thought for a while when Theo suddenly breaks the spell of road trip music and interstate cruising. "Hey Cam, want to talk to you about something. It's probably the wrong time and Piper probably agrees but I'm running out of time here."

"Yeah?" Cam says.

"I'm looking to make a change with work and wondered what you thought about my talking with Alison about how I could help James."

Cam doesn't say anything at first but seems confused. "Help James with what? You want to move into casting?"

"Probably not talent casting, although I could. I was thinking more on the side I know – directors, cinematographers, DP's, tech, animation. I don't know that there is a lot of structure around casting those positions if the production companies don't already have them lined up. I know a lot of people on the digital and tech side."

"Oh," Cam says. "To consult? I don't know if Alison has ever had a consultant, but it might be a way to consider this kind of expansion."

Theo is quiet for a moment. "Well, I would be open to that, but I was thinking as a permanent part of your team."

Now Cam is quiet. "The work we do is mostly in LA."

"Yeah, I would move to LA. But I wanted to talk to you first. Bad idea?" he asks.

Theo hears the hesitance in his own voice and isn't comfortable with it. *What is the issue? Why does Cam seem unsure of this idea?* Theo recalls that when he described the potential to Piper, she thought it sounded worthy of exploring. But Cam is not saying much. *Does he not want me in LA? Does he not think Alison will go for it? Does he not want to share the work at James?*

"I guess you should talk to her, but I'm not sure if that's where she wants to take James. We're deep in talent casting and she is pretty quiet about expanding," Cam finally responds.

"What does she say about expansion?" Theo asks.

"Well, she hasn't really talked about it with me. Chelsea said that Alison is working more than she ever has but she hasn't asked me to take anything extra on."

"Does she turn you down when you ask for more?"

"I haven't asked for more because she knows what she's doing."

"But you want more," Theo says.

"I want to be with this company for a long time," Cam says. "I want to expand into New York, I think. I want to expand how we think about the siloed talent that Simon and I talked about last night. I can't get it off my mind."

Everyone is silent. Theo is not reassured by Cam's evident hesitance. Talking with Alison is probably not the right move. And he is still very unclear why Piper was so quiet this morning. *Is she upset?* Maybe Cam is thinking about the idea of another person splitting the work at James. *Is there enough potential there? Would Alison want a third person to train when she has so much on her plate? Maybe Cam could train me? I'm spinning here.*

Piper quietly speaks from the back. "Want to know what I think?"

"Yes," Theo says. Cam looks at her in the rearview mirror.

"No one is saying what they truly think. Theo, you want a change in your career and this idea of helping James expand is exciting to you. You're holding back with Cam. You really, really want this don't you?"

"Yeah," Theo says. Cam looks over at him.

"And Cam, you need to be direct with Alison. Ask for more – step up and take the lead from her on something. She probably thinks she has to do it all herself as the managing partner of the firm."

"Agency," the guys say in unison.

Piper continues, "I know the timing isn't good because your grandparents need you right now, but my guess is Alison gets that. You can tell her that you want to do more, and you have some ideas after meeting with the New York talent director."

"Agent," they both say.

"Tell her you want to talk to her about it. I don't know Alison well, but I think she thinks the world of you Cam. I've seen the two of you together and she trusts you. Trust her enough to let her know what you're thinking."

The guys are quiet for a while and Theo says, "I want to work at James if it makes sense. And if not, I want to explore tech/crew side of hiring somewhere else."

"Talk to Alison," Cam says. "I think it makes sense. I guess thanks for talking with me about it first. It would have been strange if I heard about it after. Just call Chelsea and let her know you'd like to get on a call for 30 minutes sometime and she'll make it happen. But not this morning. Alison is in meetings with a producer for a new franchise. She's focusing on landing this project and today's meeting is critical."

"OK thanks," Theo says. He catches Piper's eye in the side mirror, and she gives him a little smile.

NORTHERN MASSACHUSETTS, TUESDAY

Theo

Cam takes I-495 around Boston and Piper packs up her laptop bag. Cam looks at her in the mirror and says, "Um, Theo, we're making a little side trip."

"I'm going to visit my Aunt Beverly and Uncle Charles in New Hampshire and let the two of you continue to Maine."

Theo turns in his seat and looks back at Piper. She's avoiding eye contact but glances up to see what is probably a sad and confused look on his face. He turns back and Piper continues.

"This has been the trip of a lifetime for me, and I've loved spending this time with both of you but I'm going to let you guys finish it up. You'll finally get the guys' trip you probably had planned before I invited myself. Thanks for letting me tag along, and thanks for dinner and the national park, Theo." He turns back to look at her and starts to say something, but she shakes her head no.

Finally, Cam says, "You didn't have to give up several days of your life to help me but thank you. Sorry I haven't been myself. And thanks for putting up with him," Cam says, pointing his thumb at Theo. Piper smiles a little and looks at the map on her phone.

"There's a restaurant just off I-93 over the New Hampshire border. Could I let my aunt know she can pick me up there? You'll just be going about 30 minutes out of your way."

"I'm still OK taking you all the way to her house. We have time and it's not that far off course," Cam looks at Piper in the rearview mirror.

She shakes her head. "No, that's OK. I want you to get to your grandparents as soon as you can."

"Where does your aunt live?" Theo asks.

"Salem," Piper tells him. Theo looks confused. "Salem, New Hampshire. The two Salems are less than an hour apart and I understand it causes some confusion for tourists." She calls her aunt and lets her know where she'll be and to take her time. "I'll grab lunch while I wait."

Theo wants to say something, but Piper chatters on about her favorite states and places she wants to visit next after this adventure. It's clear she doesn't want to talk about last night. Or she doesn't want to talk to Theo at all, he isn't sure.

"And I haven't spent a dime in days. I owe someone for hotel rooms and dinners and drinks. Please let me pay my way. I'm just not sure who to Venmo and how much."

"Yeah, let's deal with all of that later. You paid the mechanic. I may owe you," Cam says.

The Odyssey pulls into the restaurant parking lot. Cam meets Piper at the back of the van to get her luggage, but he stops and hugs her first, tightly.

"Aw, what's that for?" she asks, obviously not used to hugs from Cam.

"Love you," he says muffled into her ear. "You are probably my best friend." He kisses her cheek and asks her again if she wants them to wait until Beverly arrives.

"I'll be fine! Don't worry. Give your Grandpa Ben and Granny hugs from me. Call me if you need me. I am not sure when I'll fly home, but I'll check in with you, Cam."

She takes a deep breath and walks over to Theo, reaching up for a quick hug. He holds her tightly, not wanting to let her go. "Good luck talking with Alison. It was good getting to know you better. Take care of Cam, OK?"

Theo reaches for her hand, but she picks up her laptop bag and suitcase and heads into the restaurant. Cam looks at Theo. "You OK?"

"Yeah, give me a minute." He walks into the restaurant and stops just inside. Piper is animatedly talking with the hostess whose face is as lit up as Piper's. No idea what they've found in common in 30 seconds, but they walk away toward a table across the restaurant. Piper's laugh is the last thing Theo hears as he closes the restaurant door. *See you, Piper.*

"Was she OK?" Theo asks when they return to Massachusetts and I-495.

"Yeah, she was fine. She just wants to visit her aunt and uncle since she's this close. She's not far from Logan and can fly home when she's ready. It's Day 9 of this trip. She probably was ready for a break. I know I am."

A while later they re-enter New Hampshire for a small stretch and Theo checks his map. "Three hours to Bucksport," he announces. "Is that where you grew up?"

"Yeah, that's where my mom and Grandpa Ben's family is from."

"And your dad?"

"He's from Bangor. But he hasn't lived in Maine in a long time."

"Did you live with him part of the time or just your mom's family?"

Cam hesitates. "I haven't told you this before?"

"No, I don't think so," Theo says.

"After my mom died, I lived with my grandparents. My dad's been gone for most of that time. He was a photographer when I was growing up and traveled a lot. Then he did sales for a company and relocated to the Midwest. He came through Maine when he could. He's been in Chicago for a while though – probably about since I moved to LA. Oh wait, no he was in Pittsburgh for a while too."

Theo doesn't say anything for a minute. "I don't think I knew any of this. You never talk about your mom. Or your dad. Really just your Grandpa Ben."

"Yeah, didn't you meet my dad when he came out to LA?"

"When you drove Odysseus there? No, I remember when you moved into that apartment, but I didn't meet him. I'm sorry about your mom. I knew she was gone but I guess I didn't know the whole story."

"Yeah," Cam says, somewhat matter-of-factly. "It was a long time ago. Hard on my grandparents but they had me to focus on. I think it was hard on my dad too and that's why he left."

"How do they get along with your dad?"

"Just fine, I guess. They don't really see him. I think pretty good though. I don't really see my dad either. Never really have."

"I guess it's great that he drove out to LA with you and the Odyssey."

"Yeah, I guess so. It was a great trip. He hasn't been back to see me though. That's Grandpa Ben. You know he's been out a few times."

"Did he ever think about moving out to LA with your grandmother?"

"Ha, no, they're Mainers. They'll leave Maine on their terms, which is never. Look, I had a great childhood. Besides the drive to California with my dad, my happiest memories are with my grandparents, especially fishing with Grandpa Ben. I feel bad that I haven't been here to take care of them as they've gotten older. Granny has been battling dementia for a long time. The last time I was here she and I had a good conversation. Well, I talked to her, and she listened and smiled. I'm pretty sure she knew I was someone she loved but didn't know exactly who I was. We don't talk about my mom around her because it upsets her. So, we talked about California. I guess she probably didn't know what I was talking about. It'll be good to see her."

"What happened to your mom?" Theo asks. He realizes this is probably the longest Cam has ever talked in one stretch.

"Cancer," Cam says.

"Pancreatic?" Theo asks, assuming it is maybe hereditary.

"Ovarian. She got sick and passed quickly, I think. I really don't remember her except from photos and flashes of memories. My grandmother was the principal at our elementary school. She took off a semester to be with my mom and me, but my mom passed a lot faster than they expected so my grandmother just stayed home for a while with me. I don't remember any of this – but Aunt Ginny filled me in one time when I asked."

"How old were you?" Theo asks, not believing he has never known this about someone he considers a close friend.

"Three," Cam says. "So, I guess it's good that I wasn't older."

Theo is silent. Why had he never asked these questions before? *What kind of friend doesn't know this about another friend they've known for 10 years?* "You really don't talk about your family much."

"I feel like I do," Cam says. "Everyone knows about Grandpa Ben."

"Yeah," Theo concedes. "That's true."

New Hampshire turns into Maine, and they follow I-95 up the coast on a gorgeous fall day. "Piper would love this," Theo says.

"Really?" Cam asks.

"Oh yeah, she'd love it and would want to stop at every town. Is Bucksport near Acadia?"

"Yeah, really close."

Theo doesn't feel like looking at the map. He just wants to enjoy the views out the window. He can't see the rocky coast from the interstate, but he notices signs for whale tours, fishing boat rentals and other water activities in the area. He would love to return one day and really explore this part of the country.

But his shame grows as he realizes that Cam knows his brothers' names and what position his dad played for the Jets over 30 years ago. *Why has he never asked Cam about his family?* Probably because Cam rarely talks about himself.

"Do I stay on I-95, or do I get off at some point? I can't remember," Cam says.

"Um, you can get on I-295 or stay on 95 around Portland. It's about the same time."

"Let's get off on 295. That goes closer to the coast, right?"

"Yeah," Theo says. "295 is coming up in about 20 minutes. So, let me bring up this subject again. You're OK if I talk with Alison?"

"Yeah, I'm not sure she'll be ready to talk about expansion or adding to her staff, but you should talk to her. Maybe I'll wait until you do and then I'll talk with her about NYC and stage talent."

"Thanks. I really appreciate it. So, where do you live in LA?"

"Los Feliz," Cam says. "You haven't been to my house?"

"No. The last time I was out I stayed near campus, remember?"

"Oh yeah, I guess so. I've been at the guest house for two or three years though. I guess you just haven't been there."

"And he's an actor – the man you rent from?"

"Yeah, Jeremiah Franks was a character actor for a long time. He also did some stage and commercial work, but he's been retired for 20 years or so. He has a guest house behind his house."

"That's cool," Theo says. "How old is he?"

"I think he's 93 now. He has a full-time nursing staff but there's nothing wrong with him that I can tell. I think he likes the company. I check in on him about every day."

"Like a second grandpa?"

"Huh, yeah, I guess. I hadn't really thought of it that way," Cam says.

"And Piper lives near you?"

"Not far, about 20 minutes. She works from home most of the time, so she likes to get out as much as possible. She's over at my place more than I'm at hers. But I just see her out with friends usually. She's got the best social life of anyone I know."

"I guess growing up in LA she just knows everyone," Theo says.

"I've seen her meet someone at a club one night and then they are at brunch the next day and hiking with her friends the next weekend. She attracts people. Her dad's the same way."

"And her mom?"

"I met her mom once. Totally different from her dad. She stays at home and relies on Piper a lot."

"For what?" Theo asks.

"Seems like she doesn't do much for herself. Her settlement from Piper's dad was generous. She lives a quiet life. Maybe you should fly out to LA and meet with Alison in person."

"Yeah, I thought about that. Maybe I'll start with a call, but thanks."

Before they catch I-95 again near Augusta they stop for a sandwich, gas, and Theo suggests a quick car wash before they return the Odyssey to Grandpa Ben.

"I guess I didn't think about it but I'm going to miss this van," Cam realizes. "It's been in our family since I was in school here in Maine. I can't imagine it not being in our family, but I doubt my grandpa is going to want to keep all three of their vehicles. Maybe I should keep it?" he wonders.

"I know it's been in your family a long time but it's probably time to get something a little more practical for LA," Theo says, not wanting to offend Cam. Or Odysseus.

Theo looks at GPS. "We'll be in Bucksport in a little over an hour. So, what is the closest airport to Bucksport?

"Bangor or maybe Augusta. Probably Bangor though. Are you working on a flight now?"

"I'm just looking at options. My car and things are at the Dallas airport. I guess I need to head back there before I make any other life decisions. Yeah, I can get there from Bangor, just flying through JFK or Logan. Not a problem."

Theo starts Piper's playlist, and the guys enjoy the remainder of the ride in silence. Cam never questioned his childhood in Maine. Exits for several familiar towns, signs for lobster rolls, and green rolling hills in the distance confirm that Maine was certainly an amazing place to grow up.

Fellow Travelers – Odysseus Returns to Maine

"Going to Maryland" by The Mountain Goats
    "Maryland Memories" by Ronnie Dove
    "Maryland" by Vonda Shepard
    "Six Feet Under the Sun" by All Time Low
    "Together in Maryland" by Tony Cavallo
    "Connecticut Snow" by David Stephens
    "Connecticut" by Judy Garland, Bing Crosby
    "Kylie from Connecticut" by Ben Folds
    "The Wives are in Connecticut" by Carly Simon
    "Hotel New Hampshire" by One Bar Town
    "New Hampshire" by Sonic Youth
    "Baby, Let Me Follow You Down" by Bob Dylan
    "Boston" by Augustana
    "Boston" by The Byrds
    "Dirty Water" by The Standells
    "Escape (The Pina Colada Song)" by Rupert Holmes
    "I'm Shipping Up to Boston" by Dropkick Murphys
    "Massachusetts" by Bee Gees
    "Old Cape Cod" by Patti Page
    "Roadrunner" by The Modern Lovers
    "Rock & Roll Band" by Boston
    "The Boston Rag" by Steely Dan
    "They Came to Boston" by The Mighty Mighty Bosstones
    "U-Mass" by Pixies
    "Walcott" by Vampire Weekend
    "Weekend in New England" by Barry Manilow
    "Whoever's in New England" by Reba McEntire

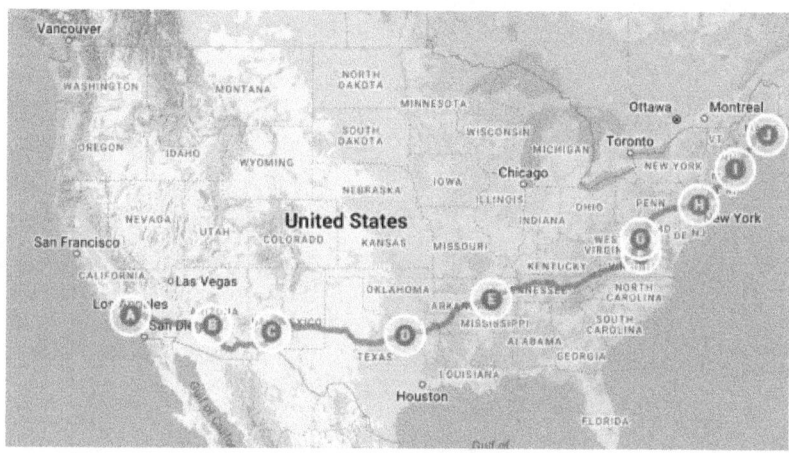

"Quick, dear boy, come in, let me look at you, look to my heart's content – under my own roof, the rover home at last."

~ Odysseus to his son Telemachus in Homer's *The Odyssey*

SOUTHERN MAINE, TUESDAY
Theo

They leave the interstate and take 15 S.

"Appreciate your coming on the trip," Cam says.

"Sure," Theo says. He looks over and notices that Cam is gripping the wheel. *He's got to be stressed as hell thinking about saying goodbye to his grandmother.* Theo has no idea if he should call an Uber and maybe find a hotel nearby to stay out of their way? He hasn't made any plans because he feels like Cam may need him. Or maybe not. But he should be there *in case* Cam needs him.

They pull into the driveway of a beautiful Cape Cod and Grandpa Ben walks out to greet them.

Theo sees the same tall man with a head of white hair that he met several years ago at UCLA. He was still working full time then and advised one of their friends on a patent question over a beer at their favorite hangout. Grandpa Ben, the legend. But this man looks 20 years older, clearly exhausted but powering through.

"Do we need to wear masks around your grandmother?" Theo suddenly thinks.

"Um, I don't know. Piper put some in the glove box." Before Theo can pull them out, Grandpa Ben arrives at his van door.

"Theo, son, how are you?"

"Good to see you sir," Theo says.

"I like that. 'Sir.'" They shake hands and Grandpa Ben grips Theo's shoulder.

"Camden." Cam smiles as he steps up to his grandfather and they hug for longer than Theo should watch so he walks to the back of the Odyssey to get his luggage out. He is not sure where he's staying tonight but he'll need his bag. Grandpa speaks to Cam in a low voice and Theo wants to give them their privacy. He hears Cam sniffle and Grandpa invites them inside.

There is a bustle of activity. Three nurses are there – one is straightening up a stack of bed sheets in the living room and one is updating a third nurse in a room with a hospital bed. They all greet the guys when they walk in and say loudly, "Mrs. Young, your grandson is here. Oh, Camden she's been looking forward to your visit. We told her this morning you were on your way."

Cam walks to his Granny and sits in the comfortable chair next to the bed. He takes her hand. "Granny, I'm here. Can you hear me?" She smiles a gentle smile and tries valiantly to open her eyes.

"Cam?" she asks.

"Yes, it's me."

Grandpa Ben walks in and takes over the introductions. "And here's his friend Theo I told you about, Elizabeth."

Theo has no idea what he should do so he walks closer and stands behind Cam. "Hello, Mrs. Young. I'm happy to meet you."

"Theo," she says. Her other hand lifts from the bed and he walks around and takes it. Has he ever held his own mother's hand as an adult? This feels intimate and like maybe this should be a family moment, but he doesn't let go until she does.

"Camden are you OK?" she asks in a soft voice.

"Yes," he says. "I'm just so happy to see you."

One of the nurses asks, "Did you have a safe trip? And where is your other friend?"

Grandpa Ben echoes, "Yes, where is Piper?"

"Um, she is with her aunt and uncle in New Hampshire. She asked me to give you both hugs."

"Cam," Granny says and squeezes his hand. Cam looks up at his grandfather, looking like he might burst into tears. Theo sees the pain and guilt on his face.

Grandpa Ben also seems to recognize the regret, worry, and sadness in Cam. He surely has battled the same feelings over the last few weeks.

"Camden, we're so glad you and Theo are here. We are happy to spend some time with you both. Theo, come with me. I've got a guest room set up for you."

Theo follows Grandpa Ben slowly up the stairs and down the hall. "This is Camden's room. And here is yours. Bathroom is across the hall. There's a Wi-Fi password and towels on the bureau. Make yourself comfortable."

"I feel like I might be intruding but wanted to be here for Cam."

Grandpa Ben sits down on the guest bed. "No, no I'm glad you are. Cam said you'd be flying home to Texas in a few days. I don't know how flexible you are, but it would be great if you could stay a few days at least. Just let us know when you want to leave, though, and we'll get you up to Bangor for your flight. Our neighbors are making dinner for us tonight and it'll be over in a couple of hours. Washing machine is downstairs if you need it."

Grandpa Ben leaves and Theo gathers his clothes to take to the washing machine. The dryer is running but the washer is free, and he starts it up. One of the nurses comes in and says, "Here, let me take care of this for you. What can I get you to drink?" she asks.

"Oh, that's OK, you don't have to wait on me."

"Are you kidding? You're family. I'm here to take care of you, too."

Theo looks at her in amazement, and maybe a little embarrassment, and asks, "How is Mrs. Young doing?"

"She's comfortable and at peace. I think she's been waiting for Camden to get here. She is not in any pain and has her family with her. Well, and she will get to see her daughter and her parents when she passes. That's a blessing too."

Theo nods, not knowing what to say in response. "Thank you for taking such good care of her," he says and stands in place, feeling utterly useless.

"The best thing that you can do is to be here for Cam. It's going to be a tough time, I'm sure."

Theo gets a glass of water and sits in the living room, trying to be available but not in the way. He sees Cam walking upstairs with his luggage. Theo goes to Mrs. Young's makeshift bedroom that he can tell was once a formal dining room. "Can I help with anything?" he asks the nurse.

"Yes," Grandpa Ben says, coming down the hall from another part of the house. "You can come out with me and get some firewood."

Theo gets his jacket, and they go out the back door. The stream behind the home is lined with conifers and hardwoods missing many of their leaves. He realizes he is dressed for a Texas fall, but not Maine. Theo gathers an armful of split wood and takes it to the fireplace inside. "We have indoor heat of course, but Liz loves a fire, so I try to keep this going during the day. I fell behind today. I had some meetings I needed to attend to."

"Are you working now?"

"Oh no, I stopped working a few years ago. I had some things I needed to make sure were taken care of before Cam arrived. We're all set. We really are glad you're here with Cam. I know it's hard for him to see his grandmother this frail. But I'm happy he's home."

Theo has so many questions but knows now is not the right time. "Do you need me to run any errands or take care of anything here at the house? I really don't want to be in the way."

"How's the van doing?" Cam's grandfather asks. He takes a seat on the couch in the living room and takes a ragged breath, closing his eyes.

Theo notices him struggle after the exertion, but Grandpa seems OK. "Good. I guess you know they had a minor problem last week but honestly, Odysseus is in great shape."

He chuckles at Theo's statement. "Good name," he says. "It would be good to have her serviced, maybe the interior cleaned as well. I want to give her to someone who can use her. I hope Cam can get a normal car for a young man living in Los Angeles. What would that be? A Prius?"

Theo laughs. "I don't know. Honda's been good to him. He may choose something else. He has never really mentioned cars to me."

Grandpa Ben looks toward the stairs and back to Theo. "And how's he doing? He always seems to be OK when we talk with him. Or I guess I should say when *I* talk with him. He's never been one to ask for advice or help, but he seems like he's happy enough. What do you think?"

I wish Piper were here, is what Theo thinks. *She knows him a lot better than I do apparently.* Theo looks toward the stairs and says, "I don't know – to be honest – I haven't seen him much since college and we only talk every few months when I give him a call. It's just a coincidence that I called right after you called him last weekend."

"And he asked you to come along on the trip?"

"Not exactly. I asked him if I could join him. I'm between projects at work right now. He agreed and picked me up in Dallas. He hasn't really seemed himself the last few days. But given the purpose of the trip, that's understandable. He did most of the driving himself. Piper, Olivia, and I all offered but he really wanted to drive."

"That's a long drive."

"I agree," Theo says.

"And who's Olivia?"

"Oh, right, she's a friend from college who lives in Memphis now. We saw her briefly on the trip."

Grandpa Ben stands up with some effort and stops, turning around to look at Theo. "What is your timeframe?" he asks, directly.

"I don't have to be anywhere. I have time."

"Could you stay through the weekend, at least?"

"Yes," Theo says. He is not clear what day today is, but he estimates it's about Tuesday. "Yes sir, not a problem."

"Don't plan anything until Sunday at the earliest, OK?" Theo nods and Grandpa Ben walks back to the dining room and his wife.

****

Dinner is salmon, salad, homemade rolls, and chocolate cake. Cam takes a little and moves it around his plate, like a kid attempting to make it look like he tried it all. He glances up at his grandfather.

"Pretty sure I was rude to the couple who brought the dinner over. They seemed to remember me, but I have no idea where they live or where I should have known them from."

"It's understandable," Grandpa Ben assures him.

Cam clears his throat and says, "I shouldn't have driven. I should have flown last weekend when you called. I should have been here."

"I'm glad you drove with your friends. It probably gave you some time to think," Grandpa Ben says. "And you got to see some great places I hear. You did the right thing and you're here safe and sound."

"How much time does she have?" Cam asks quietly, not making eye contact with his grandpa.

"Well, it's hard to tell," he responds in a low voice. "We can talk about this in the den if you'd like. The nurses are quick to point out that tension in the house affects Granny. I want her to be as comfortable as she can be."

Cam nods and walks toward the den. Grandpa leaves his meal and follows. Theo asks the nurse, Ellen, if she or Mrs. Young wants any dinner.

"No, I've already eaten. You make sure you get enough. And Mr. Young and Cam too." Theo boxes up the leftovers and places them in the fridge, alongside what looks like yesterday's leftovers. There's so much food.

Theo starts washing his and Cam's dishes when Ellen comes in. "Please leave it. It'll give me something to do when Mrs. Young's medicines kick in and she is sound asleep."

Theo hears Cam's raised voice and has no idea what he should do.

"Why don't you come join us in here," Ellen says. "Tell me about your family." She guides him to a chair in the dining room and Theo answers all her questions about the Harris's of New Jersey and Argentina. She's fascinated by his story and shares that her granddaughter played volleyball for her middle school and just made the Junior Varsity team at the high school for next year. She suddenly shifts the conversation.

"It's good that you are here for Camden. It's hard for children and grandchildren to face the reality of Mrs. Young's situation. This will be especially tough on him."

"And how is Mr. Young doing?" Theo asks. "He seems to be tired."

"Oh, he's focused on getting everything done. Taking care of us. Taking care of the house and all the details. And of course, taking the best care of Mrs. Young. She's a lucky woman to have landed such a fox like him."

Theo finds it a really odd thing to say but then he looks to see a little smile across Cam's granny's face. She said it to make her smile. And it worked.

"You're a saint," Theo says.

Ellen laughs. "Not always," she says, and Granny smiles again.

From what he can tell, Cam's grandmother sleeps around the clock, waking up to eat one or two bites, take her medicines, and sip some water. She looks like she weighs almost nothing. Her white hair has thinned and the veins in her hands are more prominent than they should be.

Cam comes into the room and walks over to his grandmother's side. He sits down next to her and rests his hand on the blanket where her hand is underneath. He's clearly upset, mad even. Theo stands up and asks if anyone needs anything and says he'll be upstairs. Cam begins murmuring softly to his grandmother and Theo wonders if he should really try to stick it out until Sunday. He feels very much in the way.

Theo finds his clean laundry folded and lying on the guest bed. He dresses in sweats and a long sleeve tee-shirt and gets ready for bed. It's 7:25. What should he do? He takes out his book and immediately closes it again and reaches for his phone.

Theo: *Did your aunt show up OK?*
   Who is this?
Theo: *Sorry, is this Piper?*
   Piper who?
Oh God, what was her last name? Something pretentious. A double name?
   Theo: *Cam's friend Piper?*
   Cam who?
OK, she got him.
   Theo: *Hi Piper it's Theo. Don't block me.*
   Piper: *I'm not going to block you. How is Cam?*
Theo: *He's taking it hard. His grandmother is frail. His grandfather says having Cam here helps.*

Piper: *Does she recognize him?*

Theo: *She's sleepy. Her eyes are closed but she said his name. Remember Little Rock and Memphis when he was stressed?*

Piper: *Yeah*

Theo: *Double that. I think he might have yelled at his grandfather tonight.*

Piper: *What? Why?*

Theo: *Not sure. He's really stressed. His grandfather asked me to stay for a few days. He asked me not to fly out until at least Sunday.*

Piper: *Very specific*

Theo: *Right*

No response from Piper and the moments tick by. Theo texts again.

Theo: *I'm not sure exactly what I did but I feel I should tell you I'm sorry.*

Piper: *That's an apology?*

Theo: *Not a good one – but honestly if I knew what I did wrong, I could*

maybe apologize better???

Piper: *Why do you think you did something wrong?*

Theo: *Because you were happy last night and unhappy this morning.*

I'm pretty sure both had to do with me.

Piper: *Arrogant*

Theo: *But true?*

No response from Piper. Then finally.

Piper: *Can you talk? I don't want written evidence of this conversation.*

Theo: *Cryptic. I think I can. If Cam or Grandpa Ben needs me, I'll have*

to go.

Piper: *Of course*

He calls and she answers. "Hi," she says.

His heart jumps in his throat. *That's a sweet hi. That's Happy Piper. That's Piper's voice from last night.*

"I think you're right," she says as an opening.

"I'm sure I am," Theo says. "But what about?"

Piper says, with a sigh, "I may be moody."

He wisely doesn't say anything. "No, you're not moody" probably would be taken as the mocking tone she pointed out earlier.

Piper continues, "No one has ever called me moody before, so I was pretty sure you were off base, but now I'm wondering if I'm moody only around you."

Again, Theo is quiet. *Let her talk. At least she's talking.*

"You have a way of making me feel like I'm doing something wrong. You call me out on my annoying traits and my friends and family have never done that. They think I'm great. You make me think about myself in a different way. Like am I steamrolling Cam? I never thought I was, and I certainly don't want to, but maybe you're right. And last night? What about last night?" Piper whispers.

"Why were you happy with me last night, from what I could tell at least, and unhappy with me this morning?" Theo asks, dying to know.

"I wasn't unhappy with you," she says. "But I guess you could see it as moody. I'm just not willing to get hurt by you I guess."

"How did I hurt you?" Theo asks, in an almost panicked voice.

"You haven't yet. But you will. And you know you will, and you seem OK with it."

Theo stands up and walks around the room but stops when he hears angry voices. "Hang on. Someone is yelling. I'm going to call you back."

Theo hangs up and opens his door. He hears Cam taking big heaving breaths. Theo is not sure if he should find them and step in.

Grandpa Ben speaks to his grandson in a patient tone. "Come here Camden. I know this is a lot to handle right now. And if you had been here the last few months it wouldn't have made it any easier. We love you and we want you to be here with us. And you are. Tomorrow I'll answer any questions you have. Do you want to get some rest?"

"Can I sleep downstairs in the dining room?"

"Yes," Grandpa Ben says. "I'll ask Ellen to help me make up a bed for you."

Theo hears them on the landing of the stairs, and he joins them. "Here let me help."

Theo and Grandpa go downstairs. Grandpa looks completely drained. Theo does not ask what is going on because that would not be any help right now.

"Theo, there's an air mattress over there. Let me get some sheets."

"Just point them out to me. I'll take care of it." Theo and Ellen make up the mattress and top it with pillows and blankets. The house is kept very warm, probably for Cam's grandmother's comfort, but blankets always help.

Cam comes downstairs, eyes red and swollen, and says to Theo, "I'd feel better if Piper was here."

Theo nods yes. "Let me give her a call," he says.

Cam looks distraught. "I'm going to take the van out for a drive. I need to clear my head."

"Do you want me to come with you?"

"No. Thanks." Theo watches Cam walk out the front door and he worries that he's in the wrong headspace to be alone. But Cam is used to being alone and he hasn't had much alone time in several days. He has had to go for a run this week to get some space.

Theo goes outside and calls Piper back. She answers, her voice clearly worried.

"Hey, uh, Cam needs you here. Can I come get you?"

"Tonight?" she asks.

"I can leave first thing in the morning."

"How far are we?" Piper asks him. Theo suddenly feels exhausted and can't think about pulling out the Maps app one more time. "I think it was like three or four hours."

"Let me see if my aunt or uncle can drive me to meet you in Portland tomorrow morning."

"Sorry Piper. I know I've complicated everything by kissing you."

"Twice," Piper adds.

"Sorry. But I know Cam wants to see you."

"Do you know what's going on?" she asks.

"I'm not really sure," Theo says. "I'll talk to you tomorrow, OK?"

***

Theo checks in on Mrs. Young and the nurse and sees Grandpa Ben there.

"Do you need anything?"

"Yeah. Come with me." It takes him a moment to stand up from the recliner. He looks like he's aged in just the afternoon since they arrived. They walk to Grandpa's home office.

"I've got a box full of papers here. Cam is going to have to go through everything when he's feeling up to it. I just wanted you to know where it all is. I'm going to give the Honda to one of the nurses, Jess. He doesn't need to take that back to California. He's not a soccer mom or a grandmother."

"Yes sir," Theo says.

"I didn't ask you. Where are you going next? You said your job in Texas was done."

"I'm moving to Los Angeles," Theo says, for the first time. He's surprised it comes out effortlessly.

"Oh good, that's really good. You can be there for Camden."

"Sir, in the morning I'm going to get our friend Piper. She's in New Hampshire right now but Cam wants her here. I'll only be gone a few hours. Is that OK?"

"Sure, sure. Yes, that's great. I know Piper. It'll be good to see her. I know Elizabeth will want to meet her too."

He roughly pats Theo's shoulder and then Grandpa Ben walks back to his wife of 60 something years. He sits in his comfortable recliner and reaches for her frail hand. He leans back, closes his eyes and Theo sees nothing but peace slide across both of their faces.

BUCKSPORT, TUESDAY
Cam

Cam drives past his old high school and the fishing supply store where he worked for three summers. He drives past the 3-mile loop that he ran most days after school, and the house where he had his first kiss at a basement party. He continues to the river, then over the bridge to one of the islands he and his friends used to frequent on the weekends. They'd build a small bonfire and drink beer, or whatever they could get their hands on. Those nights of puking up booze before returning to his grandparents' home had turned him off most alcohol for several years. Until this week.

He gets out of the Honda and looks out across the bay. He wipes his tears and his nose with his sleeve, and he calls the one person he needs to hear from right now.

Alison is driving back to the office when Cam's call comes in. "Twice this week? A record. Camden how are you?"

"Not good," he says.

"Are you in Maine? How is your grandmother doing?"

"Not good," he says again. He moves the phone away, sniffs and wipes his eyes.

"Is it your grandpa too?" she asks.

"Yeah, I think so."

"I had a feeling. I'm so sorry Cam."

"I just want to be in California right now. Attending that meeting with you. Or doing something normal. I don't want to be here."

"Are you at your grandparents' house?"

"No, I'm at the bay. I had to get out."

"Where is Piper?"

"She's in New Hampshire. I think Theo's going to get her. I don't really know. How was the meeting?" Cam asks.

"Not now, OK? Now we're going to focus on Maine."

"Sorry, I shouldn't have called you."

"Why did you?"

"Not sure," Cam says. "Needed to think about the only good thing in my life."

Alison is quiet.

"Work. James. You."

"Hang on. I'm going to pull into our lot."

"I'll let you go."

"No, just give me a second." Cam hears her park in the small lot behind the James Casting offices. "I'm sorry you're having to deal with this, but I'm glad your friends are there. What you're dealing with now is real life. And it sucks, but you can handle it."

"I wish you were here," he whispers.

"Cam..." Alison sighs.

Cam is silent.

"No," Alison says. "Look we'll deal with all the work stuff when you get back but for now, you need to take care of yourself and your grandparents."

"I'm not talking about work, and you know it," Cam says.

"Have you talked to your dad?" Alison asks.

"No, why?"

"Because he should be there with you."

"They're not his parents."

"But he's your parent and you need him."

"I probably won't call him."

"Because you think he won't come," Alison says quietly.

"I don't think he will, and if he does it wouldn't be much help anyway."

"Yeah," Alison gets it.

"Theo is going to call you about a job."

"Remind me who Theo is?"

"We went to school together. He played volleyball. He's been working with film festivals and small production companies on their digital products, marketing, and some hiring. He asked me if I minded if he called you. I said he should. He's got some good ideas about casting on the technical side. I want to talk to you too about my meeting with Simon Kaplan too. More ideas."

"Hmmm," she says. "And I've been wanting to talk to you."

"About what?" Cam asks.

"About some ideas I've had."

"I have been having those same ideas," Cam laughs.

"No Camden. I'm talking about James and your future at James."

For some reason this sparks that old fear of rejection. "My future at James is long and successful," he says with certainty, and maybe even a challenge in his voice.

"Don't get tough with me. I'm talking about possibly moving you into a managing partner role with me. Splitting the leadership in half. Expanding. I don't know. World domination."

"Yes!" Cam yells. "I'm in."

"I'm not offering you anything. I'm saying I want to talk to you."

"And I want to do more than talk to you."

Alison is quiet and Cam says, "Don't shut me out right now."

"Well, we're not going to talk about this right now. You're focused on your family. Work will be here."

"Again, I'm not talking about work."

"Well, I am. And if we're going to partner at work then we are not going to partner outside of work."

Cam doesn't respond.

"Cam, it was one kiss. And I'm your boss. I'm feeling pretty conflicted about it right now. Can you just focus on your family?"

"It was a great kiss. And why did you think something was going on with my grandfather?" he asks Alison.

She is quiet for a moment. "Do you remember that night?"

"Of course," Cam laughs quietly.

"Do you remember what you said to me and what I said to you?"

"Yeah. I told you about a conversation with my grandpa and how I didn't want to lose them like I lost my parents. But it was all hypothetical. I think I was just making a point that James is important to me. I wanted you to know that."

"You said you'd felt alone a lot in your life, and you felt like you belong at James. You said you had never thought about the possibility of a real relationship. I told you that I could see you in one, that not everyone leaves. And you kissed me. And we haven't talked about it since. I know the next days and weeks are going to be tough, but I also know you are tough. And work can wait. Listen, I'm walking into the office now for a meeting. Want my last piece of advice?"

"Yeah," Cam says walking to the edge of the bay.

"Be present. Be there for them like they've always been there for you."

Cam stifles a small sob.

"I'm going to hand my phone to Chelsea. Will you give her your grandparents' address?"

"Yeah," Cam says in a shaky breath. "Alison?"

"Yeah Cam?"

"We can do both."

Alison lets out a long sigh. He can hear shuffling of her cell phone and Chelsea's voice is the one he hears next.

"Hey Cam, are you in Maine yet?"

"Yeah, I'm here. Listen, I've got to get back to my grandparents but let me give you their address."

"I'm ready."

Cam thanks Chelsea and ends the call. And standing on the edge of Penobscot Bay, he screams. And screams. Then he and the Odyssey drive home.

BUCKSPORT, WEDNESDAY
Cam

Theo walks into the kitchen and looks surprised to see Cam with Grandpa Ben at the table drinking coffee. They have a notebook in front of them and Cam is taking down information as his grandfather talks. Cam notices that Grandpa looks tired, like he has not slept well in weeks. But Cam feels more rested and focused after his call with Alison last night.

"Morning Theo," Grandpa Ben calls out. "Could you get me a glass of water please?" Grandpa Ben massages his temple and then his chest.

The nurse joins them in the kitchen. "Have you taken your pills today, Mr. Young?"

"I was just about to," he assures her. She keeps an eye on him as she cleans the dishes in the sink and refills a cup for Cam's grandmother.

"This is our lawyer's contact information. I've known him for 40 years. He's up to speed. Now tell me about your work. I know you can't be away this long."

"Don't worry about that. My boss is aware, and I've been doing work since we left. I had meetings in Nashville and New York last week. I talked with her yesterday and everything is OK. She wants me to focus on my family."

Cam looks at Theo. "She's expecting your call, too." Theo looks taken aback.

"OK thanks," he says.

The nurse hands Theo a paper plate with lightly buttered toast and a thermal mug of coffee. "I didn't add sugar or milk."

"Black is fine and thank you. I'm leaving for New Hampshire now. Can I get the van keys, Cam?"

Grandpa motions to a sideboard with keys in an antique dish. "Do me a favor and take my car would you? I've got a guy coming over today to detail the van." Cam looks up, surprised. Grandpa waves him off. "We've got other things to do. You don't need to be cleaning a van."

Cam goes upstairs to get ready for the day. They have a meeting with his grandparents' lawyer, and he wants to sit with his grandmother when she is likely to be more awake mid-morning. He sends Alison a quick text.

"Thanks."

She texts him back, "Any time".

Well, that wasn't much of an opening to continue their conversation from last night, but he's not dissuaded. And then he remembers it's the middle of the night on the west coast. *Oops.* He straightens up his childhood bedroom. There are stacks of yearbooks and albums he wants to go through before he leaves. But first things first - the lawyer.

Cam finally locates his grandfather in the den, resting in a comfortable chair. "Grandpa are you awake?"

"Yeah," he says in a soft voice. "Just needed a break."

"What time is the appointment with the lawyer?"

"Whenever I tell him. Can you give me a couple of hours? I might take a nap." Cam notices it's barely 9 a.m. but his grandpa has been through a lot.

"Anything I can do?"

"Yeah, there's a stack of files on the chair next to my desk in the office. Can you go through them and sign where they've indicated? That'll save us time at Davis's office."

Cam pours a mug of hot tea, checks on his grandmother who is still sound asleep and then settles at his grandpa's desk. Two hours later he's gone through all the paperwork that his grandfather asked him to review.

He hasn't heard any movement from his grandparents or the nurses, so he pulls out his phone and responds to important work emails. He sends a thank you to Simon for his time as well. Too early to call Chelsea, but then he sees her response on a voiceover email thread with their largest commercial agent.

"Got time for a call?" he texts her.

Thumbs up comes back.

She answers, "How are you? How is your grandmother?"

"Wow, uncharacteristic Chels."

"You're killing me Smalls."

"OK nice," Cam says. "I'm OK. She's OK. My grandfather is exhausted but he's able to rest so that's good. Glad I'm here to help."

"Alright what do you need? I saw your responses on the three animation reviews. Do you have anything else for me? I want to help where I can," Chelsea tells him.

"I don't have anything. I wanted to know if you have anything for me."

"I'm sure Alison'll want to take care of as much as she can this week while you're with your family, but I'll try to get some smaller assignments for you to help her out. She's got a lot going on with several contracts and meetings for potentials."

"Speaking of contracts. Could you send me the latest one I signed when I was moved to Assistant Casting Director? I don't think I have it."

"Associate," she says.

"Really? Or is that an *Office* reference?"

"Your title is Associate. Yeah, when I get to the office, I'll send it to you. You sound more like yourself today."

"Yeah, I'm good. It's been a couple of weeks though."

"I can imagine. See ya," and she hangs up.

Cam sits with his Granny for half an hour, talking with the nurse about her family. He's struck by the friendliness and her comfort in someone else's home. She has been working as a hospice nurse for 11 years and he can't imagine. Her daughters are grown, and her husband is retired. She's passionate about palliative care and Cam nods, making a mental note of that word so he can look it up later. Her disposition is so positive. It strengthens his resolve to do everything he can for his grandparents at this time of their lives.

Cam checks on his grandfather who is sound asleep in the chair. He gently wakes him to see if he wants to go lay down in his bed. "No, no, I'm good," he says, groggy and pale. "Just needed a rest. Give me a few minutes and we'll head to the office."

Cam waits in the kitchen and checks his incoming texts. Nothing from Piper or Theo. Or Alison. He responds to a couple of emails while he waits for his grandfather who finally comes downstairs in his professional attire.

"Why don't you drive?" He gets a different set of keys and Cam follows him to the garage and his grandmother's Lincoln. "I try to drive it every week, but it's been a while. Let's hope it starts. Did you leave Odysseus unlocked?"

Cam laughs softly at the name. "Yes. I cleaned the rest of our stuff out this morning and it's unlocked."

"Good, Martin's guy is coming over to detail it sometime today. You remember Martin. I think his son went to school with you."

"Yeah, I think so," Cam says, not having any idea who Martin is or who his son might be. "How are you feeling? I know you've been handling a lot. I know I should have been here to help."

"We've talked about this. You're based in California. I called you when I needed you and you came out."

Cam adjusts the mirrors, starts the car, and notices his grandfather does not put his seatbelt on but lays the seat back a bit. Cam doesn't say anything about it on the short drive to his friend's law office to discuss necessary estate planning details. *Do what you want, Grandpa. You've earned the right.*

"I completely forgot about this car. I guess I always picture Granny in the minivan."

"You and your friends kept her busy after school. Track practice, getting you to your job. She loved every minute of it."

"Yeah, you know I think about her every time I get in the Odyssey. I can't help it."

"Think I'm going to offer the van to one of the nurses who's been caring for your Granny for months now. She could use it and we don't need it. That OK with you?"

"Yeah of course. Granny will be happy to hear that. That makes me feel better than selling it. I don't know why I never felt right selling it for you. It just felt like it belonged in Maine."

"Yep, I get that," Grandpa leans back and closes his eyes.

FREEPORT, WEDNESDAY
Theo

Theo checks his texts and sees that Piper and her aunt left Salem early as well. Her aunt asked that they meet at the LL Bean flagship store in Freeport, Maine. Theo responds, "See you there" and pulls in two hours later. He sends a text that he'll be inside and checks out the store, stopping first to pause at the outdoor stage being set up for some sort of activity later that afternoon.

He's in line with two sweaters when Piper walks up behind him and says a quiet "Hi". He smiles before he turns around and is about to throw his arms around her when he sees the look on Piper's face, and the imposing woman standing next to her.

"Hi Piper," Theo says. "And who is this?" he asks, shifting the sweaters to his left hand.

"Theo Harris, this is my Aunt Beverly." Theo puts his hand out to shake Beverly's hand.

"Hello Theo, thank you for meeting us here. I hope it wasn't too far out of your way."

"No, not at all. And it gave me a chance to pick up some clothes better suited to Maine in the fall. Thank you for bringing Piper half-way."

Beverly insists they get a coffee before Piper leaves again and Theo chooses not to disagree. He gives Piper a look indicating that they need to get back to Cam at some point, but if Piper sees the look, she doesn't react.

They head to the coffee shop and Theo places their order. He takes the three warm cups to their table and asks Aunt Beverly about Salem, New Hampshire. Aunt Beverly isn't interested in his charm, though.

"So, what is going on with your friend in Maine?" Her demanding tone catches Theo off-guard, but only for a second. This straightforward approach he's encountered in New England before.

"Cam is a friend from college in Los Angeles. His grandfather asked him to come out because his grandmother isn't doing well. Cam turned it into a road trip to return a vehicle."

"Yes, I understand all that. Why does Piper need to be there?"

Piper looks at her tea and doesn't contribute an answer so Theo tries to provide something that will ease her aunt's mind. "Cam was raised by his grandparents, and this has hit him harder than he realized. Last night he sort of hit rock bottom and he asked me to get Piper. Since he has such a small family, I think he wants his friends around."

Beverly looks from Theo to Piper and says, "We rarely get to see our niece. I was hoping for a couple of days."

Piper places her hand on her aunt's and says, "I know. Maybe you could come out to California this winter? I know Dad would love to see you and Uncle Charlie."

"I doubt that very much," Beverly sniffs. "But we'd love to see you, so we'll think about it. Or maybe you could come back to Salem after you help your friend?" she asks.

"Maybe," Piper says softly, looking at Theo and he agrees.

"Yes, maybe that will work out. I'm happy to drive you if you need."

"We are capable of driving up too. We don't want it to be an imposition on you and your friend."

In her soft, kind way, Piper speaks up. "Aunt Beverly, I think we need to go. It's been so lovely seeing you." Piper stands. "Let me get my bags from your car and we'll let you get back. I know you had a busy day planned. And thank you so much."

Theo is pretty sure Beverly has no idea how she is being handled at this moment. It sounded like she had more questions about the situation in Maine, but Piper's smooth way of handling difficult people came in handy. Again.

They all say goodbye at Beverly's Volvo and Theo takes Piper's luggage, guiding her to Grandpa Ben's car. Theo sets GPS back to the Bucksport house, and he starts to pull out of the parking lot. He smiles at Piper, but she is staring out the window, with what looks like a tear threatening to trickle down her left cheek.

"Hey, hey, what's going on?" Theo asks, putting the car back in the parking spot. Someone behind them honks. They probably were waiting for the parking space. *This place fills up fast for a Wednesday.* "What's wrong?" Theo asks again.

"I'm OK. I think I'm just tired. I didn't sleep much the last couple of nights, and I remembered within five minutes why I don't visit my aunt that often. She's a lot."

"She cares about you, that's for sure."

"Yeah, I don't know. She mainly talked about my dad and relatives I don't know. A lot of perceived injustices."

"Ah, got it," Theo says.

"And I'm worried about Cam." She looks at Theo out of the corner of her eye.

"Have you talked with him?" Theo asks.

"No, he knows I'm coming right?"

"Yes. He seems to be doing better today. He wanted to spend time with his grandmother, and his grandfather has some errands for them to run."

"Do you know what's going on?" Piper asks, looking at her hands in her lap.

"I'm not really sure. Cam is going to be happy to see you though."

She smiles and says, "OK, let's go."

BUCKSPORT, WEDNESDAY
Cam

The lawyer's office is a stately building converted from an older brick home. The foyer is painted in a Revolutionary blue that Cam remembers seeing in homes in the area growing up. Mr. Davis comes out and shakes both of their hands, ushering them into his private office.

"Camden, I haven't seen you in 15 years I would guess. It's great to see you. I'm sorry for the circumstances."

"Thank you, sir. How is your family?"

Cam vaguely remembers his grandfather's friend, but he has no memory of his family. *It's just a safe thing to ask.*

Mr. Davis fills Cam in on his two sons and their families along with his wife, who sounds an awful lot like Aunt Ginny. And then the lawyers turn to business.

Grandpa Ben starts, "I've got everything here that Camden signed. We have not signed over one of the vehicles yet. Someone is coming today to clean it up and I'm gifting it to a family friend. One of the nurses who could really use it."

"That would make Elizabeth happy, I'm sure," Mr. Davis says. "OK... power of attorney, living will...", as the lawyers look through all the papers Cam glances around the office and notices how much it looks like his grandfather's old office. The only thing missing is the vintage fishing decor. *I wonder where all that is now?*

"Now sadly I have to turn our conversation to the inevitable, men, and unfortunately, it's inevitable for all of us. Cam, when your grandmother passes, all her assets will transfer to your grandfather. That will happen quickly as these papers were drawn up years ago, before her disease made it difficult for her to make these decisions." He pauses, so Cam tells him he understands.

"And when your grandfather passes, he has a will stipulating where his assets will go. There are four bequeathals to the Presbyterian Church, the local humane society, the scholarship in your great uncle's name at UVA, and to your father. The rest will go to you. The legal process will take approximately 12 weeks at that time, but we have drawn up the paperwork so that it should go through without any additional hold ups. Now what questions do you have for us?"

"My father?" Cam asks, looking at Grandpa Ben.

"Yes, we never took him out of our will after your mother passed. It's not a large sum, but we want to leave something of our legacy to him as well."

"I guess I'm just surprised. Does he know?"

"I have no idea. We haven't talked to him in years. Maybe at your high school graduation? No, it was when he came to get the van. And if you'll recall he didn't stay with us the night before your trip."

"Should I tell him what's going on?"

"That's up to you, Camden. If you need him with you, then by all means."

"I hadn't planned to call him. I don't think he could come. I think he's in Chicago."

"You're not sure?" Grandpa Ben asks.

"No, not really. I haven't called him in a few weeks, and he doesn't call me that often."

The silence stretches and Mr. Davis adds, "It's good to have family with you to talk to about these things."

"Grandpa and Granny are my family," Cam says quietly.

"And I am here to help you with anything you need. What other questions do you have now though, Cam?" Mr. Davis asks.

"What will happen to your home?" Cam looks at Grandpa Ben.

"Well, if your grandfather hasn't sold it then it will go to you as one of the assets. You can then sell it."

"I don't want to sell it," Cam says automatically.

"Well, you don't have to make any decisions now." While Cam is clearly feeling concerned about the legal complexities, the overwhelming feeling is just sadness.

"I know this is a lot to think about at your age. I usually have conversations like this one with adult children who are much, much older and may even have grandchildren of their own. But I'm here for you and can help with whatever you need. You won't have to make decisions on your own."

"OK," Cam says. "Thank you."

"Why don't you take your grandfather home. You'll think of other questions later. You can call or email the office when you think of those questions, and we'll be happy to get answers to you as quickly as possible. For now, go be with your grandmother. I understand you have friends in town as well?"

"Friends from LA who made the trip with me."

"That's good. I know you've got to have friends from growing up in town too. You should give them a call if you want to reconnect."

Grandpa Ben and Mr. Davis exchange looks and then the lawyer stands up. Cam stands automatically and then reaches down to help Grandpa Ben stand as well. He has never seen his grandfather struggle. More guilt about not being here all this time.

They shake hands and leave to return to his grandparents' house, but Grandpa Ben asks if they can make a stop at the store first and then the church. They walk into the small grocery store and Grandpa beelines to the flowers. Cam stops in his tracks when he realizes why they're going to the church. Grandpa chooses a beautiful fall bouquet and Cam picks out two bouquets as well. Cam pulls out his wallet to pay for all the flowers, but Grandpa waves him off and says, "This is on me."

They drive to the church and Grandpa points around the back to the cemetery. Cam remembers walking through this space a long time ago. He helps his grandpa navigate the uneven ground until they reach a large area of grass and his mother's headstone. The men put two of the bouquets in the vase next to the headstone and stand reflecting on the mother Cam doesn't really remember.

He does the math and realizes she has been gone almost 25 years. He looks to his grandpa and says, "I didn't realize it has been 25 years."

"Almost," Grandpa says. "It feels just like yesterday you were a toddler, and she was a beautiful young mother. Harried at times but doing a wonderful job with you. Life changes fast, son." He has his hand on Cam's forearm, keeping steady.

Grandpa clears his throat. "I'm going to say something, and you may not like it."

Cam braces himself for whatever Grandpa has to say to him.

"He shouldn't have left you in California with a note and a minivan. He should have made more of an effort when you were little. You know you didn't do anything wrong, right?"

"Yeah, I do. I just wish I had memories of her. And I wish I knew him better. I know we're a lot alike, but I don't really know him that well. Can we not talk about this right now?"

"Sure. I hope you'll continue to come back here and visit your mother from time to time," he says. "God, she would be so proud of you."

"I will," Cam assures him. Left unspoken is the fact that his grandmother may be here in a short period. But it gives Cam peace that she will be with her daughter again. Cam has never thought much about the afterlife and wonders why. And why has he not been back to Maine more often in the last few years? Is he just too self-centered to think of anything but his career? He wasn't unhappy here. Why didn't he stay in touch with any of his Maine friends? It's like he cut ties with Maine when he was 18. Except for his grandparents who wouldn't allow him to cut ties with them. Isn't that what his dad did? Left after Sumner passed and didn't look back, not really? *Just another way I'm just like my dad.*

Cam feels a little guilty for standing at his mother's gravesite and thinking of himself and his father. But then, *isn't this why we visit? To reflect?* He shakes it off and places the unpleasantness behind him. "I promise I'll come back with you," he says to his grandfather.

Grandpa looks at Cam and doesn't say anything. Then he nods his head OK and says, "We love you sweet girl," and turns to walk back to the car.

Cam takes the remaining bouquet into his childhood home for his grandmother. He is in the kitchen looking for a vase when Piper walks in.

"Hi Cam," she says. He stops filling the vase with water and turns to her. Tears slip down his cheeks. She walks over to him, and he hugs her tightly.

"Thank you," he manages.

Piper sniffs and says, "It's OK. I'd love to say hello to your grandparents," she says. They walk into the dining room where the lights have been turned up. Granny must have been awake earlier this morning. He walks Piper over to his grandfather and re-introduces them.

Grandpa Ben grips Piper's hand and tells her how good it is to see her again. Piper seems a little surprised that he remembers her from the one lunch on the West Coast.

"And this is my Granny Elizabeth."

She walks over to the frail woman and touches her hand. "Hello Mrs. Young, I'm so happy to meet you."

Granny smiles a little and says, "Hello, nice to meet you," in a very soft voice. Her eyes don't open but she is present with them. Cam says he'll be back, and Piper takes a seat near Grandpa Ben. She begins asking questions about their lives together, Bucksport, and Cam as a little boy. Cam returns and breathes a sigh of relief that she is back.

Theo comes in from the backyard with a small pile of firewood. "How are you doing?"

"OK. Been to the lawyer's office, the store, and the cemetery. Unreal to be honest. But I'm OK."

"How is your grandpa?"

"I guess he's OK."

"Is he feeling alright?"

"He hasn't complained about anything. Maybe I just haven't seen him in a while."

Ellen, the hospice nurse, is stirring soup in a stock pot when Cam and Theo walk into the kitchen. "We'll have a light lunch in about 30 minutes. And there are plenty of leftovers in the refrigerator if you need something heartier."

Cam asks in a low voice, "Ellen, I know you're not Grandpa's nurse but how is he?"

"He's strong but he's tired, isn't he?" she responds, stirring the chicken noodle. "He's been very busy these last few weeks and he's with your grandmother every chance he gets. I don't think he's relaxed in a long time."

"And Granny is OK, given the circumstances?"

"She's comfortable and at peace. She is so happy that you are here. That all of you are here," she says to Theo. "I'll be leaving at 6:00 but will be back at 11:00 tomorrow. Jess is on her way to take over. But I want all of you to eat this soup. I don't want to see any leftovers tomorrow. You need to eat so you can take care of your grandparents."

"OK, and thank you," Cam says.

Grandpa Ben comes in and asks Theo to get another box from the home office. Theo retrieves it and sets it on a small table that he moved next to the older man in the dining room. He asks Cam to get a notepad by the house phone so he can pass along some more information.

Piper pulls on her light jacket and excuses herself to go for a walk and explore the neighborhood. Theo busies himself cutting more firewood.

BUCKSPORT, WEDNESDAY
Piper

Cam and Theo leave to pick up dinner from Gianni's, his grandparents' favorite restaurant. It's also the last surviving family-owned restaurant that Grandpa is familiar with. While they are out, Piper turns her attention to the beautiful dining table, now relocated to the formal living room.

She selects several platters from Granny Elizabeth's China cabinet and places them on the table. She finds good cloth napkins, a silver chest and crystal goblets. She consults YouTube to set the table correctly and fills a pitcher with cold water. Then she opens two bottles of Cabernet from the wine rack to allow them to breathe. Places are set for Granny Elizabeth and Jess as well, although she doesn't think either will make it to the table. Finally, she dims the wall sconces and sets taper candles from the fireplace mantle on the table and lights them.

Piper takes a moment to touch up her mascara and lipstick and puts on a floral top that she bought in New Hampshire when shopping with her Aunt Beverly. She brushes her dark blonde hair out and nods approval to herself in the bathroom mirror.

The guys return with the food, and they transfer everything from takeout containers to the China platters and bowls. They're pretty sure they over-ordered but everyone likes Italian.

"I remember several years ago they celebrated their anniversary at Gianni's," Cam reminisces. "They had their photo taken with the head chef and it was on the restaurant's social media. I hadn't been on Instagram in a long time, but local friends tagged me."

They invite Cam's grandparents and the nurse to dinner. Jess walks in and her eyes water at the beautiful sight.

"Well, this looks just grand. I think I'll make a plate and eat with Elizabeth," Grandpa tells them.

"Why don't we eat in here and then we can spend time with Mrs. Young. She is sound asleep. We'll save her a little of this delicious food to eat when she wakes up." Jess smoothly pulls out Grandpa Ben's chair and encourages him to join them at the table.

The conversation is lively, although in hushed tones so Granny isn't disturbed. Jess tells stories about her family including her youngest son who is graduating from middle school in May and has been accepted at a private preparatory school. She pats Grandpa Ben's hand. Piper assumes Grandpa Ben is funding the likely very expensive tuition for a much-loved family caregiver. Jess clarifies, "Cam, your grandfather wrote a letter of recommendation after meeting Logan last summer."

"A fine young man," Grandpa Ben says. "He took really good care of our lawn. I'd like to do more," he trails off and Jess shakes her head.

"Don't worry. It'll all work out," she says. "You and Mrs. Young have been so good to us."

Piper answers everyone's questions about her work because people are always curious when they find out you work for *The Herald*. She steels herself and tells the group she is thinking about a break from her job so she can write a book.

"Do it," Grandpa Ben says. "You won't regret it."

Piper smiles, "I just might take your advice."

"Or what about a podcast?" Jess asks. "That seems to be what everyone is doing these days."

Piper looks a little surprised by Jess's suggestion, but the idea is intriguing. *A podcast. Why didn't I think of that?*

"That seems perfect for you," Theo tells her. Piper is surprised again and shifts the conversation back to Grandpa Ben.

They talk about how Ben and Elizabeth met (at the movies on a blind date with mutual friends) and what their wedding was like. "It was more extravagant than I would have preferred but Elizabeth was an only child whose mother had dreamed of her daughter's wedding her entire life." Everyone laughs when he rolls his eyes at the memory.

Jess excuses herself and goes to check on Granny.

"I can't believe the Honda is back in the driveway," Grandpa Ben tells Cam.

"Odysseus has a lot of miles left in him."

"Cam's grandmother drove that van all over the state when he was in high school, running cross-country and track. She carted a whole bunch of sophomores down to Twin Brook to see the state championship race the year our upper classmen went. We taught Cam to drive in that van."

Everyone laughs and Cam smiles and shakes his head. "Granny never missed a meet, did she?"

Piper notices that Grandpa Ben has eaten very little of his pasta and none of the salad, garlic bread or his wine. He looks completely worn out. *The errands and the company have been a little too much.* Maybe some real sleep would help him get back some of his energy.

After dinner Grandpa returns to Granny, and Theo starts on the dishes. "Hey, I feel like I'm in the way here," Piper says. "Should I get a hotel?"

"I think Cam wants you here. Are you worried that he doesn't?"

"I guess I'm not worried, but I want to be sensitive that his grandmother is in her final days. Are we allowed to say that?"

"Yeah, I think everyone is pretty aware. I'm a little concerned that I don't have anything to wear to a funeral and my guess is this is going to be a proper service."

"I don't either," Piper says. "Should we go to a mall or something just in case we're here when the funeral takes place?"

Cam comes into the kitchen. "It's a good time to give them a little privacy. They are going to change my grandmother's clothes and take care of some other evening routines. Can we go out for a drink?"

Theo and Piper agree, and they finish hand washing the China and crystal. Cam reminds Jess to call him if she needs anything.

"Grandpa asked me to take his car. He sold his truck a couple of years ago. I can't get used to the idea of him driving a sedan."

"Your Grandpa doesn't strike me as a truck person," Piper muses. "Is that pretty common here?"

"Yeah, he used to fish all the time. It's better for the fishing gear." They drive to a bar with indoor and outdoor seating that looks to be full.

"Busy for a Wednesday night, isn't it?" Theo asks.

"This bar has great food too. My guess is it'll start to clear out soon." There's a table in the semi-enclosed outdoor area near a heater and they take it.

"Your grandparents are exactly as I imagined them Cam," Piper says. "I bet your grandmother was gentle but also held her own when you were growing up."

"She was a teacher and principal before she retired when the early signs of dementia became obvious. She could turn on that teacher's voice when she needed to. I spent a ton of my time with her, but my grandfather was the one I spent weekends with. He was an umpire for Little League when I was young. We camped and fished together. Spent time out on the bays and ocean. He and a friend at his law practice had a boat for a while and we would take it out to fish or during whale season."

"You fished whales?" Piper asks.

Cam chuckles, "No, to *watch* them. There are pods around here certain times of year."

"Did he want you to go into law?"

"He never said if he did. I was much more interested in movies, and some TV. I was on the AV team at the high school." Cam pauses to let Theo finish laughing. "Uh huh. I bet you were too," Cam tells him. Theo doesn't own up if he was. Piper doesn't get it but let's them have their inside jokes.

"Do you have friends who still live in town?" Piper asks.

"If they're here, I haven't kept up with them. Since I'm not on social media much either, I really only know about my grandparents. And sometimes my dad."

"And your dad's family?"

"They're in Bangor. I haven't seen them in a long time. My dad's not that close to them either."

They order a second round but Piper switches from margarita to iced tea and listens in as Theo and Cam talk shop. She's happy Theo talked to Cam about his career, and it sounds like Cam is even more on board now.

"What about Hilary though?" Cam asks him.

"Hilary?" Theo says, glancing at Piper. "That was like a year ago."

"Really? Huh. Was she the last one you dated? I remember another name, but I think it was before Hilary."

Theo says, "Yes but let's talk about you Cam."

"I date, but not that seriously," Cam says as he glances at Piper.

"Boys, go ahead and air your dirty laundry. It doesn't bother me."

Cam continues. "This summer I went out with Katharine a few times, but she was not looking to settle down."

"Are you?" Piper asks.

"No," Cam laughs, busted. "I've gone out a lot in California but to be honest it gets a little boring. If they're in the business then they want to go to store openings, events, and trendy restaurants. And the business is all they want to talk about."

"They want to stay relevant," Piper says. "I get that. Nothing wrong with it."

"Yeah, but I'm not into any of that. I also notice the women I go out with don't want to get out of LA."

"Have you gone out with anyone who isn't somehow connected to acting?" Piper asks him.

"Not a lot. Not since college," Cam says. "Where do you meet people who aren't connected to the business in LA?"

"I've introduced you to a lot. I think you might have more in common with them than you think. Martin's number is right here," she says shaking her phone. "You and he enjoyed hiking that time."

"What does Martin do?" Theo asks.

"I don't know," Cam says.

"He's in entertainment law. He works with my dad," Piper says. "And he had a good time when a group of us went hiking in August."

Cam says, "Martin is gay, or bi. Does he know I'm straight? I feel like this might be a set up. Do *you* know I'm straight?" he teases Piper.

Piper gives him a withering look. "He likes to hike, and you like to hike and the two of you took off when we went last time, leaving the rest of us in the dust. Thought you might like a hiking friend."

"Sorry, I'm teasing you."

"It doesn't bother me when you tease me. It bothers me that you might be lonely in a city of 10 million. You seem to resist all my attempts at connecting you to people."

"Ten million, really," Theo asks.

"That's the latest number I've heard," Piper says. "Three million in LA proper."

"I'm never lonely with you in charge of my social calendar," he rubs her arm. "And what about you?"

Piper reddens, and notices that Theo notices. "I haven't dated anyone seriously in a while," she says quietly.

"But lots of guys are interested. I see it when we go out," Cam says. "And weren't you engaged?" The spit-take Theo almost does is highly satisfying to Piper.

"No, I was proposed to when I was 23 but God, I was 23. No, I haven't 'gone steady' with anyone in a while. My dad's girlfriend set me up with someone over the summer, but he was dealing with a couple of issues that I didn't want to take on. And I went out with Henry Blake. You remember him, right? He was at the art show that we attended for Camille?"

"What does he look like?"

"Tall and very blonde."

"Oh right. You dated?"

"We went out and now we're just friends. I actually think he and Camille would be perfect together."

"What about Martin?"

"I haven't dated Martin. I have a lot of guy friends, but I haven't dated most of them." Piper notices Theo very clearly not looking at her.

"Another round?" Theo asks, saving Piper from Cam's 3rd degree. Or maybe he doesn't want to hear any more about her social life.

"Go ahead, I'm good," Cam says. "I want to get back soon though." Theo pays at the bar, and they take off.

Grandpa is sound asleep in the makeshift bed next to Granny. Jess tells Cam that she does not want to wake him up when Cam suggests Grandpa might be more comfortable in his bed.

"He was tired after we dressed your grandmother. He decided to stay the night with Mrs. Young. I hope that's OK."

"Yes, sure. Piper, let me get my things out of that room and I'll move to the sunroom."

Piper looks uneasy. "No Cam I don't want to kick you out of your room. Why don't I go to a hotel. If one of you can take me, I'll be just fine."

"No just stay here, we'll make it work."

Piper walks over to Cam. "Cam, please, I don't want to cause any stress. Let me fix this. I'll go to a hotel."

Cam realizes she's serious and says, "I really want you here."

Jess steps in and says, "I changed the sheets in the master bedroom when your grandpa went to bed down here. Someone should stay there. Fresh towels in the master bath too."

"Perfect, thank you. I'll sleep in my grandparents' room. Please stay, Piper."

"OK. But only if you let me know when I'm in the way."

Piper and Theo take turns in the guest bathroom. Once Cam shuts the master door, Theo steps into Cam's childhood bedroom where Piper is staying. He pulls the door to and leans back against Cam's dresser. "Hey. I'm happy you're here," he whispers.

"Me too," Piper whispers back.

Theo walks toward her slowly. "Can I put my arms around you?" Piper glances toward the hallway and says yes. They stand wrapped in each other's arms for a minute and Theo pulls away. "See you tomorrow," he kisses the top of her head and leaves.

Piper gets under the covers, checks her emails, responds to everything she can and then sends her editor an email.

Can we set up a time to talk on Thursday? I sent in tomorrow's "Ten" earlier tonight and I'm waiting to hear back on the Getty direction. Anything else you need me to do? I'm in Maine now.

She turns off the light and drifts off to sleep thinking about hiking, karaoke, long kisses, and forest lined highways.

Fellow Travelers – Odysseus Returns to Maine

"A Tombstone Every Mile" by Dirck Curless
"King of The Road" by Roger Miller
"Long Time Sunshine" by Weezer
"Nothing but Time" by Jackson Browne
"Portland, Maine" by Donovan Woods
"The Reach" by Dan Fogelberg

BUCKSPORT, THURSDAY
Theo

Theo wakes up at 3:40 a.m. to muffled voices. His first thought is that Piper and Cam are talking but then he realizes it's Jess, the nurse.

"Camden? Cam, can you hear me? I need you to come downstairs."

Theo sees Cam pull on a t-shirt as he opens his grandparents' bedroom door. "Jess?"

"Yes, can you come downstairs?"

Cam stops in the bathroom quickly and then runs downstairs leaving the bathroom light on. Theo goes to Cam's bedroom and sees Piper sitting on the edge of the bed. He joins her and they sit together until Cam is ready for them.

"How long has she been bed-bound, do you know?" asks Theo.

"No, I'm not sure. She's such a sweet soul. I have no idea how to be helpful here." Piper lays her head on Theo's shoulder, and he reaches for her hand. There is plenty of noise downstairs, but Theo feels rooted to the room. He isn't sure if they would be in the way.

Cam jogs upstairs and looks into the guest bedroom but must notice Theo isn't there. He looks in his old room and sees his friends sitting on the bed together. "An ambulance is coming," Cam says. "I've got to get dressed and go with him to the hospital."

"We'll come too," his friends stand up.

"No, could you stay here with Jess and Granny?" Theo and Piper are both confused.

Theo says, "Wait, your grandfather is going to the hospital?" Piper is shaking her head trying to process.

"Grandpa was not breathing. Jess thinks he may have had a heart attack. He's breathing now."

Sirens sound in the distance and then stop as they enter the neighborhood. Cam dashes out to change and grab his things. Piper and Theo look at each other. *What is happening?* Theo thinks to himself. They go downstairs to offer their help.

Two hours later Jess takes a call and delivers the news that Grandpa Ben has peacefully passed away. Indications are that he had a heart attack and did not wake up after. Piper and Theo get the keys to Grandpa's car and drive to the hospital. Theo doesn't understand why he feels so numb. *Maybe it's too early in the morning? Or maybe it's just disbelief.*

He follows the GPS directions and looks over at Piper who is visibly upset. "I can't imagine how Cam is feeling," she says.

They park at the ER and are directed to a waiting area just down the hall. Two nurses are talking with a hospital administrator who walks over to Piper and Theo. "Are you with Mr. Young's family?"

"Yes, we're with his grandson, Cam," Piper responds.

Theo hears muffled crying further down the hall. He grips Piper's hand and then lets it go. "I think that's Cam."

"I guess you know that Mr. Young passed away. We are so sorry for your loss. I know Cam will be glad to see family. When he is feeling a bit better, we can answer any questions you have."

"Where is Cam?" Piper's asks in a shaky voice.

"He's with his grandfather right now. A nurse will let him know that you're here. Why don't you wait in this empty room until he's ready. I'll get you both some water as well."

A few minutes later Cam stands at the door to the room, pain written all over his face. Piper rushes to him and hugs him and they both cry together. Theo lets them have some time and then he walks to his friend and puts his arm around his shoulders. "I'm so sorry, man."

Cam sniffs and Piper hands him a box of tissues that she picked up somewhere. "I can't believe he's gone. We were just with him last night."

They sit in the uncomfortable chairs in the hospital room and let Cam talk. "I can't believe he's left me. I know that sounds crazy but it's what keeps going through my head. He's left me too." Cam tries not to cry but can't help it. He bends over and lets the tears fall. Piper rubs his back and cries quietly with him.

He sits up and says, "How is Granny? Is she OK? Oh God, I can't believe he's not going to be with her."

"Jess is with her, and another nurse was coming too. She was sleeping peacefully when we left," Theo tells him.

"I have no idea what to do. I cannot believe this. I'm so sorry you had to be here through all of this. I never should have brought you here," Cam wipes at his tears.

Piper stops crying and says sharply, "What are you talking about? This is exactly where we need to be. You can't go through this alone. Cam, we wanted to be here for you, no matter how hard it was going to be."

"Yeah, but I shouldn't have let you." He sniffles and reaches for another tissue. "I need to talk with the doctor about what to do next. I don't have any idea what I'm supposed to do. Why don't I just see you back at the house. Thanks for coming. You didn't have to." Cam gets up and walks toward the nurse's station.

"We are not leaving him," Piper says in a serious tone to Theo.

"No, of course not," Theo reassures her. He kisses her temple and puts his arm around her, then thinks better of it. *This is not the time to let Cam know we got closer one night. And it's not the time to let Piper know I'd like to continue that conversation.*

"I'm so happy I got to see him again," Piper says and leans into Theo's side.

"Yeah, me too. He was so pale yesterday. And he barely ate last night. We should have known something was off."

Piper gets up and walks to the nurse's desk and Theo joins her. Cam is providing information to a nurse completing paperwork. "Someone from the funeral home will be in contact with you in a little while. I'll give them your number."

Cam looks up and says, "Oh I thought you were going back."

Firmly Piper says, "Not yet. Cam, do you want to sit with your grandfather?"

"I just said goodbye," he clears his throat and wipes his eyes again. "I want to be with Granny now." He finishes the necessary paperwork, and they return to the parking lot and to the quiet home.

BUCKSPORT, THURSDAY
Theo

Cam and Piper have been at the funeral home all morning. Mrs. Young has not woken up yet today and another nurse, Maryann, is with her now. Theo assumes they won't tell her that Grandpa Ben has passed away. *But won't she know if he's not there?*

He checks in with Maryann and then goes out for a walk. He's been gone for an hour or so when his mom pops up on Facetime.

"Hola Mami," he says, continuing his walk. They talk about Theo's job and his mom catches him up on how his brothers are doing. Theo lets her know he is on a trip with his college friend Cam when Mrs. Young's car pulls up next to him. He realizes he's walked further away from the house than he meant to.

"Do you want a ride back?" Cam asks.

"No, I'll walk back, but thanks."

"Can I join you?" Piper asks. She looks at Cam for permission at the same time.

"Yeah sure," they both say. She jumps out and waves goodbye to Cam.

"Uh, Mami, yeah I'm back."

"Oh!" Piper says, not realizing he had been on the phone this whole time.

"Yeah, this is Piper." He holds up the phone to let the two women meet each other and Piper automatically brushes down her bangs with her hand.

"Hello, I'm so sorry. I didn't mean to interrupt your call."

"Hello Piper," a beautiful woman with Theo's light skin and dark eyes says. The only difference is Theo's mom has gorgeous long dark hair. "And who are you?" she asks in a friendly voice with a trace of an accent. "A friend from school too?"

"Ah, no I'm Piper, a friend of Cam's. Um and Theo's. I live in Los Angeles. I am on a road trip with Cam. We're friends." She is nervous and talking in circles but isn't sure what Theo's mom knows.

"I'm Angela, Tio's mother. It's nice to meet you, Piper."

"Mucho gusto," Piper says, pulling College Spanish out of a seldom accessed part of her memory.

"Ah, mucho gusto," Angela says. "Tio was telling me about Cam's family situation. This was unexpected, I know. But it's good that you both are with Cam. There is so much to do in the days following a loss. Can you both be with him for a few more days?"

"Yes," they say in unison.

"Good. And Tio?"

"Yes?" he answers, looking at her video on the screen, but really looking at the smaller video of himself and Piper standing together on the sidewalk in Maine.

"Be good to your friends and call your brothers. They miss you. Tell me when you decide on your next trip. I miss you and can't wait to see you. Maybe you bring Cam? And Piper?"

"Ok, ciao Mami." He blows her a kiss as Piper melts on the sidewalk.

"Tio?" she asks.

"Theodore is a family name on my dad's side, and he really wanted to use it. But "TH" is not that common in Spanish, so she has always called me Tio, and the entire family does too. Maybe one day Nathan or Marco will have kids and it'll come in handy."

"You seem really close to your mom."

"Really? I only see her once a year. I don't feel like we're all that close."

"I see my mom three times a week, and she knows almost nothing about my life. Maybe I don't try hard enough. We just have so little in common, and I feel like I'm the parent half the time."

"What about your dad?"

"My dad and I see each other at least once a week but we don't talk about serious things. Work, golf, latest gossip, best new restaurants, his latest girlfriend. I love him but I wouldn't say he knows me that well either."

Theo reaches for Piper's hand as they re-enter the Youngs' neighborhood. They let go as they turn the final corner back to the house. "It's a terrible time to talk," Theo says, "but I'd like to find a good time."

"OK," Piper says. "Maybe later tonight?"

They check in the dining room, but it seems Cam's grandmother is still asleep. Maryann is setting out the lunch that a neighbor brought by after hearing about Mr. Young's passing. *News travels fast, it seems.* Piper goes upstairs to check her emails and freshen up. Theo looks for Cam who he finds sitting outside.

"Hey, I'm really sorry about your grandpa. He was truly a great man. I wish I had gotten to know him even better."

"He is pretty great," Cam says. "I'm having trouble processing this, I'll be honest. It does not seem real that he's gone."

Theo has no idea what to say, so he chooses just to sit with his friend in silence.

Cam speaks first. "Hey, we haven't talked about your plans. I am not sure how long I'll be here," he says, looking towards his grandmother.

"There's no rush."

"And you didn't want to go to New Jersey?"

"No, I just talked with my mom today and I'll check in on the family in Jersey this week. I don't want to get in the way, but I want to be here to help you."

"Yeah OK," Cam nods, "God, I need a nap and a shower." He gets up and walks back to the kitchen and makes a plate of food – chicken casserole and green beans. He eats a few bites and checks on his Granny before returning upstairs. Sleeping in his grandparent's bed probably feels even stranger than it did before, but Theo knows his friend is completely exhausted.

BUCKSPORT, THURSDAY
Piper

Cam bumps into Piper coming out of the guest bathroom, her wet hair in a towel and wearing fresh clothes. "Oh Cam," she says, hand on his arm, "How are you?"

"I guess it really hasn't sunk in yet."

"Sorry - I am trying not to say the wrong thing."

"It's OK," Cam smiles softly. "There's lunch downstairs. I need to crash for a couple of hours. Maybe you could sit with my grandmother?"

"Yes, I will!" Piper dries her hair as quickly as possible, so the noise doesn't disturb Cam, and adds just a little makeup. She gets a plate of food and settles into the chair next to Cam's grandmother. Maryann lets Piper know that she is being replaced by Ellen in a few minutes and that there is more food in the fridge that another neighbor just delivered. Piper looks shocked.

"Oh, I'm afraid there's going to be a lot more."

"We can't possibly eat all this food."

"Just say thank you and if it's something like cookies or cake, you can display it when people come over to offer their condolences. Offer them coffee and a cookie. You'll likely have a lot of people stopping by in the next few days. Did Camden determine when the service will be?" Maryann asks quietly so Mrs. Young can't hear.

"No, not yet. He needs to check with the minister at his church. I'm not sure he's done that yet. He's taking a nap."

"Good. It's going to be a busy few days."

Piper decides she can't stomach any food, washes her dishes, and returns to the dining room and Granny Elizabeth. She retrieves her phone from her back pocket and scrolls through her work emails. She has an invitation for a phone call at 3:30 Maine time with her editor. Time to jot down some notes on what she wants to talk about.

Theo comes in, dressed in jeans and one of his new LL Bean sweaters, hair wet from his shower. "I think Cam is still asleep," he says.

"Would you sit with Mrs. Young? I need to finish tomorrow's article and I've got a meeting with my boss in a little while. I'll be able to help afterward. Ellen is on her way."

"Yes, go ahead. I'm reading *Cold Mountain* that I found in Mr. Young's office. I'll sit here until Cam needs me. I'm going to stay for a while, by the way. He kind of asked me to and I don't have any other commitments." Piper gives him a small smile and heads upstairs.

At 3:30 she calls into the conference call with her boss, Alex.

"Piper, how are you?"

"I'm OK, Alex. As you know, I've come on this trip with my friend Cam Anderson because his grandmother is in hospice care."

"Yes, and you're in Maine now, right?"

"That's right. He actually lost his grandfather overnight from a heart attack, so I wanted to let you know that I'll be here at least a few more days."

"Oh my - I'm sorry to hear that. Caregivers often have health issues after years of caring for a loved one. I know we went through that with my in-laws, too. How is his grandmother?"

"Sleeping a lot, but I don't think she's experiencing any discomfort."

"It's got to be hard seeing your grandparents decline like that. I'm sure Cam is grateful that you're there."

"Yes, it's tough for sure," Piper says. "I emailed you last night before everything happened because I want to talk about work."

"I received your article for tomorrow. Thanks for keeping up with the article while you've been gone and looking into the Getty information."

"You're welcome, but that's what I wanted to talk to you about. I'd like to take a sabbatical, and maybe try my hand at a book. Something I've been toying with for a while, and I have felt that desire a lot more in the last few days."

"A sabbatical? We don't exactly have a precedent. What were you thinking of?"

"The 'Ten' has been a great opportunity for me and you've allowed me to make it my own, which I appreciate. But I need a change of scenery. I am happy to help out with other pieces, but I want to write, and maybe travel, and can't do that with a full-time job. What are my options?"

"Any way I could interest you in part-time, so we don't have to replace you fully?"

"How would that work?"

"I don't know, can I think about it? If you're open to the idea, then I am sure we could come up with something. I'd like to keep you Piper, but I also think you'd be a terrific novelist. Is it a novel you want to write?"

"Thank you, Alex. Likely non-fiction but I am not sure. I need to dig a little into it. I appreciate your time and I appreciate your thinking about options. I'll be here until the funeral at least - I am not sure yet when that will be, but I will keep you updated. And if you need anything, please let me know."

"OK, let me talk with Stephen and maybe someone in HR and I'll get back to you tomorrow, OK?"

"Great, thank you."

Piper signs off and feels lighter than she has in months.

BUCKSPORT, THURSDAY
Theo

Cam, Piper, and Theo attempt the semblance of dinner later that evening. Warmed fried chicken, mashed potatoes and gravy, and bacon wrapped green bean bundles look and smell delicious, but no one seems to be able to eat more than a few bites. Piper wraps up the remaining food and puts it in a bag in the fridge for Ellen to take home to her family when she finishes her shift.

"Cam, did you talk to the minister?" Piper asks.

"Yes, he called while I was sleeping, and I called him back. He's also already talked with my grandfather's lawyer and the funeral home. My grandfather has instructions on the service for himself and/or Granny. I had no idea people put a plan in place, but I guess it makes sense."

"What do we need to do tomorrow?" Theo asks.

"I need to go back to the funeral home and make some final decisions. They've determined the service will be on Sunday at 2:00. The visitation will take place from 1:00-2:00. There will be a reception after at the church. We won't have people back here like I've seen in movies. There's so much to think about, but they already made a lot of the choices."

Piper cringes a little and says, "What about the obituary, Cam?"

"It's written," he says.

"What?" Theo and Piper both ask.

"Yeah, the basics for the obituary were already written. The lawyer emailed it to me earlier today. I'm able to add whatever to it I want, but the structure is there. I am going to call my Aunt Ginny tonight and let her know, but also ask her to help with the obituary. It's important and I want her thoughts."

"I can't believe we didn't think to call Aunt Ginny today," Piper says.

"Any other family to contact?" Theo asks.

"I'm not sure to be honest. I'm going to ask Aunt Ginny to contact them and let them know about the service date and time."

"What can we do?" Piper asks.

Cam looks at her with such softness in his eyes. "I know you don't want to hear this, but I understand if you need to go. This is a lot to deal with and you both have done enough. I mean, this isn't your family."

"Why are you saying this, Cam?"

"You helped the van and me get here to Maine. You've taken care of me for more than a week. You didn't sign up for all of this."

"I think she's been taking care of you for a long time," Theo says.

Piper gives him a sarcastic look and reassures Cam. "This is where I want to be. I talked with Alex earlier today and he knows I'll be here for a few more days. You'll have to kick me out, but I'm not going anywhere if I think you need me. OK? And if you have family who are coming and you need the room, please let me know and I will go to a hotel."

He nods and Theo hopes it's the last time they discuss this topic.

Cam checks on his Granny and walks to his grandfather's office where he makes the difficult call to Aunt Ginny.

Theo hasn't moved from the kitchen table, not sure what to do at this point. "I guess we should sit with his grandmother now?"

"Let's do that for a little while and then maybe we can go out after, get Cam out of the house?" They both greet Ellen and Granny Elizabeth, and Piper lets Ellen know they'll be going out later, but the dinner is boxed up for her when she is ready for it.

"How is she doing?" Theo asks quietly.

"Her breathing is regular, and she is responsive when we give her meds and change her. She has not talked today, but that happens sometimes."

"I have no experience with hospice or home health care, but I can see how helpful it is to Cam and his family. Thank you," Piper says.

Theo mumbles a thank you as well, not sure how to engage in this conversation, but wanting to. Ellen looks at Theo. "Do you have any experience with end-of-life care, Theo?"

"My grandparents lived near us when I was growing up. I don't remember my grandmother as much, but my grandfather passed away when I was 14. He came to all our events. He had a stroke and was in a nursing home for the last year or two. It was hard to see him there and he didn't really want to be there, so it was hard on everyone. We weren't with him when he passed one night."

"Yes, it's hard to know the timing and family often feels guilty but the family member wouldn't want them to. We're all just doing the best we can for those we love," Ellen tells him.

Theo nods and swallows a lump in his throat. "I don't know how to ask this but how long do people usually stay in hospice care?"

"Oh, it really depends. Hospice is a general word and sometimes people are cared for in the hospice world for months or years. As far as Mrs. Young, it's hard to know. She's comfortable and she has all of you here, so she is content."

Piper chokes back a sob and quietly asks, "Do you think she knows?" Theo reaches for Piper's hand, but she is busy wiping away her tears. "Sorry," she says quietly with a small smile.

"I don't know," Ellen says. "I understand that they were together last night, and they talked into the night. Jess stayed in the living room to give them some quiet together. It's the way I would want to go, sweetheart. Surrounded by people who love me. And now Mr. Young is waiting for her, getting things ready."

Piper lets out another sob and goes to the powder room to pull herself together.

"She's a real sweetheart," Ellen says to Theo.

"She is," Theo agrees.

Cam joins them in the dining room and says goodnight to his grandmother. "I've got to work on a few things for the minister and then I'm going to bed." He says goodnight to Piper through the bathroom door.

"Hey Cam," Theo says, jogging after him. "Do you mind if I take one of the vehicles and maybe get a drink or go for a short drive?"

"Sure," Cam says, "but can you take Piper too? I think she might need a break from all of this."

Piper and Theo ask Ellen if she needs anything before they leave, and Piper gives Ellen a long hug. They get in Granny Elizabeth's car and head to a bar only 10 minutes away. Theo says he doesn't feel up to a restaurant and Piper says she honestly doesn't care where they go.

Once their drinks are half-downed, Piper takes a cleansing breath and says, "I talked with my boss today. I let him know that I want to take some time off from work, maybe think about writing a book."

"Wow, what did he say?"

"He's trying to find a solution where I don't leave, I think. He's looking into part-time options and will get back to me tomorrow."

"Would that work because it sounds ideal?"

"Maybe. I know women who have tried part-time, especially after having kids, and it's hard to maintain. The workload and expectations sometimes don't change, but the pay does. I don't know if *The Herald* has had staff writers try it, so we'll see. And what about you? Have you talked to anyone at James?"

"No, it hasn't felt like the right time. I think I'll call Chelsea, who I did not sleep with," he says to Piper with a pointed look, "and see if she can set up time for a call with Alison. I'm not convinced she'll want to work with me but it's worth a shot."

They finish their drinks. Theo orders a second round, and the silence grows.

Piper meets Theo's eyes, and he says, "Hi." She tries to stop herself from smiling, but she really wants to laugh.

"This is absurd," she says.

"Yes," he agrees.

"We should be focused on Cam and the service and his grandmother and what the hell is Cam going to do now?"

"We are," Theo reminds her.

"You and I didn't like each other a few days ago."

"We grew on each other."

"Or something," Piper says.

"So just one night then? Is the idea of something more than that freaking you out?"

Piper takes a long drink and says, "Nothing's freaking me out. It doesn't make a lot of sense, and I worry that we're being a little self-centered even thinking about it right now. But I'm not freaked out."

"I need to know, what happened the morning after? I don't understand why you called your aunt and uncle. What did I do that scared you? Or upset you?"

Piper looks uneasy but eventually looks up into Theo's eyes and relaxes a little. "I woke up early that morning and started thinking about how this could end terribly, and I was the one who would end up getting hurt. From what I saw in LA, you were happy with one night hook ups. That's just not me. I didn't know if you were going to go back to Hostile Theo or if you were going to completely ignore me. I just wanted to get myself out of the situation I guess."

"OK, yeah, I can see that." Theo sips his beer. "Does it help to tell you that I stopped by your hotel room before I went down to breakfast, but they were already cleaning it? I wanted to spend a minute with you before we had to face Cam. And I was OK with telling Cam that day if you were."

Piper stares at Theo, somewhat stunned. Her guarded eyes soften, and she lets out a breath it seems like she's been holding onto. "OK, I guess I overreacted a little. That makes me feel a lot better."

"So where do we go from here?" Theo smiles.

"No clue," Piper chuckles. "Honestly, no clue. I mean, where do *I* go from here? Do I quit work for six months and write a book? Or do I fly back on Sunday night and return to my life?"

"Yep," Theo says. "I've got a car in a parking lot in Dallas, and I need to call my dad and brothers tomorrow, but otherwise, I don't have much of a plan. Do I go to LA and look for work, or do I accept another assignment and return to my nomadic life?"

Piper looks at Theo for the answers, but he's quiet.

"Another drink?" Theo asks.

"Not for me," Piper says, checking her watch. "Do you think Cam needs us?"

"No, I don't. I think he'll call or text if he needs us."

"Then let's talk," Piper says. She orders a hot tea, and the server looks at her, confused. "Or just a glass of water," Piper adjusts. "And one for him as well." Theo orders a third beer but gamely drinks the water first.

"So, here's what I know. I want to write, and I want to travel," Piper starts. "I have a trust that my grandfather left me, and I haven't touched it. It's supposed to be part of my retirement nest egg, so I haven't wanted to touch it but now I want to take out a little money to add to my savings and spend six months traveling and writing. Would you want to sublet my apartment in LA for six months?"

"Yes!" Theo says without hesitation. "I would."

Piper tentatively reaches her hand across the table and Theo gently takes it. "I'd like to explore deeper things. I'd like to meet people and have deeper conversations than I usually have with my family. And I'd like to learn more about the US by traveling to a lot of places I've never been to. I know I'm a big help to everyone in my life, but I'd like *not* to be for just a little while. I doubt I could let go of that side of myself completely, but I like that side of myself."

Theo rubs his thumbs over her hand, encouraging her to continue.

"I usually live by a plan, but I also want room for exploring. And spontaneity. And surprises. Like you. I think I'll be a better journalist when I return to the real world, whether that's at *The Herald* or somewhere else. So that's me. And I don't know what that means for where we go from here."

She finishes her water and signals their server. "Could I please have a refill when you have time?" The server smiles at her and returns one minute later with two fresh glasses of water. Piper thanks her.

"Hold that thought," she says to Theo and slips off the stool to go to the restroom. Theo pulls out his phone and emails Chelsea.

Chelsea, Cam gave me your email address. Would you mind setting up a 30-minute call for Alison James and me in the next week? I can be flexible on time - my main responsibility is to Cam right now. Thanks. Hope to see you soon. -Theo Harris.

Piper returns and folds her hands on the table, looking at Theo patiently. "I think you should do all of that," he tells her. "Whether you take off work or work part-time, whether you travel on a plan or not. I think you should do it. I just sent an email to Chelsea asking her to set up time for me with Alison. Now that Cam is OK with it, it doesn't hurt to explore possibilities, right? I want to move to LA. I have friends there, there is a lot of work there given my experience, and you are there. I want to explore LA and I want to see what happens with us. That's what I want."

They finish their drinks and leave the bar, along with a generous tip. They walk hand in hand to Granny's car. Piper leans against the door that Theo reaches to open for her. He leans in and kisses her, and she kisses him back.

BUCKSPORT, FRIDAY
Cam

The days before the service are filled with final details and another meeting with the lawyer. Piper drops off the suit Cam brought with him at the dry cleaner to be pressed. She and Theo make a quick stop at a shopping center for a dress and shoes for Piper and dress pants for Theo. They take turns spending time with Granny Elizabeth who has not changed much since the young people arrived. Ellen, Maryann, and Jess's responsibilities have not changed. They are also keeping a close eye on Cam, whom they seem especially concerned about.

Aunt Ginny arrives Friday afternoon. Her cousin Betty picks her up at the Portland airport and they arrive at the Young's home to visit with the family. Ginny spends time with Granny Elizabeth, and they spend a lot of time with Cam.

"Give me three assignments Cam," Aunt Ginny gently requests over coffee.

"Can you call the vocalist who is going to sing 'Amazing Grace'? It was in Grandpa's instructions. The church contacted her, but I haven't talked to her. And how much do you think I should give the pastor, vocalist, and pianist? Is $100 the right amount? I have no idea and I don't want to mess this up."

"Yes, I think that is OK. Do you need help getting those checks together?"

"No, I think I have it."

"Betty and I are going to pick up some appropriate thank you notes as well, and we are going to stop by the church to see if there is anything else. What time do you want us at the church Sunday?"

"12:00? The minister said to set up items from Grandpa's life like awards and framed photos. Also, when you speak to the church, can you ask if there is anything we need for the reception after? I haven't asked."

"It sounds like you've thought of a lot."

"The director at the funeral home and Piper have been very helpful with details."

"Flowers?" Aunt Ginny asks.

"The funeral home has ordered them based on the instructions that Grandpa and Granny had written up. The obituary was very well done. Thanks for your help with that. I just want to make him proud."

"You always have, Cam. Betty and I are going to take off and I'll take care of these assignments." Cam gives her the pastor's phone number and Aunt Ginny pauses.

"Cam, I know this is all very unexpected, but I am so glad you were here. Did you have time with your grandfather this week?"

"Yes, we had some time together, just the two of us. I wish I had gotten here sooner, but I don't know if there ever would have been enough time." Cam gives his aunt and her cousin a hug and is relieved when he has a moment to himself.

Theo and Piper return with their purchases, and they all meet in the kitchen to catch up.

"Aunt Ginny and her cousin Betty were here. She's going to call the vocalist and minister. I think everything else is caught up. Or maybe it isn't. I have no idea. I also met with Grandpa's attorney today. God, there's so much to do. I'm just trying to think about what else we need to do before Sunday."

"Hey Cam, have you talked to your dad?" Piper asks.

"No, do you think I should?"

"Well, I don't know, but I think so, yeah. He would want to know, and he should be here for you. Doesn't his family live nearby too? Wouldn't they want to know?"

"I don't think so," Cam says. "I don't know that they even know my grandparents really."

"When was the last time you saw his family?" Piper asks.

"I don't remember. I was young."

"Maybe they would want to be here for you."

Cam shrugs, "Maybe, I don't know. It's a lot to ask them. OK, let's think about everything we need to do tomorrow. I need to talk with the funeral home about the program. I scanned a photo of my grandfather from his law school days. They are using that in the obituary."

"It's online," Piper says.

"What?" Cam asks, reaching for his phone.

"The King and Sons website has the obituary up."

"I thought it was going in the local paper."

"It is probably in today's paper too, but the funeral homes also post the obituaries on their sites."

Piper hands him her phone and he reads the summary of his grandfather's life. "He was a remarkable man," Piper says.

Cam's eyes fill with tears, but he doesn't shed any. "Yeah," he agrees. "Can you both help me get some things from his office and bedroom to set up at the church?"

They fill a box with framed family photos, local awards, and two fishing trophies. Cam goes to his grandparents' bedroom and gets a framed photo of their wedding day and a photo of an infant Cam and his parents to add to the box. It looks like the nurses maybe have cleaned up the room a little. The curtains are open, and the bed has been expertly made as well.

"These nurses deserve a big Christmas bonus," Piper says. "They're amazing."

Cam realizes he has no idea of the number of things that are probably obvious to others but not to him. "God, I wish you could stay here after all this is over because I have no idea what I'm supposed to do. Aunt Ginny is getting some thank you notes. Who all do we write them to?" Cam asks, looking slightly panicked.

"People who brought over food, I think. And people who send flowers to the funeral," Piper says.

"We already ordered flowers," Cam reminds her.

"People will also send them to the funeral. Or at least that's what I've seen at funerals I've been to," Piper says. Cam rubs his face with his hands and sits down hard on the bed.

"Please don't worry," Piper says. "We'll help you, your Aunt Ginny too, and even the nurses. Let's ask all of them to give us pointers on what to do since this is so new. I'm not even sure I have all of this right."

"No, I'm sure you do," Cam says. He asks a question that has been on his mind since the hospital early Thursday morning. "What do I do with his wedding ring, glasses, and watch? They gave them to me. Do they go with him?" A tear escapes Cam's eye and Theo sits down on his other side.

"I don't know," Piper says quietly. "Let me do a little research and I'll let you know, OK? Do you want to keep them?"

"Not if they're supposed to go with him," Cam whispers and wipes his eyes.

"I know you're concerned you're going to do the wrong thing, but there is no *right* thing Cam. We'll figure it out, I promise you."

"Theo, can you get them? I can't touch them right now."

"Sure, where are they?"

"Ellen said she put them in the top drawer of the desk there," he says, pointing to the roll top desk in the corner of his grandparents' bedroom.

Theo pulls out the items. "I'll put them in the guest bedroom for the time being." Then he looks down and sees a pill case with the days of the week on it. He takes that as well.

Everyone lets the silence fill the room. Finally, Cam says, "I had a thought last night. You are going to think it's ridiculous."

"We won't Cam, what is it?" Piper asks him.

"No matter how hard I try, you're not going anywhere are you? Either of you?" Cam says, looking up at Theo.

His friends are quiet, and Cam eventually continues.

"In my experience, people don't usually stick around. And even though I brush it off, it's a little painful when they leave. Even someone I just went out with a couple of times that I thought might work out. I just assumed the two of you were temporary people in my life, like everyone else. Except for James and my grandparents."

Piper lays her head on Cam's shoulder.

"When you both walked into the hospital the other night, it hit me hard. You're my people."

Piper stands up and walk a few steps toward Theo. She turns around and looks at Cam. "I'm glad you finally got it. Now stop pushing us away." She smiles and wipes her eyes.

"This would be even harder without you both," Cam says.

"We're here for you, Cam," Piper says. "And so are other people like Olivia, your Aunt Ginny, Chelsea, Jeremiah..."

"And maybe even Martin?" Cam asks, attempting humor.

"It may be too late for Martin," Piper smiles. "I have a call that I need to return to the paper. Are you going to be OK?"

"Yes," he says, "I'm going downstairs to sit with Granny. Thanks."

When Piper finishes her call, she joins everyone downstairs. Theo stands up and says, "Hey guys, got a minute?" He motions to his friends to join him on the back patio.

"I wasn't going to say anything, but I feel like I should," Theo says. They're all hugging their arms in the cool night air. "When I got your grandfather's items from the desk, I found this pill case. I don't know if it's one he used recently, but the pills have not been taken since Friday. See? Saturday through Wednesday's pills are here. Do you think this is an old pill case that he put in his drawer? Do you know if he took medication?"

Cam stands frozen, staring at the pill case. Piper turns her attention to Theo. "It's probably an old case, Theo. If they were his current pills, wouldn't they be in the bathroom? Cam, was your grandfather sick? Or maybe they were your grandmother's pills?"

Cam can't move. He's just staring at the case. "Come inside," Piper says.

"Hang on," Theo says. "I didn't want to say this in front of the nurses or family."

Cam reaches for a patio chair and sits down. "I don't want to talk about this right now," he says.

"OK," Piper agrees. "It's not a big deal." She looks at Theo again, frowning.

"Don't say anything to anyone Theo," Cam says quietly.

"I wasn't sure what to do but thought I should tell you."

"Don't say anything to the nurses or Aunt Ginny, OK?"

"What? No, of course not. I'm not saying anything to anyone but you two."

"Yeah. Thanks," Cam says as he gets up and goes inside, shutting the door behind him.

Cam hears Theo and Piper talking loudly through the kitchen door.

"I think I'm doing the right thing here," he says to Piper.

"Yeah, I get that," Piper says, "but you could learn something about timing. He's got a ton to deal with over the next couple of days."

"I should have kept my mouth shut?"

"I don't know. Maybe if you talked to me, we could have found a time to talk to him about this when he isn't exhausted and on the verge of tears."

They go into the kitchen and pull food out of the refrigerator for dinner and relieve Jess so she can get a quick bite and take care of a few things before she starts Granny Elizabeth's nighttime routine. Piper gets a plate of food and takes it to Cam who sets it on the table next to him and tells her thanks. "Will you sit with me?" he asks her.

"Of course." Piper sits down and Cam takes her hand. He looks up at Theo who he knows is watching with concern and gives him a little shrug. Theo gives Cam a supportive nod and goes into the living room.

BUCKSPORT, FRIDAY
Piper

Piper leaves Cam with his grandmother and walks out front when her manager calls back. "Hi, Piper, how are you?"

"I'm OK. We're in the middle of planning Cam's grandfather's funeral service so you can imagine how melancholy we all are. But I'm OK. Thanks for calling me back."

"Piper, we'd love to have you stay on and handle the two projects you're currently doing but work part-time. Instead of asking you to take on additional features, we'll move you to part-time for six months and you can just focus on the 'Tens' article and the Getty assignment."

"So, how is that different than what I am doing now? I'm not sure I understand."

"Well, we won't add additional articles to your workload. And you can write or fill your other time in whatever way you want. It would be helpful if you were available for the occasional meeting at the office, but otherwise you would be free to travel. That's what you said you wanted, right?"

"Yes, you're right. But the responsibilities are not that much different than what I am doing now. I guess if the work is not going to change, then there's no motivation to move to part-time pay."

"It's really your choice, but we think it can be done part-time which would be a good compromise and would allow you that flexibility you would like."

Piper is not sure it's in her best interest but also doesn't want to make a decision at such a difficult time.

"I really appreciate your looking into this for me. Could I get back to you on Monday, after the funeral and after I've had some time to think?"

"Yes, of course. Take care, and let's talk on Monday."

They hang up and Piper decides to do what is in her best interest instead of worrying about the paper so much. She has until Monday to figure out exactly what that move should be.

Theo waits for Piper to finish her call and joins her outside. "Chelsea sent an invitation for me to meet with Alison on Tuesday on Zoom."

"Oh, that's great," Piper tells him.

"Yeah, it'll give me a few days to put some thoughts together before the call."

"I just got off the phone with Alex and I've got some thinking to do as well. I told him I'd call him back on Monday."

"It's kind of nice to be thinking about work and life changes right now."

Piper agrees with him, "It is. How is Cam doing?"

"I don't know. I know my timing wasn't great. And maybe it's nothing. But I think Cam is processing it. Hey, did he really think he didn't have any friends? I mean, real friends?"

"It kind of makes sense. Cam doesn't make a lot of effort to keep track of people in his life. He's probably been avoiding rejection all this time. He knows we're here for him though. God, I'm exhausted, how about you? This grief thing is not for the faint of heart."

"Come on," Theo says. "Let's go see what we can do to help."

BUCKSPORT, FRIDAY

Cam

Cam changes into sweats and a light jacket and lets Piper know he's going for a run. She is about to mention how incredibly dark it's gotten, but Cam doesn't need her to take care of him at this moment. She heads to her room to research potential articles for Monday's 'Today's Ten' article and wrap her head around her work options, one of which could be life changing. Without taking Theo into consideration. Or Cam. She needs to think about what is best for her.

Instead of a run, Cam walks through the neighborhood and calls Alison. She texts back.

In a meeting, I'll call you in 20 minutes.

Cam continues his walk and ends up at the park he grew up playing in. He sits on the picnic table and waits for Alison's call back.

She calls, out of breath, "Cam, hi."

"Hi," he says, smiling at the sound of her voice.

"I've been worried about you. And I'm so, so sorry about your grandfather."

"Thanks," he says. "Remember how you thought there was something going on with him, you said you had a feeling? I may have found out for sure today. I'm not sure how to handle it."

"Chelsea said your grandpa had a heart attack. Has someone asked you about it?"

"Theo found his pills. He hasn't taken any in days."

"What kind of pills?" Alison asks, her tone clipped, ready for battle.

"I don't know. I didn't know he was taking any. I can probably find the bottles and do some research. But I think I knew all along that he wanted to be in control here. I think you had the same suspicions, right?"

"Well, it was just a feeling. So, Theo thinks the same thing? Is he going to say anything?"

"No, he won't. And Piper probably is thinking about it too. Should I talk to his attorney about it? Or my great aunt?"

"Is that his sister?"

"No, she was married to Grandpa Ben's brother who died a decade ago. I don't know what to do and I'm feeling kind of panicked about this. I just wanted to talk to you."

"Maybe there is nothing to do. Was he with family?"

"He was with my grandmother. We had a great dinner that evening. Piper set the table with Granny's fancy dishes and lit candles. We talked for a long time. He passed basically in his sleep."

Alison sighs deeply. "I can't imagine a better end to a long and full life. Are you upset with him?"

"Shouldn't I be?" Cam asks, his voice catching as tears threaten again.

"Are you?" Alison asks again.

"No, not really."

"Then let him have this. Talk to the attorney under privilege if you want to. Otherwise, give this gift of a peaceful passing to your grandparents and to yourself."

Cam chokes back a sob and sets the phone down to walk away. He comes back and says "Sorry" to Alison.

"No, I'm sorry. I really don't know what I'm doing here. I have very little experience with what you are dealing with."

"Yeah, but you always have your shit together. I needed your level-headedness tonight."

"Are you kidding me?" Alison laughs. "I never see my family in Oregon, I work 100 hours/week, I spend any free time I have scrolling shelter websites dreaming of a dog that I don't have time to take care of, and I've got feelings for a man that might likely ruin a professional relationship. And that I'm probably too old for. I need to lose 10 pounds but no matter how much I swim I can't get them off even though I haven't had sugar in a year. No one has all their shit together Cam. Especially not me."

"I might be the answer to all your problems," Cam says quietly.

Alison sighs again. "Yeah, I've thought of that. Or you may absolutely devastate me. I'm not sure I can take that. Hell, until a week ago I thought you and Chelsea had feelings for each other."

"What?! Theo said the same thing."

"When she told me that you were driving to Maine with a friend, she added, 'and just so you know, Cam and I are not interested in each other.'"

Cam laughs quietly.

"Goddammit," Alison says, "Chelsea knows everything before I do."

After a long pause, Cam takes a deep breath and says, "Can I say something to you that I really need to say? It seems like it's my day for confessions."

"Oh Cam, I don't want to hurt you, and I don't want to get hurt."

Here goes. "Alison, I know I belong at James, but I think I also belong with you." Cam realizes he's bracing himself for Alison's gentle rejection.

Alison quietly says, "I don't think we want the same things. We might be at different points in our lives. And that's OK. It doesn't change anything. We are good, Cam."

"I want to try. I have never wanted that with someone. But I do with you. I have never wanted to risk getting close to someone. But I want to risk it with you. Even if it doesn't work out, and I think it will. You are worth the risk."

"God, Cam, I don't know what to say. Let's not talk about this right now. There is so much happening in your life. Let's talk when you get back, OK?"

"Yeah, I get that. But will you think about what I'm saying to you, and not just write me off?"

"I'm not writing you off. I hear you and I will be thinking about you this entire weekend. I hope you feel better."

"I do. I really do."

BUCKSPORT, SATURDAY
Cam

Cam returns from the funeral home in time to talk with his Granny in her most aware moments in the last few days. He places his hand on her hand, and she softly says, "Love you," and gives him a little smile. Maryann lets him know that she was able to sip water and have a few bites this morning, and she had some color back in her cheeks.

"I love you Granny." She gives him another little smile and returns to sleep. It's hard to tell if she is actually sleeping, but she is no longer responsive to his words.

He finds Theo and Piper at the kitchen table. "Can we go out to lunch before more family starts arriving? Need to talk."

They pile into Granny's car and are quiet on the way to a diner that Cam grew up eating in with his parents, and then his grandparents. They order (burgers for Theo and Cam, chef salad for Piper) and Cam starts.

"I have a lot to say," Cam informs his friends. "I have said that a lot in the last 24 hours." Piper's face encourages him to continue, but he sees the concern in her eyes. He reaches over for her hand. "I left a voicemail for my dad last night. I asked him to let his family know, and I asked him to come to the funeral, which I didn't realize was as big a deal to me as it ended up being. I don't think he'll come, and I'm going to be Ok with that. But it was important for me to ask him for help, which I've never done."

Cam pauses before continuing. "I know that it's been a lot and you've got to get back to your lives, but I really, really appreciate your being here with me through the service tomorrow."

The food arrives but no one touches it. Piper starts to fill the silence but stops herself.

Finally, Cam says, "Can we not discuss the pills? I don't want to talk about it, and I don't want to talk to anyone else about it. I'm pretty sure I knew this could be coming. He tried to talk to me about it when we got here, but I got angry before he could really say much. I think my Aunt Ginny might have suspected as well. I feel bad that I brought you both here with this in the back of my mind. I think it's why I kept suggesting an airport. I'm sorry."

Piper and Theo let him pause and gather his thoughts.

"I don't know if those are his pills or if his heart just gave out. And does it really matter? It was his life. I'm not mad at him for leaving when he did. *If* that's what happened. I don't feel like he abandoned me. He's taken care of me my entire life and allowed me the freedom to do what I wanted with my life. I'd like to offer him the same."

No one responds, but the looks across the table are clear. There is no one to blame.

"I never asked him to stay even though I really wanted to. I guess I wanted to support him more than I didn't want him to leave me." Cam smiles at that sentence construction. "I think you know what I mean. And I can continue to show them how much they mean to me by taking care of Granny."

"I understand," Theo says. "And I'm not mad that you brought me here. So don't worry about that."

"Well, I'm sorry I haven't been a good friend to either of you. It never occurred to me that you'd both stick around. It was almost confusing at times – especially you," Cam points at Piper. "But I realized today that you are both family, and I will try to do a better job of making sure I don't disappear."

Piper pushes her salad around with her fork and studies her plate while tears flow freely from her eyes. Cam does not notice, but Theo, sitting next to her, does and reaches for her other hand in her lap. Cam notices that though and says, "So what is going on with you two?"

Theo laughs and shakes his head and Piper looks up startled. "Nothing."

"Ok," Cam says, picking up the top bun from his burger and removing the tomato.

Piper starts, "Cam this trip has really changed me. I'm talking with Alex about taking some time off, maybe. I want to write and travel, and I'm finally able to say out loud that I am no longer inspired at work. We're working through part-time or a sabbatical, or some sort of option, but I'm going to make the choice that is best for me."

"That's smart," Cam says.

"Maybe?" Piper says. "It may be professionally stupid, but I need to figure out what makes me happy and go after that."

"Yes, you deserve that. What would Piper say to you?"

"Go for it," she quickly says, smiling, brushing away the tears.

"Then go for it. And what about you?" Cam asks, looking over at Theo who is still holding Piper's hand under the table.

"I'm going to move to California. No plans just yet, but I do have a call with Alison on Tuesday, so we'll see what she thinks. There are plenty of options in LA though."

"And just work?" Cam asks.

"Maybe not," Theo says and bites a fry in half.

"Not ready to talk about anything else," Piper says, cheeks blushing.

"I have a lot of questions," Cam teases her.

"Nope," Piper says.

"Oh yes. When did this start?"

"Nope," Piper says again at the same time Theo says, "Knoxville." Piper looks at Theo in astonishment.

"I would not have said that early," Piper says quietly.

"Maybe earlier," Theo says, grinning at her.

Cam looks just as surprised. "Really? Wait is that why you passed up a chance to go to the football game, so you could hike with Piper?"

Theo looks stumped. "Uh, I don't really know why I didn't go to the game with you and Liv. I haven't thought about it. Growing up I went to a lot of games with my dad. I mean, I didn't know Piper was going to the park. Maybe I just wanted to explore a little?"

"Yeah, I bet you did," Cam grins.

Piper focuses on her salad, willing the red to disappear from her cheeks.

"Enough," she says.

"Anything else we need to discuss?" Theo asks.

"I have more questions, but for now, no. Sounds like we've all got a lot going on."

Piper asks, "Has anyone let Olivia know about your grandfather?"

"Oh, I didn't think about that," Cam says.

"Want me to contact her for you?" Piper asks, happy the focus is shifted elsewhere.

"No, I've got it," Cam says.

"When are you leaving, Cam?" Piper asks, knowing it's a tough subject given his grandmother's health.

"I don't know."

"I don't want to leave if you need me."

"If you can help me get through tomorrow, I would really appreciate it."

Theo says, "I'm happy to stay longer. I know you have a lot to do. And there's your grandmother too."

Cam pushes his plate away, takes a big inhale and lets it out. "I am not sure how much longer my grandmother has, but I will be here for her. I think you both should look for flights on Monday and get back to your lives. I can handle it."

Piper reaches for Cam's hand with her free hand and squeezes it. Cam says, "I'm not holding your hand Theo."

"Yeah, not necessary," Theo says.

Piper smiles at the two guys, squeezes both of their hands, and finally digs into her salad.

"But the great leveler, Death: not even the gods can defend a man, not even one they love, that day when fate takes hold, and lays him out at last."

~ Athena to Telemachus, in Homer's *The Odyssey*

BUCKSPORT, SUNDAY
Piper

The service is lovely. Grandpa Ben and Granny Elizabeth planned the service together, the funeral home director mentioned. They chose the flowers, the music, the scriptures, the service order, and the burial arrangements. Of course, they probably thought Granny would go first, but fortunately they wanted the same arrangements. More than 200 friends fill the church, and many attended the visitation ahead of time to personally pay their condolences to Cam.

Surprisingly, George Anderson makes it just in time for the service. He sits with Grandpa Ben's extended family in the row behind Cam, Aunt Ginny, Piper, and Theo. During the reception after the service, Cam introduces his father to his friends. Theo asks how he likes living in Chicago and George launches into a rather long story about the work he does. He also tells the group about his latest adventure to Banff and Calgary that previous summer.

Everyone notes that George and Cam look a lot alike with their dark hair, green eyes and runner's builds. But it is evident Cam inherited much more from his grandparents.

Piper watches the interaction between estranged father and son. George does not seem to realize he has not been in the same room with his son in years. Nor does he seem to be aware of how this must have been hard for Cam the last two weeks, as he would likely be losing both of his grandparents in quick succession. George agrees to go to the burial with close family that afternoon, but only after Cam lets him know he would really like him to be there.

When George returns to the buffet table to get a refill on his coffee, Piper follows him. "Mr. Anderson, I wondered if any of your family was here today? I know Cam would love to have family around at this time."

"No, no they couldn't make it today."

"Well, I hope to see you again soon. Maybe you could come out to California to visit sometime. We can show you the sights."

"Cam asked me to come out too," George tells her.

"He did? Oh great!" Piper exclaims, surprised that Cam would risk another rejection from his father.

"Work is pretty busy but yeah, maybe I can do that." George starts to tell Piper the story of his decision to buy a motorcycle after they drove the van to California, but Piper cuts him off.

"I'm sorry Mr. Anderson, but I think the family is heading to the cemetery now." George looks around and notices many people are shaking Cam's hand and leaving. "I know you must be so proud of your son," Piper says.

"Oh yes, definitely," George says, and adds sugar to his coffee.

That evening Aunt Ginny, Cam, Piper, and Theo sit in the dining room with Granny Elizabeth. Aunt Ginny lets Cam know who all the family were in attendance and how they are all related.

"What a turnout," Piper says. Theo is sitting next to her with his hand resting on the back of her chair.

Cam notes the easy affection and shakes his head in mild disbelief. "I still can't get used to that," he says.

Piper sees what he's talking about and shakes her head, looking down at her hands. Theo, on the other hand, is in no way embarrassed and doesn't find the need to apologize for it.

"When are you returning to California?" Aunt Ginny asks Piper.

"Um, actually I am going to Dallas tomorrow afternoon and then we are driving to LA."

"Together?" she asks.

"Um, yes," Piper says.

Cam laughs out loud and shakes his head. "Oh, it's a long story, Aunt Ginny," who doesn't think it's that long at all.

"I hope you'll come back to Virginia to visit me sometime."

"I would love that," Piper says genuinely. "I may take you up on that sooner rather than later."

"OK! I will give you my number before I leave tonight."

"What time is your flight?" Cam asks. "Now that I know you're flying together," he adds sarcastically.

"3:30 p.m. out of Bangor. Are you able to take us?" Theo asks.

"Yeah, I can do that."

"And what about you Camden?" Aunt Ginny asks.

"I'm staying here for a while," he nods at Granny. "She is my priority now. I have no idea what I need to do other than be here with her, but I'm sure the lawyer will let me know. I'll keep up with work the best I can. Piper, can you please check on Mr. Franks as soon as you get back? He's the one I'm most worried about in LA."

"Yes, I will. My car is there so it'll be my first stop."

"And you can stay at my place if you want Theo." Piper blushes again and Cam says, "Um, that's if things don't work out, I guess." The guys laugh and Piper shakes her head and looks up at the ceiling.

"This is never going to get old," Cam says.

Aunt Ginny looks fondly at her nephew and his friends. "You know, you're lucky to have each other. I'm so thankful to the two of you for being here for Cam."

Piper and Theo smile but Cam says, "I didn't realize how much I would need these two. And I still feel bad that I wasn't here longer."

Aunt Ginny pats Cam's hand. "I know. But I also think the timing was exactly what your grandfather wanted."

Piper sees Cam's eyes fill with tears as he looks at his grandmother, but there is more a sense of peace in the room.

"So, what happened to your grandmother's minivan?" Aunt Ginny asks.

"Grandpa signed Odysseus over to one of the nurses who has three kids and fosters dogs. She was so grateful. Her name is Jess. I'm not sure if you've met her yet."

"Oh, what a lovely gift. Your grandmother must be so pleased." She pats Granny Elizabeth's arm gently.

Piper decides it's time to do a little work and hugs Aunt Ginny goodbye after storing her number in her phone. "I've loved getting to know you," she says. "Thank you so much for everything."

"You take care of each other," she says and Piper nods.

After getting ready for bed, Piper pulls out her laptop and sends off a quick email.

"Dear Alex - I can't thank you enough for your flexibility. After much thought, I would like to continue as things are. But I would like to take you up on your suggestion to travel and write when I am not needed at the office. I am hopeful that this solution will work for both of us, and if not, then I will happily provide my letter of resignation to you. I am flying to Dallas on Monday and will be back in LA by Thursday at the latest. I'll have the 'Tens' to you each day. Please find tomorrow's article attached here. Best regards, Piper Nelson-Keller."

"No need my unlucky one, to grieve here any longer, no, don't waste your life away. Now I am willing heart and soul to send you off at last."

~ Calypso to Odysseus in Homer's *The Odyssey*

BANGOR, MONDAY

Cam

"Two weeks," Cam says to Piper as they pull into the departures drop off area.

"God, it feels like a lot longer than that," Piper says. She hugs Cam tightly and says, "You know I love you. Take care of your granny and take care of yourself. Call if you need to talk, OK? I will always be here for you."

"I know. But you focus on you right now, OK?" She shakes her head yes before taking her laptop bag and suitcase from Theo and stepping aside.

Theo and Cam do a guy's half-hug and Cam says, "Don't screw this up."

Theo says, "Please," in his smug tone and Piper rolls her eyes. "I'll call you in a couple of days," Theo says.

Cam waves goodbye and watches his chosen family walk away. Before he gets back into his grandmother's car, he watches Theo kiss Piper and ask her, "Ready?"

"Yes," Piper says confidently.

"Let's go," Piper smiles up at him and they take off.

***

Cam drives to the cell phone lot at the airport and places two calls.

"Hi Cam," Olivia answers. "I'm sorry we've been missing each other. And I'm so sorry to hear about your grandfather. How is your grandmother?"

"About the same. She is resting a lot and seems peaceful when she is awake. I'm going to be here for a while."

"I know you're going through a tough time right now."

"Hey, did I say thank you?"

"For what?" Olivia laughs.

"Just everything. Insisting I take a break. Taking me to a football game and introducing me to your intimidating family. Being my friend when you were really Theo's friend."

"You're welcome for all of it."

"Hey guess what," Cam says. "Theo and Piper are in love."

"What??? Did they tell you that?" Olivia screeches. Cam hurries to adjust the volume on his phone.

"What, no, but they can't keep their hands off each other and Piper hasn't stopped blushing."

"I had my suspicions, but I think they were fighting it," Olivia says. "Well, good for them."

"Yeah, I'm happy for them but I'm keeping my eye on him."

"Yes, please, he's going to need your help on this one."

"I'm on it. Take care, Olivia. Come out to LA sometime and see us. I've missed you."

"I'd love it. Bye."

***

Next Cam calls a number his Aunt Ginny gave him. His dad's older brother, Uncle Stan, still lives in Bangor. Cam has no idea if he will remember Cam or want to talk to him, but it's worth a shot to maybe meet more family while he's in the state.

"Hi, is this Stan Anderson?"

"Yes," the gruff voice responds.

"Hi, this is Cam. George's son?" Cam suddenly questions his decision to call. *Well, too late to turn back now.*

"Yeah. Cam," Uncle Stan says in an unenthusiastic tone.

"I am in Maine, and my aunt gave me your number."

"Ok. He says it's Cam," he says to someone with him.

"Um, I just thought I would call and say hello. I don't know when we last saw each other. If this is a bad time, I can call you back."

"Cam. Camden! I was confused there for a second. The last time I saw you, you were in grade school, I think. Hang on a second." Stan says something to someone and comes back on the phone.

"I'm going to put you on Speaker. Helen is here."

"Cam? It's so good to hear from you. We just heard about your grandfather this morning, and we are so sorry. How are you doing?" a sweet voice asks.

"Oh, I'm OK. It's been a hard couple of weeks but I'm OK. My friends were here and some of my mom's family. My dad also came to the service. I just hadn't seen you in a long time and my great aunt thought I might like to reach out. I hope it's a good time."

"Yes, yes!" They both say in unison, now very enthusiastic. "Where are you?"

"I'm at the Bangor Airport. I just dropped off my friends. They are returning to Los Angeles where I live now. But I'm here for a while. I'm not sure if you knew but my grandmother is not doing well."

"No, I am so sorry, we had not heard that. Do you have time to come by so we can see you?"

"I'd like that. I want to get back to my Granny soon but if it's a good time, I can leave the airport now."

"Yes, now is great! We can't wait to see you," Aunt Helen says.

"I don't know how long you'll be in the area, but we would love to take you out fishing if you have time. It's perfect weather right now," Uncle Stan adds.

"Oh Stan, stop talking about fishing," Aunt Helen tells him. Cam smiles.

"OK, OK, we'll talk about that later. We'll text you the address. See you in 15 minutes!"

Cam puts the car in gear and takes off to meet his family.

LOS ANGELES, MONDAY
Chelsea

Alison opens the door to James Casting and plops down on the little sofa in the brightly decorated reception area.

"How did it go?" Chelsea asks her, typing while talking per usual.

"Good, I'm just not sure we can take on one more project this month. But I want it, so we're going to say yes if it comes our way."

"Absolutely, we'll make it work. What else is on your mind?"

"Oh, nothing. Hey, I said I needed to go to New York for the series final calls. Can we move that to this week?"

"Yes, I can move everything to Wednesday in-person and then you can handle anything critical via Zoom on Thursday and Friday. Does that work?"

"Today's Monday? Yeah, that works. Actually, let's see if we can get the red eye tomorrow night and set up the meetings for Wednesday, with Thursday on hold just in case."

Chelsea searches for flights to New York and glances up to see Alison mulling something over. She hides her smile and waits for Alison to come to a decision.

"Ok I've got you set up for Tuesday night's red eye."

"Hmm," is all Alison says in response, clearly still mulling.

"So, I guess you want to return on Thursday evening or Friday morning?"

"Or?" Alison ponders.

Chelsea pauses her search and looks at her boss. "Or?"

"Or I could leave New York Thursday morning and fly to Maine for a few days." Alison glances at Chelsea to gauge her reaction.

Chelsea smirks. "Bangor it is," and begins typing away.

The End

Fellow Travelers – Odysseus Returns to Maine

"Born to Run" by Bruce Springsteen

"Drive My Car" by The Beatles

"End of the Line" by Traveling Wilburys

"Hit the Road Jack" by Ray Charles

"Holiday Road – National Lampoon's Vacation" by Lindsay Buckingham

"I'm Gonna Be (500 Miles)" by The Proclaimers

"Interstate Love Song" by Stone Temple Pilots

"Life in the Fast Lane" by Eagles

"Life is a Highway" by Tom Cochrane

"Ramblin' Man" by Allman Brothers Band

"Runnin' Down a Dream" by Tom Petty

"Running on Empty" by Jackson Browne

"Shut Up and Drive" by Rihanna

"The Golden Age" by Beck

"Two of Us" by The Beatles

About the Author

"Medicine, Law, Commerce, Engineering...they are noble and necessary races to dignify human life. But poetry, beauty, romance, love are things that keep us alive." ~ Dead Poet's Society, 1989

Bonnie Elise did not grow up thinking she was creative. She traveled the U.S. and Europe as an Army brat, studied languages in college, and spent most of her career in corporate human resources. While raising a family and exploring different hobbies, she found creativity after all. Her passions for bringing people together, books, movies, and travel have led to some much-needed imaginative outlets. She leads a Wine Club and the Litwits book club, hosts a travel podcast, a RomCom movie podcast, and always has two or three trips to new places lined up. While she calls the South home, she currently lives in the Midwest with her husband of 30 years, her two sons, and two very pampered pups. This is her first book, but it won't be her last.